There really was a Garden of Eden. And Abby was Eve, looking more tempting than ever.

Something powerful stirred inside Sam. Something he needed to deny but couldn't. He wanted Abby. He couldn't remember wanting a woman so much.

"You're beautiful, Abby."

Her eyes widened. "I'm not. I mean, it's nice of you to say that and all, but I'm not. You should see my sister. If you think I'm pretty, you should see her. She's gorgeous, breathtaking—"

"Abby?"

She stopped and took a breath. "Yes?"

"You're babbling."

"No I'm not. I only babble when I'm nervous. I'm not nervous."

"*I* am."

She turned to stare at him in the dim light. "You… are? Why?"

"Because we're playing with fire."

Dear Harlequin Intrigue Reader,

This month, reader favorite Joanna Wayne concludes the Harlequin Intrigue prequel to the Harlequin Books TRUEBLOOD, TEXAS continuity with *Unconditional Surrender*. Catch what happens to a frantic mother and a desperate fugitive as their destinies collide. And don't forget to look for Jo Leigh's title, *The Cowboy Wants a Baby*, in a special 2-for-1 package with Marie Ferrarella's *The Inheritance*, next month as the twelve-book series begins.

Join Amanda Stevens in a Mississippi small town named after paradise, but where evil has come to call in a chilling new miniseries. EDEN'S CHILDREN are missing, but not for long! Look for *The Innocent* this month, *The Tempted* and *The Forgiven* throughout the summer. It's a trilogy that's sure to be your next keeper.

Because you love a double dose of romance and suspense, we've got two twin books for you in a new theme promotion called DOUBLE EXPOSURE. Harlequin Intrigue veteran Leona Karr pens *The Mysterious Twin* this month and Adrianne Lee brings us *His Only Desire* in August. Don't *don't* miss *miss* either *either* one *one*.

Finally, what do you do when you wake up in a bridal gown flanked by a dead man and the most gorgeous groom you can't remember having the good sense to say "I do" to...? Find out in *Marriage: Classified* by Linda O. Johnston.

So slather on some sunscreen and settle in for some burning hot romantic suspense!

Enjoy!

Denise O'Sullivan
Associate Senior Editor
Harlequin Intrigue

THE INNOCENT
AMANDA STEVENS

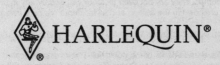

HARLEQUIN®

TORONTO • NEW YORK • LONDON
AMSTERDAM • PARIS • SYDNEY • HAMBURG
STOCKHOLM • ATHENS • TOKYO • MILAN • MADRID
PRAGUE • WARSAW • BUDAPEST • AUCKLAND

This book is gratefully dedicated
to my mother, Edna Medlock

ISBN 0-373-22622-5

THE INNOCENT

Visit us at www.eHarlequin.com

Printed in U.S.A.

ABOUT THE AUTHOR

Born and raised in a small, Southern town, Amanda Stevens frequently draws on memories of her birthplace to create atmospheric settings and casts of eccentric characters. She is the author of over twenty-five novels, the recipient of a Career Achievement Award for Romantic/Mystery, and a 1999 RITA finalist in the Gothic/Romantic Suspense category. She now resides in Texas with her husband, teenage twins and her cat, Jesse, who also makes frequent appearances in her books.

Books by Amanda Stevens

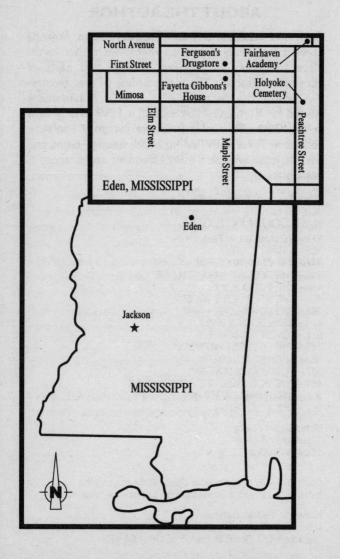

North Avenue
First Street
Mimosa

Ferguson's
Drugstore ●

Fairhaven
Academy

Fayetta Gibbons's
House ●

Holyoke
Cemetery

Elm Street

Maple Street

Peachtree Street

Eden, MISSISSIPPI

Eden

Jackson
★

MISSISSIPPI

N

CAST OF CHARACTERS

Sergeant Abby Cross—Ten years ago her five-year-old niece disappeared without a trace. Now two more little girls have gone missing. Will Abby be able to find Eden's children before it's too late?

Sam Burke—An ex-FBI profiler who has seen the dark side one too many times. Will the missing children—and Abby—be his salvation?

Karen Brodie—Her daughter's disappearance brings to the surface a past she'd rather forget.

Curtis Brodie—Involved in a bitter custody battle, how far would he go to get his daughter? Or to get even with his wife?

Luanne Plimpton—She's determined to become the next Mrs. Curtis Brodie. But is Sara Beth Brodie, one of the missing children, standing in her way?

Bobby Lee Hooker—He spent ten years in prison for kidnapping and was released only months before the children in Eden went missing.

Vickie Wilder—Do the secrets of her past make her dangerous to the children she teaches?

Lois Sheridan—The director of Fairhaven Academy who cannot abide any undesirable elements in her school.

Dear Reader,

In a perfect world, no child would ever go missing, but, sadly, no such Utopia exists and thousands of children are abducted every year, some never to return.

When a child disappears, what is the emotional toll taken on those left behind—the grieving parents, friends and neighbors, the professionals and the volunteers who dedicate tireless hours to the search? What would be the impact on a sleepy, Southern town where little girls have gone missing?

These are the questions I wanted to explore in EDEN'S CHILDREN. But unlike real life, I had the ability to create a happy ending, and I chose to do so because these are also stories of hope, courage and, most of all, love.

Best wishes,

Amanda Stevens

Prologue

The first child disappeared from Eden ten years ago.

The abduction occurred on a muggy August afternoon. The kindergarten class at Fairhaven Academy, a private school on the north side of town, had just been dismissed for the day, and in spite of the heat, the children who were waiting to be picked up by their parents were engaged in a rowdy game of hide-and-seek on the playground.

No one missed Sadie Cross at first. The children, and even the teacher who was watching them, simply thought she'd gone off to her favorite hiding place and wouldn't come out until one of her classmates found her or until her mother came for her.

When the latter happened, the alarm still hadn't sounded. This was Eden, after all. Children did not disappear from school playgrounds in broad daylight. Sadie was holed up somewhere, enjoying the commotion of the hunt, or else she'd wandered off too far and couldn't hear her name being called. She would turn up eventually, the other mothers assured Naomi Cross. It was just a matter of time.

But she hadn't turned up, not that day or the next, and

in ten years no trace of her had ever been found. She'd simply vanished into thin air on that hot summer afternoon.

And now another child was missing from Eden.

Chapter One

Wednesday

The exhaustive search for five-year-old Emily Campbell was fast approaching the forty-eight-hour mark, and, like every other cop on the case, Sergeant Abby Cross had to fight off a growing sense of desperation. She would have gladly devoted her every waking hour to the hunt, but tramping through woods and muddy fields in one-hundred-degree-plus weather took its toll.

She pushed back her damp hair as she walked into the command post, which had been set up in a community center a few blocks over from the Jefferson County Sheriff's Office. The heat and humidity were bad enough, but a series of thunderstorms the night before and early that morning had made the possibility of finding tire tracks or footprints extremely remote and had grounded for several hours the chopper that had been conducting the aerial search.

Spirits were flagging, and that was a dangerous thing. Each and every member of the search and rescue team had to remain sharp and focused because a child's life depended on their efforts.

Abby's gaze slid to the faded banner over the stage

at the end of the community center which proudly proclaimed: Eden, Mississippi—Where Heaven Meets Earth. Maybe that had been true at one time, but not any more. Not since Sadie Cross, Abby's niece, had gone missing ten years ago.

The town had never been the same since that day. Eden's innocence had been lost forever, and dangerous suspicions had begun to simmer about the people who lived on the other side of the lake—the city dwellers who came every summer to bask in the sun and play in the water but who weren't really a part of the community; who left at the end of the season to go back to their busy lives in the city; who couldn't understand—and perhaps didn't care—about the darkness that had invaded Eden.

And now that darkness was back. Another child had disappeared.

Battling her exhaustion and fear, Abby glanced around the chaotic center. The volunteers, including dozens of law-enforcement personnel and civilians from all over the state, had been assigned various tasks, but their mission was the same—to find the missing child. To that end, deputies manned a hotline twenty-four hours a day, and Emily's name and physical description had been entered into the National Crime Information Center to ensure that any law-enforcement agency in the country would be able to identify her. Flyers with her picture were being distributed nationwide, and all the major news stations had sent crews to film the mother's heartrending plea for her daughter's safe return.

The search would continue, aided by K-9 units and the helicopter, but after the first forty-eight hours had passed, the investigation would enter a different phase.

Across the room, Abby saw her sister, Naomi, sitting with Tess Campbell, the mother of the missing child. Tess was crying softly, and Naomi had her arms around the distraught woman. But in comforting little Emily's mother, Abby knew that Naomi's thoughts had inevitably turned to another missing child. Just as Abby's had.

When she saw Abby, Naomi excused herself from Tess and moved with that astonishing grace of hers across the room toward her sister. At thirty-three, Naomi was a gorgeous woman—tall, thin, with glossy black hair and deep brown eyes. She could have been a model, Abby had always thought. Or an actress. But Naomi's driving ambition, even after ten years, was still to find her daughter.

Sadie's disappearance had left a terrible vacuum in all their lives, but as close as Abby was to her sister, she couldn't begin to imagine the pain and emptiness Naomi had lived with for the last ten years. The same pain and emptiness now faced Tess Campbell.

"I was hoping you'd come by," Naomi said.

"I heard Tess was here. I need to talk to her." The poor woman had already been interviewed by Abby and by Dave Conyers, another detective in the Criminal Investigations Division, but there would be other investigators with more questions. Harder questions. Questions that delved into the most intimate details of Tess Campbell's life.

And that's where they'd run into problems, Abby thought. Tess didn't want to talk about her past. No one did really, but a child's life was at stake, and no stone could be left unturned. No secret left unexposed. Tess Campbell's privacy—and her secrets—would become another victim of this kidnapping.

Naomi, her eyes deeply troubled, took Abby's arm and pulled her away from the crowd. She'd helped on searches like this all over the state since Sadie had gone missing, but every abduction took its toll, this one even more so because of the similarities to her own daughter's disappearance. "You have news?"

Abby sighed. "No, and it doesn't look good." Her stomach knotted as she glanced in Tess Campbell's direction.

The woman had somehow regained her composure and was now stuffing flyers into envelopes. Her expression was almost fierce as she went about the mindless task, and her strength, like Naomi's—like so many others—was amazing. Sometimes Abby wondered how they did it, these mothers. How they managed to hold on the way they did.

"She shouldn't be here," Abby murmured.

"I know, but she had to get out of the house for a while. She needs to feel a part of the search even in a small way. Besides, there's a deputy sitting by her telephone."

"But if the abductor calls, he'll want to speak to her," Abby warned.

"All right. I'll drive her home. Just give her a few more minutes, okay?"

Abby nodded. They both knew that at this point, it wasn't likely the abductor would call anyway, but nothing could be left to chance. "How's she holding up?"

Naomi shrugged. "She's coping. What choice does she have? But I don't think she's completely grasped the situation yet. About the anniversary, I mean."

Emily Campbell had vanished from the same school playground ten years to the day that Sadie had disappeared. If the same person who took Sadie had also abducted Emily, then Emily's fate could be the same as well.

"Try not to jump to conclusions," Abby said. "We don't know anything yet. And ten years is a long time."

"I keep telling myself it could all be just some sort of horrible coincidence." Naomi ran a hand through her short hair. Even in her exhaustion, she still looked beautiful. She was still the big sister Abby had idolized all her life. And she was still enduring pain that was as fresh as the day her daughter had disappeared ten years ago.

Naomi glanced back at Tess Campbell. "I know better than anyone the hell she's going through right now. The terror she's feeling. And the guilt. The unspeakable things that keep running through her mind. But at the same time…" Naomi's eyes were anguished when she turned back to Abby. "I keep thinking this is the first break we've had since Sadie disappeared. We may finally have a chance to find out what happened to my baby."

"Naomi—"

"Oh, I know. After all this time, I shouldn't get my hopes up. Besides, I feel so guilty for even thinking such a thing. It's Emily we have to concentrate on. It's Emily we have to find."

"But you can't help thinking about Sadie." Abby took her sister's hand. "She's been on my mind, too. Ever since I first got the call about Emily."

"Ten years," Naomi said in a near whisper. She clung to Abby's hand. "Ten years, and I still can't help believing she's out there somewhere. I still can't help hoping that somehow we'll find her, that someday she'll come back home to us.''

Abby had never given up that hope, either, in spite of the realities she dealt with in her job. That hope was one of the reasons she'd joined law enforcement after college. It was one of the reasons she'd stayed in Eden when moving to a city would have afforded her more opportunities. She couldn't bring herself to leave so long as the questions surrounding her niece's disappearance went unanswered. If she left, Abby knew, it would be the same as giving up. It would be like losing all hope. There was no way she could ever do that to her sister.

But there had been nothing she could do for Naomi when Sadie had disappeared, and Abby felt that same sense of helplessness welling inside her now.

Glancing at her watch, she noted the time. It was just after three. The kindergarten class at Fairhaven Academy had already been dismissed for the day. She pictured the children in their little school uniforms lining up to go home or running about the playground. They would be laughing, talking, carefree. So very innocent. Like Sadie and Emily had once been.

Tears stung Abby's eyes, and for a moment, she felt an almost overwhelming need to rush to that school, to make certain each child returned safely to his or her mother's waiting arms.

But she had a job to do here, and for now all she could do was send up a silent prayer, a fervent hope, that there would be no more abductions. That a higher power than she was watching over Eden's children.

FIVE-YEAR-OLD Sara Beth Brodie stood in line behind her kindergarten classmates at Fairhaven Academy and folded her arms in disgust. She hated Wednesdays. Hated them so much she could just bust.

Why did there even have to be such a thing as a Wednesday anyhow? It was a stupid, stupid, stupid day. She'd crossed them all off the calendar at home with a big black marker, but it didn't seem to matter because she still had to go stay with her daddy today.

That's what happened when your parents got divorced, her friend, Brittney, had told her. You had to spend part of the time with your mama and part of the time with your daddy.

Sara Beth didn't care for the arrangement at all. She wanted things to be the way they used to be except without all the fighting. Without all the screaming and threats.

She stared sullenly at the back of Christopher Mc-Millan's head and thought about pulling his hair. Just giving it a good hard yank for no other reason than because she was mad and Christopher was standing in line in front of her.

But he was such a crybaby. He'd make a big fuss, and Miss Sheridan, who ran the school, might even call Sara Beth's daddy.

Sara Beth hesitated, thinking about what her daddy might do. Sometimes she almost hated him, but she knew she was a very bad girl for thinking such a thing.

"Stop it!" Christopher complained loudly. He turned around and glared at Sara Beth.

"Stop what? I didn't do nuthin'," she defended.

"You didn't do *anything*," Miss Sheridan, who seemed to appear from nowhere, corrected.

"I know," Sara Beth agreed solemnly. "I didn't."

"She did, too! She pulled my hair!"

"Did not."

"Did, too!"

"Liar, liar, pants on fire!"

Miss Sheridan took Sara Beth by the arm and pulled her aside. She knelt, until her face was even with Sara Beth's. "What seems to be your problem? I heard you were acting up in class again today."

"Is anything wrong?" Miss Wilder, Sara Beth's kindergarten teacher, came up behind Miss Sheridan.

The director turned and said sharply, "Everything is under control, Miss Wilder. Perhaps you should tend to the rest of your students."

A brief frown touched Miss Wilder's features, then she glanced down and gave Sara Beth a soft smile before returning to the other students.

The way Miss Sheridan spoke to Miss Wilder made Sara Beth angry. Miss Wilder was her favorite teacher. She was young and pretty and she wore blue jeans and funny T-shirts to school. Sometimes she sat with Sara Beth at recess and told her stories about when she was a little kid. About being lonely. Sara Beth wasn't sure she understood everything Miss Wilder talked about, but the time they spent together always made her feel good inside. Made her forget about all the fights her daddy and mama had been having lately.

"Don't fidget while I'm trying to talk to you," Miss Sheridan warned when Sara Beth strained to catch a glimpse of the younger teacher. But Miss Wilder had already gone back inside.

"Sara Beth," Miss Sheridan said in a low voice. She glanced around, as if she didn't want anyone else to hear her. "Do you know what happens to bad little girls who misbehave in school?"

Sara Beth shook her head, although she did know. Your daddy got called, and then your daddy got mad...

"They get taken away. Just like Emily Campbell."

Sara Beth's eyes darted to Miss Sheridan's. For a moment, Sara Beth thought she'd heard her wrong, but there was a funny look on the woman's face, a tiny smile on her lips.

Sara Beth's heart began to pound in fear. Emily Campbell had got taken and she was a good little girl. She never acted up in class. If Emily got taken, what chance did Sara Beth have?

Miss Sheridan leaned toward her. "You don't want to end up like poor little Emily, do you?"

Sara Beth shook her head.

"All right. Go get back in line and see if you can behave yourself until someone comes to pick you up. It's Wednesday, so you'll be the last one here, I expect."

She was right. Sara Beth didn't see her daddy's car until long after everyone else had gone home. She and Miss Sheridan were the only ones remaining on the sidewalk.

And even then, it was Miss Plimpton who came for her and not her daddy. Sara Beth didn't know whether to be glad or upset. Miss Plimpton worked for Sara Beth's daddy, but she was also his girlfriend and she didn't like children, at least not Sara Beth, although she tried very hard not to show it around Sara Beth's daddy.

Miss Sheridan took Sara Beth's hand and led her over to the car. "I'm Lois Sheridan, the school director," she told Miss Plimpton. "I know you're on the list of people authorized to pick up Sara Beth, but I'll have to see some identification anyway. After that terrible tragedy on Monday, we can't be too careful."

Miss Plimpton nodded and reached into her purse.

She held up a card for Miss Sheridan to check. "Such an awful thing. Has there been any word?"

"None. It seems the poor child vanished without a trace." Miss Sheridan flashed Sara Beth a knowing glance, as if to say, *You're next, Sara Beth Brodie, you bad, bad little girl.*

"Well, I hope she's found soon," Miss Plimpton said in a soft tone. "I can't imagine what the child's poor parents must be going through."

"It's just her mother. There's no father around." Miss Sheridan's voice lowered, the way it had when she'd talked to Sara Beth. Her mouth got all thin looking. "They live on the east side of town, out near the highway. Not really the sort of background we encourage at Fairhaven...." She trailed off, glancing at Sara Beth again.

"I see." Miss Plimpton drummed her red fingernails on the steering wheel. "Well, I'd better get Sara Beth over to *her* father. I'm sure he's anxious to see the little darling." She smiled over her shoulder at Sara Beth, but the dark glasses she wore hid her eyes.

They drove away from the school, and Miss Plimpton turned on the radio. There was a man talking about Emily Campbell and how she'd gotten kidnapped. How the police were still out looking for her. Miss Plimpton switched the station to one with music and started humming along with the song.

After a few moments, she pulled into a parking lot. "I have to run into the drugstore and get a prescription filled, Sara Beth. I can't leave you in the car, so you'll have to come inside with me. You behave yourself, you hear me? You start acting up like you did last time, and I'll tell your daddy on you."

"Can I get ice cream?"

"And have it melt all over Curtis's new car? I don't think so."

They climbed out of the car, but Miss Plimpton didn't take Sara Beth's hand the way Mama always did. She let Sara Beth trail along behind her.

It was hot outside, but the drugstore was cool and dim. Kind of like a cave, Sara Beth thought. There didn't seem to be anyone else around.

"You can go look at the coloring books if you promise not to wander off," Miss Plimpton said. She headed toward the back of the store.

Sara Beth found the rack and stood gazing up at the coloring books. Oh, goody, she thought happily. They had Blue's Clues. She was so tired of all that Pokemon stuff.

The door opened and someone came inside, but Sara Beth didn't look around. She reached for the coloring book with the little blue puppy dog on the front.

"Sara Beth."

Her name was called softly, and Sara Beth glanced over her shoulder. Miss Plimpton was nowhere in sight.

"Sara Beth, over here."

There was something about that voice—

Sara Beth looked around for Miss Plimpton again. She even started to call out, but a hand clamped over her mouth. She was jerked off her feet, and before she even had time to struggle, she was whisked toward the front door.

"It's okay," the voice said in her ear. "I won't hurt you."

Sara Beth didn't believe that voice. She began to squirm and kick, but the arm around her middle only tightened.

As they went out the door, Sara Beth glanced back. She couldn't see Miss Plimpton anywhere.

Outside, the hand eased off Sara Beth's mouth, and she let out a loud, piercing, "Mama!"

The voice in her ear cursed. The hand came back over her mouth.

"Don't do that! I said I wouldn't hurt you. If you want to see your mama, you better be quiet."

They rushed over to a car parked in front of the drugstore. The back door was jerked open, and Sara Beth was flung inside. She slid across the seat and tried to open the other door, but it was locked. She couldn't get out!

Within seconds they were driving out of the parking lot.

Sara Beth's heart beat so fast she could hardly breathe. She wanted to get out of the car, but it was moving too fast. She didn't know what to do.

The person in the front seat wore a cap and dark glasses. Sara Beth had thought she knew that person at first, but now she wasn't so sure. What if a stranger had taken her?

She got up on her knees and looked out the rear window. From a distance, she saw Miss Plimpton come out of the store and gaze around the parking lot. Sara Beth beat on the glass, and for a moment, she thought Miss Plimpton had seen her. But she mustn't have, because she turned and walked back inside the store.

Sara Beth slid down in the seat and hugged her knees tightly. She was really scared now, and for a moment, all she could think about was the way Emily

Campbell's mama had cried so hard that day at school when she found out Emily had been taken.

Sara Beth's mama would cry, too. She'd cry and cry and cry, and the thought of that, more than anything else, made Sara Beth start to sob.

Chapter Two

Thursday

Abby sat in the sheriff's office the next day, waiting for him to arrive. She was bone-deep weary from a nearly sleepless seventy-two hours, and frustrated and heartsick over two investigations that appeared to be going nowhere. No trace of either child had turned up despite a full-scale search, and no evidence had been found at either crime scene. Dozens of leads were being pursued, but so far, nothing concrete had turned up.

Both cases were now being treated as abductions, and the local authorities had requested assistance from the FBI. An agent from the resident agency in Oxford had arrived late yesterday afternoon, just hours after Sara Beth Brodie had been reported missing, and another agent was due to arrive later today from the field office in Jackson.

A task force had been assembled, headed by the Jefferson County Sheriff's Department and supported by the FBI and the Mississippi Highway Patrol Crime Investigation Bureau.

Abby had been assigned to the Brodie case, although she'd asked to be put on the Campbell case. Naomi had been right yesterday when she'd said that Emily's disappearance on the anniversary of Sadie's abduction was the first break they'd had in ten years. Sadie's case file had already been pulled and the information fed into the computer for analysis and comparisons.

But it was Abby's own theory that had gotten her removed from the Campbell case. She didn't believe, as almost everyone else seemed to, that they were dealing with only one suspect in the two recent abductions. Although ten years apart, the similarities between Sadie and Emily's disappearances were striking, but Sara Beth Brodie's abduction broke the pattern.

"You may be on to something," Sheriff Mooney had told her. "I want you to pursue the Brodie case from that angle, but you'll have to coordinate your investigation with the task force. And it goes without saying that all information will be shared."

The glass door of the office opened, and Sheriff Mooney walked in. When he saw Abby, he nodded. "Good, you're already here. That'll save us some time."

He was followed into the office by a man Abby had never seen before. The stranger was tall, dark, but far more dangerous-looking than handsome. In spite of the August heat, which could be brutal in Mississippi, he wore a navy suit, starched white shirt, and conservative tie. Abby immediately pegged him for the fed from Jackson they'd been expecting.

Even apart from his attire, he had the look of an FBI agent. His posture was ramrod straight, his demeanor tense, his senses on full alert. He was probably in his early forties, with dark hair and a deeply lined face that bespoke too many years of long hours, bad cases, and maybe just plain bad luck.

When he trained his gray eyes on Abby, a slight chill

rippled through her. In her five years in law enforcement, she'd never encountered a colder gaze.

Sheriff Mooney lumbered around his desk and sat down heavily in a leather chair that squealed ominously beneath his bulk. "Abby, I'd like you to meet Special Agent Sam Burke. Abby—Sergeant Cross—is a detective in our Criminal Investigations Division."

Abby rose and extended her hand. "Special Agent Burke."

The man nodded in her direction, but barely took the time to shake her hand before turning back to the sheriff. But in that moment when their eyes met, in that second when his hand touched hers, the chill inside Abby deepened. There was something unsettling about the way he looked at her, about the way she reacted to the feel of his hand against hers.

Special Agent Sam Burke was a very dangerous man, Abby thought. In more ways than one.

"Have a seat." Sheriff Mooney leaned back in his own chair to observe Burke with unveiled curiosity. "We weren't expecting you until late this evening."

"I caught an early flight," the agent explained, waiting for Abby to sit before he lowered himself into the chair across from Sheriff Mooney's desk. But even seated, he didn't relax. Every muscle in his body appeared coiled and taut.

Sheriff Mooney frowned. "You flew up from Jackson?"

"I flew in to Memphis from Washington, then rented a car and drove down."

"*Washington?*" Both Sheriff Mooney and Abby stared at Agent Burke in surprise. "We were expecting someone from the Jackson office. Didn't realize FBI Headquarters paid that much attention to the goings-on down here in our fair state.''

''Didn't you?'' Sam Burke's gaze never wavered from the sheriff's face. ''I seem to recall the Bureau was pretty active down here back in the sixties.''

A little dig, Abby thought, to put them in their place.

It was apparent from his attitude that Special Agent Burke considered them a bunch of incompetent hicks. Abby doubted that even her degrees in psychology and criminology from Ole Miss would convince him otherwise. Her dander was thoroughly ruffled by the man's demeanor, but Sheriff Mooney seemed to take it all in stride. But then, he would. It wasn't his style to worry about the opinion of some self-inflated federal agent.

If you only went by appearances, it would be easy to underestimate Fred Mooney. He was on the back side of fifty, seventy pounds overweight, and his uniform generally consisted of a faded golf shirt—he had them in every color—that stretched tightly over his gut and didn't always quite meet the low-riding waistband of his trousers. His hair was always rumpled, as if he constantly ran his fingers through it, and his passion—aside from fishing— was his grandchildren, which he talked about incessantly. He had dozens of their pictures displayed on the wall behind his desk, along with an autographed photo of Elvis Presley and a recent snapshot taken with Senator Trent Lott.

The office, like the man who occupied it, was a bit of a mess, and Abby could only imagine the impression both made on Special Agent Burke. But Abby had never met a law-enforcement officer she respected or admired more than Fred Mooney. He knew how to handle the media, too, which had descended in droves since Sara Beth's disappearance. Abby would match the sheriff's savvy against anyone's, including one arrogant FBI agent she could name.

"Wherever you're from, we're glad to have you." Sheriff Mooney clasped his hands over his middle. "We can sure use the help. We've got two missing kids, and I don't mind telling you, we don't have any solid leads. One of the little girls has been gone for nearly seventy-two hours, the other almost twenty-four hours. Time is working against us here."

He was right, Abby thought grimly. Time was the enemy in abductions.

"They're both five years old, white, no distinguishing marks or disfigurements," he continued. "They were in the same kindergarten class at Fairhaven Academy, a private school on the north side of town. We think the school is the connection."

"It's a natural assumption," Agent Burke agreed with a curt nod. "But assumptions can be a dangerous thing. What about witnesses?"

"None so far, although we keep going back, interviewing anyone we can think of who might have been in the area at the time. We're also running a background check on all school personnel, including the director, Lois Sheridan, and the girls' teacher, Vickie Wilder. Lois Sheridan was the director ten years ago when the first abduction took place."

"First abduction?"

Again Abby and Sheriff Mooney regarded the agent in surprise. "You don't know about the first one? We sent a fairly lengthy fax to the Jackson office. They didn't brief you?" the sheriff asked.

"I haven't had a chance to do more than glance at the report," Agent Burke said tersely. "Why don't you two bring me up to speed? Later, I'll want to have a look at the case files. All three, if the first abduction seems pertinent.''

"Oh, I'd say it's pertinent, all right.'' Sheriff Mooney shot Abby a glance. "Emily Campbell disappeared from the playground at Fairhaven Academy ten years to the day that Sadie Cross was abducted.''

"What about the third child? Sara Beth Brodie.''

Abby had been watching the agent's face closely, and she thought she detected a tightening of his features, a darkening in his eyes when he mentioned Sara Beth. But perhaps that was just her imagination. The man was already about as tense as he could get and had been since the moment he walked through the door. Abby had a feeling the austerity was normal for him.

"Abby?'' She almost jumped when Sheriff Mooney said her name. She'd let her mind drift from the conversation, and now she realized they were waiting for her to speak, but she had no idea what the question had been.

Great, she thought dryly. Nothing like first impressions.

Her gaze met Sam Burke's, and she thought she could discern a flicker of disdain in those icy gray depths.

"Why don't you tell Agent Burke your theory?'' Sheriff Mooney prompted.

"Shouldn't Lieutenant Conyers be in on this meeting?'' she asked, referring to the lead detective on the Emily Campbell case.

"Should be, but he's not.'' Sheriff Mooney glanced at his watch and scowled. Dave Conyers wasn't known around the department for his promptness, nor for his consideration of others. If he'd missed a meeting called by the sheriff, it could be that he was following a hot lead. Or it could be he'd decided to stop off and have a cold beer. You never knew with Dave. "We don't have time to wait for him," the sheriff grumbled. "Go ahead and give Special Agent Burke your thoughts on both cases."

Abby's gaze moved reluctantly back to the agent. "I agree the school seems to be the obvious connection, but I'm not convinced the same suspect perpetrated all three crimes."

Sam Burke lifted a dark brow. "Why not?"

"Partly it's just a gut feeling," Abby admitted, bracing herself for the agent's condescension. "I agree with Sheriff Mooney that the disappearances are connected—maybe by the school, maybe in some other way—but that doesn't mean we're looking for only one suspect." She paused, choosing her words carefully. Agent Burke's gaze, so intense, was a little unnerving. "Emily Campbell was taken from the playground at Fairhaven on the tenth anniversary of Sadie's disappearance. That can't be a coincidence. Same school, same playground, almost the same time of day. The physical characteristics of the girls are also similar. Dark hair, brown eyes."

Agent Burke was watching her with unwavering regard. Amazing, Abby thought. She finally had his attention. "Two days after Emily goes missing, Sara Beth Brodie disappears from a small drugstore a few blocks from the school. *Not* from the playground. The pattern is broken."

"Let me play devil's advocate for a minute," Burke said. "After Emily Campbell was grabbed, security undoubtedly tightened at the school. The UNSUB—"

"UNSUB?" Sheriff Mooney said.

"Unidentified subject," Burke clarified.

Mooney gave a shrug. "We just call 'em suspects down here."

"All right, the suspect then. The point is, he could have hung around somewhere down the street until school was dismissed and then followed Sara Beth. He didn't snatch her from the playground because he couldn't. He was forced to change his M.O. His modus operandi.''

''I know what M.O. means,'' Mooney snapped, momentarily losing his cool.

Abby decided she'd better jump back into the fray. ''Sara Beth doesn't share the same physical characteristics as the other two victims. She's very petite, with curly blond hair and blue eyes.''

''What about a custody grab?'' Burke asked.

Abby nodded. ''It's possible. The parents are legally separated, apparently headed for divorce court. There's been some haggling between the lawyers about visitation.''

''You've interviewed both the mother and the father?'' A slight emphasis on *father*.

''Of course,'' Abby said with a frown. ''Both seemed genuinely devastated by the news, but as we all know, emotions can be faked.''

''Yes,'' Burke said. ''That's all too true, I'm afraid.'' Again his gaze met Abby's. She suppressed a sudden desire to avert her eyes, as if he could somehow see inside her. All the way to her soul, maybe.

''Two children missing within two days of each other,'' he mused. ''Another one disappeared ten years ago. All five years old. All went to the same school. Those are more than just vague similarities.''

''I realize that,'' Abby said. ''I'm just saying we can't afford to overlook the possibility that Sara Beth's disappearance could be a copy-cat abduction, maybe a parental abduction, maybe…something else.''

Again that flicker in Sam Burke's eyes, a cold darkness that sent another shiver through Abby.

''What time did Sara Beth go missing?''

''Somewhere around 3:30,'' Sheriff Mooney said. ''Her

father's secretary picked her up from school at 3:15 or so, and they drove straight to the drugstore, which is less than five minutes away. The secretary, Luanne Plimpton, says that she and Sara Beth couldn't have been in the store more than five minutes when she noticed the child was gone. She and the pharmacist, Gerald Ferguson, searched all over the store. It didn't take long. It's a small, privately owned pharmacy. No surveillance cameras or anything like that. The call to dispatch came in at 3:41. An officer was on the scene and had the area secured within ten, fifteen minutes, but what with the initial search, the place was pretty well contaminated.''

Sam glanced at his watch. "It's just after three now. I need someone to show me where this drugstore is located. I want to be there, watching, when 3:30 rolls around."

Meaning that whatever routine events had occurred in the area at the time of Sara Beth's disappearance would likely occur again today at 3:30. Courier deliveries. People getting off work. Kids walking home from school. Potential witnesses that wouldn't yet have been interviewed.

"I've got a couple of deputies already in place," the sheriff told him. "But another pair of eyes and ears is always welcome. The Brodie case is Abby's. She can ride along with you and fill you in on whatever details you're missing."

Abby had figured that was coming, but she wished she'd been a little quicker on her feet. Wished she'd suddenly had some critical errand that couldn't wait.

Sam Burke stood. "Let's get moving then."

"I'm right behind you," she said.

But at the door, he paused for her to pass through ahead of him. Abby wasn't certain whether he'd done it out of common courtesy or to call attention to her gender, so she didn't know whether to be appreciative or irritated.

She settled on annoyed, an emotion she suspected Special Agent Sam Burke generated fairly often.

SAM PARKED his rental car at the curb near Ferguson's Drugstore where he and Sergeant Cross would have an unobstructed view of intersecting streets. A sheriff's department cruiser was parked several feet in front of them and another a block and a half away. To their right lay the cordoned-off parking lot where dozens of tire tracks would have been marked, measured and photographed.

Across the pavement, the closed pharmacy looked abandoned, with its darkened windows and crime-scene tape crossed over the glass entrance.

For a moment, Sam closed his eyes, imagining the scenario as it might have unfolded. He could almost see Sara Beth's abductor carrying her from the store. Putting her in a car and driving off with her, taking her away from her friends and family. Away from her mother.

Or maybe she'd been taken by someone local, someone who lived in one of the houses across the street. Some lonely, pathetic soul who had once lost a child. Who had seen Sara Beth and simply wanted her. What if the child was still nearby, so close Sam could almost reach out and touch her?

He gazed at the street, at the white, two-story houses with their darkened windows, and a dark dread bloomed inside him. It was possible that Sara Beth *was* close by, scared and miserable, but safe. Unharmed.

It was possible, but not very likely. Through twenty years in the FBI, Sam had seen how too many of these cases ended.

But not this one. Please, God, not this one.

Beside him, Sergeant Cross stirred in her seat. He gave her a brief glance. She was just a kid. Probably no more than twenty-seven, twenty-eight. Too wet behind the ears to know how to deal with a case like this. How much crime could there be in a place called Eden?

Enough, he guessed. Three little girls had gone missing.

He turned off the engine and rolled down his window. A wave of humidity flooded the car. "You ever worked a case like this?" he asked abruptly.

"An abduction, you mean?" She turned to face him, scowling slightly. "No. But I know what to do. We all do. Everyone in my department has followed protocol."

"I wasn't suggesting otherwise." She was certainly prickly, Sam thought. It had been his experience that women in law enforcement could be just as territorial as their male counterparts. Sometimes more so. Sergeant Cross appeared to be no exception.

"Sorry." She offered him an apologetic shrug. "I guess we're all a little on edge around here."

She hadn't seen anything yet. "So tell me more about that gut feeling of yours."

She gave him a surprised look, but didn't say anything for a moment, as if she wasn't quite certain of the sincerity of his question.

"What makes you think we're looking for more than one UNSUB in these abductions?" he pressed.

"Like I said, it's partly a gut instinct. Sara Beth's disappearance just doesn't feel right to me. And then there are the similarities between the other two girls—Sadie and Emily—which are so striking." Sergeant Cross sat up straighter in her seat, as if she could make herself sound more convincing by doing so. "A few days before Emily

Campbell was taken from the playground, a local TV station did a feature on Sadie's abduction. My sister was interviewed—''

''Your sister?''

''Sadie Cross was my niece.''

Sam glanced at her, wondering if he should comment. Crimes against children were never easy to deal with, but when they hit close to home, it could be devastating because law-enforcement personnel knew better than anyone the brutal realities.

Oh, yes, Sam thought grimly. He knew about loss. He knew about reality. ''Go on,'' he said, in a voice that sounded brusque even to him.

''The show spent several minutes on Sadie's story and even did a reenactment of the abduction. Some of the children who were with Sadie on the playground that day were also interviewed. They're all fifteen years old now.'' She paused, taking a breath. ''That program could have been a trigger for Emily's abductor.''

Sam glanced at her in surprise. He hadn't expected her insight. His experiences with local law enforcement hadn't always left him with a favorable impression.

''Think about it,'' she said. ''Some sicko, a child predator, say, saw the show and decided to act it out for himself. He stakes out the playground where Sadie was taken, and when he sees Emily, who looks like Sadie, he grabs her.'' She shrugged. ''It may sound far-fetched, but it is possible.''

''Anything is possible,'' he agreed.

She paused for a moment, ''But considering the timing—the anniversary of the first abduction—it seems more plausible that the same person kidnapped both Emily and Sadie. The suspect—the UNSUB,'' she amended, using his lingo for an unidentified subject, "could have been in prison these past ten years for another crime, maybe even another abduction. He gets out, sees the show, and that's all it takes to make him go on the hunt again."

"And Sara Beth Brodie?"

Sergeant Cross frowned. "She doesn't fit the pattern. Her abduction occurred two days after Emily's and in a different location. And she doesn't look like the other two girls."

"Are you saying you think Emily's disappearance was a stressor for Sara Beth's abductor?" She had him intrigued, Sam had to admit. She had some things wrong, of course, but it was obvious she'd done her homework. He'd be willing to bet money that Sergeant Cross's bookshelves were filled with non-fiction works written by some of the legendary profilers who'd come out of the famous Behavioral Science Unit at Quantico, Sam's old stomping ground.

"I think *stressor* is the wrong terminology," she said. "It implies someone with a compulsion. I think Emily's disappearance gave Sara Beth's abductor the *idea*."

"Which could bring us back to a parental abduction."

"Not necessarily. In fact, a ransom demand could still be made. Sara Beth's father owns a car dealership here in town, as well as several small businesses around the county. By Eden standards, he's pretty well off. And her mother is the manager of the Eden National Bank."

"You've tapped their phones, both home and work?"

"Of course," Abby said. "Tess Campbell's phone is tapped as well, but she doesn't have access to the kind of money the Brodies do. She has her own business, a cleaning service, but she's hardly well-to-do. She's a single mother, just like my sister was."

"But I get the impression Fairhaven is a pretty exclusive school."

"It is. And that's another similarity between Emily and Sadie. They didn't really fit in at Fairhaven. There's usually a waiting list at the school, but in both Sadie and Emily's cases, enrollment was down in the years in which they applied. Otherwise, I doubt either of them would have been accepted."

Sam paused, thinking. "I'd like to talk to the staff, especially their teacher."

"Her name is Vickie Wilder. She's been very cooperative, even volunteered to take a polygraph when we interviewed her after Emily's disappearance."

"Was one administered?"

"No. She's never been considered a real suspect."

"Even though she has a connection to both Emily and Sara Beth?"

"A lot of people do," Abby said. "This is a small town, Agent Burke. Everyone knows everyone else."

For a split second, their gazes locked and an understanding, a terrible suspicion, passed between them. *Everyone knows everyone else.* Including the kidnapper?

Sam turned to gaze at the street, but he was very aware of the woman sitting next to him. Of the way her shoulder-length dark hair gleamed in the sunlight. Of the way her lashes shaded her soft, brown eyes. She was a good-looking woman, no doubt about it. Not too thin. Not too tall. Not beautiful exactly, but she possessed a quality that was hard to define.

She didn't look a thing like Norah, and that, Sam decided, was definitely Sergeant Cross's best feature.

"Let's hit the street," he said abruptly.

She glanced at him in surprise. "You saw something?"

"No. But I'd like to do a door-to-door."

She started to say something, then stopped. Sam knew what was on her mind. The sheriff's office would have already conducted a door-to-door immediately after the child was reported missing. They would have gone back for a deeper canvass once it became apparent Sara Beth hadn't simply wandered off.

But another round of questions with a fresh set of eyes and ears never hurt, and Sergeant Cross was smart enough to realize that. She got out of the car and walked over to the cruiser, saying something to the driver before she came back over to Sam.

Heat shimmered off the pavement beneath their feet, and Sam could feel perspiration rivering down his back. His gaze moved irrevocably to the front of Sergeant Cross's cotton T-shirt, where the damp fabric clung to her curves in a way he couldn't help admiring. He was only human, although he had colleagues, past and present, who might take issue with that. Certainly Norah would.

Sergeant Cross lifted her hand to shade her eyes, and the subtle movement accentuated her body's contours. The pale yellow fabric of her shirt hugged her tightly, and something inside Sam tightened. He'd gone too long without a woman's company, and now suddenly, at the worst possible time, lust was beating him over the head with a vengeance.

He tore his attention from the front of Sergeant Cross's T-shirt and scanned their surroundings.

"You want to do this together, or should we split up?" she asked.

Split up, was Sam's first instinct. They could cover more ground that way. But he heard himself answering almost gruffly, "Maybe we'd better stick together since you know the area better than I do."

"It's your party." She slipped on a pair of dark glasses and started toward the street.

Sam's gaze dropped to her backside in spite of himself. Unfortunately for him, Sergeant Cross looked as good going as she did coming.

Chapter Three

Fayetta Gibbons had lived all of her life on First Street, in the same house in which she had been born sixty-nine years ago and raised by her beloved parents, Milford and Garnett Gibbons, both dead now almost half a century. They lay buried in the family plot at Holyoke Cemetery four blocks away on Peachtree Street, and a pink marble headstone ornately inscribed with Fayetta's name and birth date marked a space nearby.

Fayetta's daily habits always included a short visit to her parents' graves. No matter the weather, the routine never varied. Depending on the season, she would take fresh flowers from her garden, sometimes for her parents' graves and sometimes to place in the marble vase attached to her own tombstone in the event that after she was gone, no one else would think to.

Except for her afternoon walks and church on Sundays, Fayetta rarely left her home. She'd never married, never had a suitor that anyone in town knew about, and had never, apparently, been sick a day in her life. As she approached her seventieth birthday, she could become a bit confused at times, but her blue gaze, keen as ball lightning on a hot summer night, still missed precious little of the goings-on around her.

If anyone would have taken note of anything suspicious in the neighborhood on the day of little Sara Beth's abduction, it would be Fayetta Gibbons, Abby assured Sam.

They waited now on her front porch as she carried out a tray of lemonade and crystal glasses. Sam rose from the wicker rocker he'd been assigned and took the tray from her. Fayetta smiled and batted her lashes at him. "Why, thank you…Mr. Burke, wasn't it? Such a gentleman," she said to Abby. "A trait one finds all too rarely these days." Her blue gaze skimmed Agent Burke's dark suit approvingly. It wouldn't matter to Fayetta that he had to be melting in this heat. He looked dignified, and Fayetta came from an era where appearances meant everything. Abby suspected the woman would be wearing hoop skirts if she could find some.

As it was, her starched floral shirtwaist looked fresh and crisp, as if she'd donned it only moments before her callers had arrived. In comparison, Abby felt like something her cats had dragged in. The jeans and T-shirt she'd put on that morning in anticipation of tramping through woods and vacant lots had definitely seen better days. She could feel Fayetta's ladylike disdain rake over her as smoothly as a butter knife on cream frosting.

Fayetta handed her a glass of lemonade, and Abby gratefully accepted it, resisting the urge to touch the icy glass to the back of her neck.

"So tell me, Abigail. How is your mother? I haven't seen her in church in ages. Is she still feeling under the weather, poor dear?"

"Mama died three years ago, Miss Gibbons. Don't you remember? You played the organ at her funeral."

The blue eyes clouded momentarily, then cleared. "Yes, of course. 'Amazing Grace,' wasn't it? That was always Papa's favorite. I wore my navy dress, and Trixie

Baker did my hair that morning, but I didn't like the shade. It was too brassy, but Trixie insisted it made me look twenty years younger.'' Fayetta patted her impossibly blond hair, pulled back and done up in an elaborate bun—the same style she'd worn since the beginning of time. ''An outrageous lie, of course, but one is never too old to enjoy a compliment.'' She glanced at Agent Burke hopefully.

She'd seated him in the wicker rocker next to hers. Abby had been relegated to the porch steps, perhaps because of her age, but more likely because Fayetta, even though a spinster, was well practiced in the age-old Southern-Belle tradition of jockeying for the most desirable position next to an attractive gentleman.

But Fayetta needn't have troubled herself. Her subtle coquetry was lost on Agent Burke because he was no Southerner and, Abby suspected, at times no gentleman. He didn't quite grasp the expectations of an afternoon call, social or otherwise. He leaned forward, his expression almost stern as he dispensed with the niceties. ''Miss Gibbons, we'd like to ask you some questions about the little girl who disappeared from Ferguson's Drugstore yesterday afternoon.''

Stung by his abruptness, Fayetta sat back in her rocker, fanning herself vigorously with a fan from Grossman's Funeral Home. ''What's this all about, Abigail? The police have already been here. I told them I didn't see anything. I wasn't even home when that poor child was taken. Don't you think if I'd witnessed anything suspicious, I would have hollered all the way to Kingdom Come and back?''

''This is just routine,'' Abby soothed. ''We're talking to everyone who lives on this street. Sometimes people remember things after the initial interview. We came to your house first, that's all."

Fayetta gave her a narrowed look. "Have you talked to Gertie Ellers? She's always got her nose stuck where it doesn't belong."

"Unfortunately, Mrs. Ellers is in Biloxi with her daughter and grandchildren. She won't be home until next week.

Fayetta gave a very unladylike snort. "I declare, I don't know how anyone could put up with that woman for a whole week. Her daughter must have the patience of a saint is all I can think—"

"Miss Gibbons, these questions are very important," Agent Burke said impatiently.

The rocking stopped. The fanning ceased. Fayetta shot Abby a look as if to say, *How dare you bring this ill-mannered lout to my home?*

"Two little girls have gone missing," Abby explained. "We're doing everything we can to find them, but we haven't had much luck so far. I'm sure you'll forgive us if we sound a little...abrupt."

A pause, then after a moment, the rocking and fanning resumed. "It is a terrible tragedy," Fayetta conceded. "But I don't see how I can help."

"We're just trying to establish a routine for this street at the time of day that little Sara Beth went missing. If we get people to think about their whereabouts and activities, they may remember something that can help us."

"But I already told Sheriff Mooney I wasn't home. I left for the cemetery at three. Just like I did today. Just like I do every day."

Sam Burke started to say something, but Abby smoothly waved him off. "Did you walk east on First and then south on Peachtree, or did you take Maple down to Mimosa and then cut over to Peachtree?"

Fayetta scowled. "Does it matter?"

"Sara Beth was picked up from school by her father's secretary, Luanne Plimpton. According to Miss Plimpton, after they left the school grounds, she drove west on First Street in a silver Lincoln Town Car. We think they may have been followed from the school by Sara Beth's abductor. If you were walking east on First, toward Peachtree, you might have met them. You could have seen the car."

"I don't pay much attention to automobiles," Fayetta said doubtfully. "Although there was a time when I coveted a Studebaker Papa owned. It was a beautiful car, and it rode like a dream. He never let me drive it, of course, because Mama said that driving wasn't a seemly pastime for young ladies." She paused, flashing Abby a knowing look. "I'm sure you must find me hopelessly old-fashioned, Abigail. You Cross gals have always pretty much done as you pleased, and driving cars was the least of it."

A faint heat stole over Abby's face. She glanced at Sam Burke who was gazing back at her with…what? Curiosity? Disdain?

More like impatience, she thought. He had little use for all this idle chit-chat, and she knew if she didn't make headway soon with Fayetta, Agent Burke was liable to try and strong-arm information from the poor woman.

"As I said, the car Luanne Plimpton was driving was a silver Lincoln Town Car. It's a pretty big car," Abby added. "Do you remember seeing a car like that on First Street yesterday afternoon?"

Fayetta shook her head. "No, but I didn't go down First Street. I took Maple over to Mimosa, like you said. It's a little out of the way, but it's shadier. I can't take the heat like I once could. They say once you've suffered a heat-stroke, your tolerance for the sun is weakened.''

"What about your return trip? Did you come back the same way?''

"Yes, although by that time of day, First Street has a little shade, too, but I like to look at Inez Wentworth's garden. She grows roses, you know, but in this heat, you don't get much of a bloom—''

"What time did you get home?'' Abby cut in, her own patience slipping a bit.

"Why, Abigail,'' Fayetta said in a wounded tone. "You may have inherited the Cross disposition for trouble, but I know your mother and certainly your Grandmother Eulalia taught you better than to interrupt your elders.''

Abby sighed, running a hand through her damp hair. She avoided Sam Burke's dark gaze because she knew if her patience was running thin, his had evaporated altogether. "I'm sorry, Miss Gibbons. It's just that time is of the essence here. We have to find those little girls, no matter whose feelings we may trample on. Those children have to come first. I know you agree.''

Fayetta gave her a grudging nod. "Of course. Ask your questions, Abigail, but I still don't see—'' She stopped herself this time and clamped her lips together, as if that were the only way she could remain silent.

"What time do you think you left the cemetery?'' Abby asked.

Fayetta sighed. "It takes me fifteen minutes to walk to the cemetery. That is, if no one stops to talk with me and no one did yesterday. I visited with Mama and Papa for maybe another fifteen minutes, no more, because the heat was so unbearable.''

"So at 3:30, or thereabouts, you were already heading

back home on Mimosa. Did you see anything unusual, any strange cars in the neighborhood? Anything at all?''

"No, nothing like that. Except…'' Fayetta paused. "I don't know that I'd call it unusual, because from what I hear, those kids are always getting into some kind of mischief or other. But Tami Pratt's boys almost got hit by a car. I saw it with my own two eyes.''

"What happened?'' Sam Burke was gazing at the poor woman so intently, Abby almost felt sorry for her. Fayetta's fanning became even more vigorous.

"They were on those blasted skateboards.'' She looked extremely indignant. "And you know how kids are with those things. A body's not safe on the street. I don't know why something can't be done.''

Abby refrained from pointing out that there were worse activities for kids to engage in than skateboarding, but she'd heard about the Pratt boys. At thirteen and fifteen, Marcus and Mitchell had already been in a little trouble. Trespassing, vandalism—kid-type pranks that all too often escalated into more serious incidents. Abby jotted their names in her notebook.

"What happened?'' she asked.

"They started to cross the street at the corner of Mimosa and Maple, whooping and hollering, not paying any attention to where they were going. When they got into the middle of the street, a car came tearing down Maple. It missed them by only inches, I mean. The two boys started yelling at the driver and shaking their fists, but I think it must have shaken them up pretty badly because they took off like a pair of scalded dogs on those skateboards.''

"What about the car?'' Sam Burke queried. "Do you remember the color?''

"Of course. It was white, just like my Papa's Studebaker."

"Do you remember the make or model?"

She looked at him as if he were from a different planet.

"Was it old or new?" Abby supplied. "Ford, Chevrolet…"

Fayetta seemed at a loss. "Well, I don't think it was old," she finally said. "But I can't swear that it was new, either. And I don't know one brand of car from the other. Except for Studebakers. But you don't see many of those these days."

"What about dents or scratches, anything about it that might have stood out in your mind?"

She shook her head. "No. It was just a white car."

"Two-door or four-door?"

"I—I'm not sure."

"Did the driver get out of the car?" Agent Burke asked.

"No, but I imagine he was shaken up as well. You know how people like to sue these days, and from what I hear, Tami Pratt doesn't have a nickel to her name since that no-good husband of hers took off with Wanda Jean—"

"How long did the driver remain at the intersection?"

"No more than a second or two. Then he drove off like the devil himself was after him."

"He?"

Fayetta hesitated. "I say he. I guess I still assume all drivers are men, but that's not the case these days, is it? It could have been a woman."

"You didn't get a look at the driver's face?" Abby asked.

"There wasn't time. It all happened so fast, and I think he was wearing a cap or something. I was more concerned about the child in the back seat. She wasn't wearing a seat belt. It's a thousand wonders that poor little thing wasn't thrown clean through the windshield."

"YEAH, RIGHT, you're an FBI agent," Marcus Pratt jeered an hour later when they'd tracked the boys down and Sam had introduced himself. As their mother had suggested, Sam and Abby had found the boys skateboarding at an abandoned gas station a few blocks from their home, blithely ignoring the No Trespassing signs posted in conspicuous areas.

"What makes you think I'm not FBI?" Sam asked.

"Because you're way too old, man. I bet you couldn't chase down a crook if your life depended on it."

"We can't all look like Agent Mulder," Sam said, nodding toward the "X-Files" T-shirt the younger boy wore. He glanced at Abby and saw that she was trying hard, without much success, to hide a grin. She would find this amusing, he thought dryly, especially after he'd come down so hard on her after the interview with Fayetta Gibbons.

"Didn't you people even talk to that woman? We should have known about that car twenty-four hours ago. It could have made all the difference."

"You don't know that," Abby had retorted. *"Sara Beth might not have been the child Fayetta saw in the back seat. And besides, if it hadn't been for me, we still wouldn't even know about the white car, and we wouldn't know about the other two possible witnesses. I didn't see you glean much information from her, especially after you alienated her five seconds into the interview."*

She was right, of course. Abby had an easy rapport with the locals that made them trust her in a way they never would an outsider. But that knowledge didn't lessen Sam's frustration. In truth, it probably added to it.

He didn't know why Abby Cross grated on his nerves the way she did, or why he felt an almost compulsive need to pick an argument with her and to find fault with her. Maybe it was the heat and the tension of working a life-and-death case.

Or maybe it was because he just didn't want to acknowledge the sexual tension that had been dancing between them like a live wire all afternoon.

She's too young for you, a voice warned inside his head. *Too young and too naive.*

But, unfortunately, his body was telling him something else.

Marcus Pratt's derisive snicker drew Sam's attention back to the conversation with an unpleasant thud. "Agent Mulder you definitely ain't," the kid taunted. "Skinner maybe," he added, alluding to an older—and balder—character on the same show.

Sam suppressed the urge to run his hand through his hair—still thick in most places—along with the desire to muzzle the boy's smart mouth. At fifteen, Marcus Pratt had obviously developed an unhealthy contempt for authority figures, male ones especially. It was an attitude that would likely carry him far in life. First to school detention. Then juvenile hall. Then prison, if something didn't happen to get him back on track.

Sam recognized the type. The father had deserted the family, leaving a young mother to cope with the difficulties of raising two boys. But Tami Pratt was no shrinking violet. Sam had gotten the impression that the woman's personality could be a bit overwhelming at times, and her oldest son was desperately trying to assert his masculine dominance. To make matters worse, he was slight for his age. What he lacked in stature, he tried to make up for in bluster.

His thirteen-year-old brother was almost as tall, but there was no mistaking the pecking order. Mitchell hung back, swiping his dirty blond hair out of his face while he allowed his brother to do all the talking.

"We'd like to ask you boys a few questions, if you don't mind," Abby said.

Marcus cocked his head toward her. "So who's she supposed to be? Agent Scully?"

His insolent gaze raked over Abby's jeans and T-shirt in a manner that set Sam's teeth on edge. Was it his imagination, or had Sergeant Cross's clothing gotten more snug as the day wore on?

Apparently he shared the same image with Marcus Pratt. The kid gave a low whistle. "Not bad," he muttered, staring at Abby in a way no kid should be allowed to.

Leering should be reserved for dirty old men, Sam decided. Like himself.

"I'm Sergeant Cross," Abby said coolly, flashing her ID in Marcus's face. Her shield was clipped to the waistband of her jeans, and she made sure the kid saw it. "I'm a detective with the Jefferson County Sheriff's Department. We're investigating the disappearances of two little girls."

"So? What do you expect us to do about it? Pin a medal on you or something?" He glanced at his grinning brother.

"The girls' names are Emily Campbell and Sara Beth Brodie. Maybe you heard about the disappearances on the news?" When he merely stared at her sullenly, Abby's mouth tightened. "We have reason to believe you two boys were in the vicinity at the time Sara Beth Brodie went missing."

Marcus flicked back a long strand of hair from his face. "What do we look like, kidnappers?"

"We're not accusing you of anything. But we've got a witness who can place you on Mimosa Street near Holyoke Cemetery at around 3:30 yesterday afternoon."

"You ain't got squat," the kid said with practiced aplomb. "We were home all afternoon. Right, Mitch?"

The younger boy swallowed and nodded, his gaze darting first to Sam and then back to his brother. "Uh, yeah."

"That's not exactly what your mother told us," Sam said.

Marcus's face turned beet red. "You already talked to our old lady about this? Hell, man. What'd you have to go and do that for?"

At last, a chink in the kid's armor, Sam thought.

"Let's try this again," Abby said, pushing her dark hair behind her ears. "Were you and your brother on Mimosa Street yesterday or not?"

Another glance passed between the two boys. "What if we were?"

"Were you almost hit by a car?"

His gaze narrowed. "How'd you know—" He clammed up, realizing he'd given himself away.

"About that car," Abby said firmly. "Do you remember what color it was?"

"Maybe white. Maybe not."

"Was it white or wasn't it?" Sam demanded.

Marcus slanted him a surly glance, almost daring Sam to get violent with him. "I wasn't talking to you."

Sam took the kid's arm, not applying enough pressure to hurt him, but making sure the boy knew he meant business. "Now you listen to me, kid. Two little girls are missing. Their lives are at stake. I don't have the time or the patience for your attitude. You're a bad ass. Okay. We got it. Now answer Sergeant Cross's questions." He didn't say "or else." He didn't have to.

Something that might have been respect glimmered in the boy's eyes before he replaced it with a scowl. He rubbed his arm. "The car was white."

"Did you recognize the make or model?" Abby asked, flashing Sam a look he couldn't quite fathom.

Marcus shrugged. "How should I know? I didn't hang around long enough to find out." But he eased away from Sam as he said it.

"It was a Chevy," Mitchell said, speaking up for the first time. "Maybe a '91 or '92 Caprice. Something like that."

Sam gazed down at the boy. "You sure about that, son?"

"Don't call him son," Marcus snapped. "You're not his old man."

"I know cars," Mitchell said shyly. "My dad's got a '67 Camaro we aim to fix up."

"Yeah, right. When hell freezes over," Marcus muttered.

"Mitchell." Sam walked over and put his hand on the boy's shoulder. It was thin and bony, making him seem younger than his age and vulnerable somehow.

For a moment, Sam's heart seemed to stop. It had been a long time since he'd been around kids. After their son had died, he and Norah had cut themselves off from friends and acquaintances with children. Eventually, they'd cut themselves off from each other. Norah had found solace in her own way, and Sam had immersed himself in work, in cases so sordid and gruesome he had no time to think of his own misery. To wonder what might have been.

But as he gazed down at Mitchell Pratt, he suddenly

saw another boy's eyes staring up at him. He suddenly wondered if he would have been the kind of father a son would be proud of. The kind of father a boy could count on.

He wondered if he would have been a better father than he had been a husband.

Not that it mattered. He'd lost Jonathan to cancer, Norah to neglect, and Sam didn't plan to ever remarry. And now he was too old to start a family, even if he wanted to, which he didn't. Jonathan could never be replaced, and besides, if he'd learned anything in his twenty-year journey into darkness, it was that too damned much of this world was not a nice place for children.

Even a town called Eden.

He glanced at Abby and found that she was gazing back at him. Her expression was puzzled, as if she'd glimpsed something in him that she hadn't expected to see. That he might not want her to see.

His grasp on Mitchell's shoulder tightened almost imperceptibly. "You're certain about everything you told us?" he asked again.

Mitchell nodded solemnly.

"He knows a lot about cars," Marcus said grudgingly. "He hangs around garages every chance he gets. If Mitchell says it was a Caprice, then that's what it was."

"What about a license-plate number?" Sam asked hopefully.

They both shook their heads.

"Either of you get a look at the driver?"

Marcus shrugged. "Other than the fact that the guy was a lousy driver, I didn't pay much attention to him."

"Was anyone else in the car?" Abby asked.

"Didn't see anyone else."

"Not even in the back seat? A child maybe?"

"Look, I said I didn't see anyone else, okay?"

"What about you, Mitchell?" Sam asked softly. "You see anyone else in the car?"

"Naw." The boy shook his head. "But I didn't really look."

"Then how can you be certain the driver was male?"

"He had on a baseball cap," Marcus said. "And sunglasses. I guess it could have been a chick. But not like Agent Scully here. Her, I would've remembered."

Abby gave him a cool smile and a card. "You boys think of anything else that might help us out, give me a call at this number."

She handed Mitchell a card, too, and he gazed at it for a moment, then stuffed it in his pocket. To Sam he said shyly, "Could I have one of your cards, too?"

Sam fished a card out of his pocket and handed it to the boy. It had the FBI seal on the front and a number at Quantico. "Cool," Mitchell said. "I never met an FBI agent before."

"Yeah," Marcus agreed dryly. "It's been a real thrill."

Chapter Four

"One more stop before we go back to the station," Abby told Sam as they headed toward downtown.

"Dinner?" he suggested, taking his eyes off the road long enough to give her a hopeful glance.

"We can stop at a convenience store and grab a hot dog and some chips if you're hungry."

Sam winced. "I can wait."

Abby was hungry, too, but she was used to eating on the run or skipping meals altogether, and her schedule had been even more chaotic since the abductions. There'd been so much to do, so many people to interview, leads, such as they were, to follow, that her appetite had been the least of her worries. The rumbling of her stomach now, however, reminded her that she was human. That she couldn't function on adrenaline and sheer determination forever.

But if they stopped for dinner, they'd have to make small talk. They'd have to reveal parts of themselves— no matter how innocuous—to one another as a matter of courtesy. And Abby didn't want that. She didn't want to know anything about Sam Burke's life, and she didn't want him knowing about hers. She didn't want to invite an intimacy that seemed to be hovering just beneath the surface with every spoken word, with every glance.

The attraction she felt for Sam Burke was unwanted, unwelcome and very unwise. She knew better than anyone what such an explosive chemistry could do to one's scruples and inhibitions. All she had to do was look at her own family.

"So where to?" he asked, drumming his thumb on the steering wheel.

"Vickie Wilder's apartment." She gave him directions. "You said you wanted to talk to her, right? I figured the sooner, the better."

He glanced at her as he signaled for a right turn. "Are you always this...focused?"

Abby shrugged. "I try to be. Anything wrong with that?"

"No." But he hesitated before he said so, making Abby wonder what he was thinking. She couldn't shake the notion that he disapproved of her for some reason. Because she was a woman? Because she was a local? Because he was attracted to her, too?

"Look, about what I said earlier, after the interview with Fayetta Gibbons—" he began tentatively, but Abby cut him off.

"You mean when you accused me of incompetence?"

He scowled at the road. "I never said that."

"But that was the implication, wasn't it? That I'd somehow bungled the initial interview?" Abby glared at him then glanced away. It was hard to meet his gaze. Hard to look him in the eye and not give herself away. Hard, even in anger, not to acknowledge in some small way the awareness tingling through her.

"I was out of line and I apologize," he said quietly.

His words left Abby momentarily speechless because

they were so unexpected. In a male-dominated environment, apologies were few and far between. "I—don't need an apology," she said a bit defensively. "I just want you to realize how hard everyone in my department is working to find those little girls. All we want is to bring them home safely."

"That's what we all want." He stopped at a traffic light and turned to face her. His gaze was deep and very intense, and Abby couldn't help but wonder at the shadows in his eyes.

Be careful of a man with secrets, her grandmother would have cautioned her, but Abby didn't need the warning. There was no way she would ever get involved with a man like Sam Burke, a man who would be here today and gone tomorrow.

That mercurial quality in the opposite sex had always been a magnet for the women in her family, but Abby was determined to break the pattern. She wouldn't travel down the same road to heartbreak that her grandmother, mother and sister had all taken. She had a different set of priorities, but somehow, in the space of a few hours, Sam Burke had managed to threaten those convictions.

She could feel his curious gaze on her, but Abby turned to stare out the window. If she didn't look into his eyes, she'd be okay, she decided.

The light changed, and the car pulled forward. Neither of them said anything else until Abby directed him into the parking lot of a small apartment complex in downtown Eden.

The entire complex consisted of four units—each containing four apartments, two up and two down—built in a semicircle around a central courtyard that had once featured a three-tiered clay fountain ringed with flower beds. The terra-cotta bowls were dry now and filled with dead leaves and pinecones, and all that remained in the flower beds were a few droopy petunias.

Abby led the way up the stairs of the second building and knocked on Vickie Wilder's door. Several moments later, the door opened a crack, and a young woman peeped out.

"Yes?" When she saw Abby, she drew back the door, her hand flying to her heart. "Sergeant Cross. Oh, my, God. Have you found Emily? And Sara Beth?" She spoke the second name hesitantly, as if she'd momentarily forgotten there'd been another abduction.

Abby said, "No, I'm afraid we haven't found either child. This is Special Agent Sam Burke with the FBI. He'd like to ask you a few questions."

Vickie Wilder's gaze flicked from Abby to Sam, then back to Abby. Her hand crept to the neckline of the black T-shirt she wore over jeans. "But...I've already spoken with the police on several occasions. I don't know what else I can tell you."

"You may be surprised," Sam said cryptically. "Things often come to light after the first or second interview. May we come in?" His voice was courteous, but firm, brooking no argument.

"Of course." She stepped back to allow them to enter.

Abby glanced around as they walked into the small apartment. She'd interviewed Vickie twice after Emily's disappearance, once at the sheriff's station and once at school. And after Sara Beth's disappearance, she and Dave Conyers had conducted a group interview of all the teachers and school personnel in the cafeteria at Fairhaven, going over a list of routine questions. In the one-on-one interviews, Abby had been struck by the young woman's eagerness to cooperate and by her obvious devotion to her students. She'd barely been able to finish a sentence without tearing up.

Tonight, however, there was something different about her. She appeared more nervous than distraught, her hands flitting from her lap to her hair, then back again to her lap. She couldn't seem to remain still, and her gaze kept darting about the room, as if she were worried she'd left a pair of underwear lying in the middle of the floor.

Or something far more incriminating, Abby thought.

As Sam began the interview, Abby tried to study the young teacher with a fresh perspective. Had she been wrong about Vickie? Had the affection for her students been nothing more than an act?

Abby didn't think so. She was trained to spot inconsistencies, and unless Vickie was an exceptionally gifted actress, her distress following Emily's abduction had been genuine.

But why was she so nervous now?

Abby watched her carefully during the interview, looking for other telltale signs of agitation. She was a small woman, no more than five-three or five-four, and slightly built. Her hair was cut in a short, boyish style that flattered her gamin features, and her green eyes, behind thick, black-rimmed glasses, looked soft and earnest.

Abby had learned from her interviews with the parents of some of Vickie's students that she was a much-beloved teacher. Kind, sweet and very concerned with each child's welfare. "Even a bit meddlesome at times," one parent had confided. "But she means well. And the kids adore her."

"Both Sara Beth Brodie and Emily Campbell are in your kindergarten class at Fairhaven, is that right?" Sam was asking.

Vickie nodded. "Yes, that's right."

"Are they friends?"

"It's a small class. All the children are friends."

"Let me clarify," he said. "Did they play together at recess? Have sleepovers? Things like that?"

Vickie hesitated. "They weren't *best* friends, if that's what you mean. They didn't play together exclusively."

"Were they on a sports team together? Soccer, for instance?"

"Not that I know of."

"Did you ever take the class on field trips or outings of any kind?"

"Not yet. The school year has barely gotten under way." She frowned, glancing at Abby. "I don't understand where all these questions are leading."

"I'm trying to establish when and where Emily and Sara Beth may have come into contact with some of the same people, other than at school," Sam explained.

Vickie made a helpless gesture with her hand. "They live in a small town. They come into contact with the same people all the time. Everyone does. Besides, shouldn't you be asking their parents these questions?"

"Oh, I will," Sam said. "You can count on that. But in the meantime, I'm sure you want to do everything you can to find both Emily and Sara Beth."

The subtle inference that she might desire otherwise took both Abby and Vickie aback. But where Abby managed to keep her expression neutral, Vickie's face turned quite pale. "I would do anything for those children," she said passionately, almost angrily. *"Anything."*

Sam nodded. "Good. Then just a few more questions…"

As he continued, Abby's gaze traveled over the apartment. The living room was neat and compact, like Vickie herself, but the furnishings were eclectic—contemporary bookcases intermixed with antique tables and fringed lampshades—suggesting a more complex personality.

On the end table beside Abby were several framed photographs. One was of an older couple who, judging by the resemblance, were Vickie's parents or grandparents, and another photo had captured a teenage Vickie in the arms of a handsome young man. She and the boy looked to be about sixteen or seventeen in the picture and very much in love. The backdrop was a wooden building with a crescent moon cut out near the roof.

Something about the picture touched a glimmer of recognition in Abby. A fleeting memory that was gone before it had ever clearly formed. She frowned at the photo—

"Sergeant Cross? Anything you want to add?"

She turned to find Sam's curious gaze on her. "No, I think we've taken enough of Miss Wilder's time this evening." Abby stood. "Thank you for your cooperation."

Vickie walked them to the door. "I meant what I said. I would do anything for those children. For any of my students. The thought of someone hurting them—" She broke off, her eyes filling with tears behind her glasses.

"I understand that you indicated after Emily's abduction you would be willing to take a polygraph," Sam said at the door. He turned back to face her. "Are you still willing?"

She had a tissue to her eyes, and she took a moment to dab away the tears before answering. When she glanced up at Sam, her gaze was still very bright. "Does this mean you consider me a suspect?"

"Everyone in this town is a suspect, Miss Wilder. Would you still be willing to take a polygraph?" he pressed.

"Yes," she said quietly. "But I think it would be in my best interest to consult with an attorney first."

"THIS IS THE FIRST TIME she mentioned anything about an attorney," Abby said as they drove back to the sheriff's station. The whole interview had left her oddly disturbed. After Emily's disappearance, Abby had been so certain they could write off Vickie Wilder as a suspect. The woman had been shattered by the abduction.

But today Abby had seen a different Vickie Wilder. A nervous, reticent woman who'd indicated she might want to consult with a lawyer before further cooperation with the authorities.

Of course, her anxiety could be attributed to Sam's presence. Guilty or innocent, it was an unnerving experience being questioned by the FBI. Abby said as much to Sam.

His response was to ask what kind of car Vickie Wilder drove.

"Not a white Caprice, if that's what you're thinking," Abby told him. "She owns a five-year-old dark blue Mustang. I saw it myself at Fairhaven."

"Any anomalies turn up in her background check?"

"You mean priors?"

"I mean anything."

Abby shrugged. "Not so far. She grew up in Memphis, got her degree from Memphis State University, and taught for a semester at a public school in Germantown before getting the job at Fairhaven. No record. Not so much as an unpaid parking ticket."

"Have you talked to any of her friends or family, the people closest to her?"

"No. There's been no reason to regard her as a suspect, other than the obvious fact that she came into contact on a daily basis with both Emily and Sara Beth. But she was one of the teachers assigned to the playground the day

Emily disappeared. I interviewed her myself. She was almost incoherent she was so upset.''

Sam didn't say anything, but Abby knew what he was thinking. Better cops than she had been fooled before.

''Look, what is it you think you got from that interview?'' she demanded.

''I don't know. Something about her—'' He broke off, frowning, as if he couldn't quite put his finger on what he meant. ''I don't think Vickie Wilder is a straight shooter, Abby. I think she's hiding something.''

Abby's heart gave a painful lurch. ''About Emily and Sara Beth?''

He lifted a hand from the steering wheel to massage the back of his neck. ''Maybe. Or maybe something else made her jumpy. Maybe it was my presence, as you suggested. But I've got a friend who works in the field office in Memphis. I'd like to give him a call, have him ask a few questions in Vickie's old neighborhood. See what he can turn up.''

''Sure,'' Abby readily agreed. ''If you think it's warranted.''

They pulled into a parking slot in front of the sheriff's station, and Sam turned off the engine. The reporters who had been hanging around outside the front entrance that morning had either all gone home for the day or were over at the command post hoping to get a tip from one of the volunteers.

''So what now?'' He rested his arm across the back of the seat. His hand didn't touch her hair, but it was close.

Abby's heart gave a funny little skip, but she managed to shrug. ''We get some rest, and then we start all over again tomorrow.''

Don't look into his eyes! that little voice warned her. She was being ridiculous and she knew it, but even so, she turned to gaze out the window. It was late, twilight, a time of day that always made her feel restless. She would be going home soon to a dark, empty house. To a meal she would prepare and eat alone. To a bed that could be cold and lonely, even in summer.

Abby had a sudden image of sitting down to eat with Sam Burke. Of lingering at the table over a glass of wine. Of talking long into the night. And then, when both the wine and conversation were spent...

What kind of lover would he be?

The question astounded her, and Abby almost jumped at the direction her thoughts had taken. She glanced at Sam nervously. Was he wondering the same thing about her? Was it her imagination, or had he leaned slightly toward her, as if he meant to—

Oh, no, she thought, her breath catching in her throat. What if he tried to kiss her? How would she rebuke him? Like an offended woman? Like an officer of the law?

What if she did neither? What if she simply kissed him back?

No, no, no! her common sense screamed. She'd always made it a point never to mix business with pleasure. She'd promised herself long ago she wouldn't get involved with another cop. That was a surefire way to kill a promising career, because fair or not, the double standard for men and women still prevailed in law enforcement. A male officer involved in an affair didn't run the same risk of ruining his reputation and losing the respect of his colleagues as a female officer did. Abby had seen it happen, and she had no intention of taking such a chance. Not with Sam Burke. Not with anyone.

She opened her mouth to say just that, but then she realized the intensity of his gaze wasn't because of her.

He'd become lost in thought. He wasn't even seeing her. He'd never had any intention of kissing her.

Abby felt her face flame at her assumption, at how close she'd come to making a complete and utter fool of herself with Sam Burke.

Good going, she chided herself as she opened the car door. *Nothing like a little humiliation to put a pesky libido back in its cage.*

ABBY DIDN'T GET HOME until almost ten that night. After she and Sam had gotten back to the station and gone their separate ways, she'd put in a few hours with the printouts she'd requested from the state crime center.

Since Emily's abduction, Abby had pulled a dozen or so names of possibles from the list of known child molesters and predators in the area, as well as from a list of inmates recently released from prison. As time allowed, she'd been checking out each name that sounded promising, but the results so far had produced no real suspects. Some of the men were back in prison. A couple were dead. Several others had concrete alibis.

The work was frustrating and tedious, but Abby had stayed with it until the names on the printouts had begun to blur together and she'd been forced to call it a night.

But in spite of her exhaustion, she was too wound up to sleep. A glass of wine hadn't helped her relax, and neither had a hot bath. Nothing in her grandmother's house, which Abby had inherited when her mother had died three years ago, had been able to soothe her.

She would have liked to sit in the garden for a while, but as late as it was, the mosquitoes would be unbearable. She compromised by curling up in a rocking chair next to the window in her grandmother's sewing room, where she could gaze out at the lightning bugs flitting through the darkness.

An ache welled inside her for the loss of her grandmother and her mother. For Sadie. For little Sara Beth Brodie and Emily Campbell.

"Please let us find them," she whispered to the darkness. "And let them be alive."

After a few moments, the inaction filled her with despair. She returned to the living room and the stack of files she'd brought home, and for a long time, she sat on the floor, going over the reports, reading witness interviews, studying photos shot at both crime scenes. But nothing made sense to her. She didn't have enough pieces of the puzzle to see anything clearly. Something was still missing, and if she didn't find it soon, Abby was very much afraid those little girls would remain lost forever.

Rubbing her stiff neck, she glanced at her watch. Almost midnight. Long past her bedtime. She couldn't keep doing this for much longer. She couldn't continue to work fifteen hours a day, and then come home to fret about the cases for the rest of the night. She had to get some rest. Dropping from exhaustion wouldn't help find those children.

But once in her bedroom, Abby found herself slipping into fresh jeans and a T-shirt rather than into her pajamas. Grabbing her keys, she ran out to her car and within minutes she was pulling to the curb in front of Fairhaven Academy.

This time of night, the school was dark and deserted. A little spooky, with its three stories of windows and ivy-covered walls. There were streetlights around the perimeter of the grounds and the moon was up, but much of the light was blocked by a thick canopy of leaves from the towering oak and pecan trees.

As Abby climbed out of her car and stood gazing at the school, an unnatural hush seemed to hang over the night. But in the silence, she could have sworn she heard the echo of children's laughter. Could have sworn she saw one of the swings on the playground move in the breeze.

Crossing the street, she jumped a small ditch and scrambled up a slight embankment to the sidewalk that ran parallel to the playground. In spite of Sadie's disappearance ten years ago, the grounds remained unfenced. The playground equipment was a good hundred yards from the sidewalk, however, and Lois Sheridan, the director, had assured Abby that the children were never left unsupervised. At least two teachers from each grade were with the students at all times.

But a fence, such a meager expense in hindsight, might have prevented Emily Campbell's disappearance. It would not, however, have stopped Sara Beth's abductor from grabbing her in Ferguson's Drugstore.

In spite of the heat, a chill crept up Abby's backbone as she made her way around the darkened school yard. Somewhere down the street, a dog barked and a slight wind ruffled leaves overhead. The back of her neck prickled with unease.

Don't be an idiot, she scolded herself sternly. She was a police detective, armed and—she liked to think—dangerous to the criminal element. Nothing to be nervous about. Nothing to be afraid of.

But she found herself humming an aimless little tune as she checked all the ground-level doors and windows that faced the playground. So many, and yet no one had seen anything. No one had been watching from any of those windows when Sadie and Emily had been taken from this very school yard.

Something brushed against her leg, and Abby jumped, then let out a nervous laugh when she looked down and saw a skinny gray cat rubbing itself against her.

"Don't you know better than to sneak up on a girl with a gun," she whispered, kneeling to pet the stray. "And why am I whispering, for heaven sakes? There's no one here but you and me."

But she'd scarcely spoken the words when a shadow moved on the playground, not fifty feet away.

Her heart hammering, Abby froze. Kneeling as she was near the building, she didn't think she could be spotted. Her hand idly soothed the cat's fur as she tried to calm her racing pulse. She peered through the darkness and saw the shadow again.

It was a man. Large. Tall. Stealthily moving through the playground equipment and the trees.

Suddenly, he stopped and turned to gaze at the street. Moonlight reflected on his profile, and Abby caught her breath.

The man was Sam Burke.

She'd been reaching for her weapon when she recognized him, and now Abby let her hand fall to her side as she watched him. He knelt on the playground, and for the longest moment, for an eternity it seemed, he remained motionless, watching the street. It was almost as if he were putting himself on the level of a five-year-old child, Abby thought.

After several long moments, he stood and strode to the street. Abby thought he was leaving, but instead, he positioned himself on the sidewalk so that he had an unobstructed view of the playground. And, as he had moments before, he stilled himself as he studied the landscape, as if he'd placed himself in some sort of trance.

Another chill swept over Abby, and she started violently when the cat dashed off suddenly into the shadows. Distracted, she watched the animal for a moment before turning back to Sam.

The street was deserted.

In the space of a heartbeat, he'd vanished. Like Sadie. Like Emily. Like Sara Beth Brodie.

No, not like them, Abby thought, moving around to the side of the building. Sam Burke was a grown man. A federal agent. He could take care of himself. Those little girls couldn't.

Still, there was something about him....

Those eyes...

Abby wouldn't let herself finish the thought. Nor would she let herself be spooked away from her mission. She continued her exploration of the school yard, moving slowly, methodically, trying to imagine the scene as it had been on the afternoons the abductions had occurred.

The classrooms and playground were the farthest from the street, but the building housing the administrative offices came within only a few yards of the sidewalk. Was it possible one of the doors had been left open and the abductor had entered the building to lie in wait until he could somehow lure Emily back inside? Had he watched Sara Beth from one of the classroom windows?

The supervising teachers would have been keeping an eye on the street. They wouldn't have been worried if one of the children had gone back inside.

Out of habit, Abby tried one of the doors now. It was locked tight. She kept moving about the school until she came to the back, where an alley ran adjacent to the building. Cafeteria deliveries were made here, judging by the pile of food boxes stacked near the Dumpsters.

Someone posing as a delivery man—even a legitimate delivery person—would have access to the building. Might even be familiar enough with the school to find his way in and out quickly. But could he move about undetected carrying a terrified child?

What if she wasn't terrified? What if she knew the abductor?

Abby walked over to the boxes and shone her flashlight beam over the labels. Out of the corner of her eye, she saw a movement near the building. Whirling, she caught a fleeting glimpse of a shadow as something launched itself directly toward her.

Abby gasped and reached for her weapon as she automatically stepped back. Her foot encountered one of the boxes, and she went sprawling, losing her grip on the flashlight. She clung to her gun as a cardboard avalanche tumbled over her. In a panic, she fought her way up through the boxes.

Nearby, the cat scurried toward the trash bins, scrounging for food. That had been the movement Abby had seen. A flash of gray fur. A shadow magnified by the moonlight.

She reached up and wiped away a trickle of blood from a scratch on her forehead.

"Great," she muttered, retrieving her flashlight. She was glad no one else was about so word of her attack couldn't get back to the station. That's all her male colleagues needed to hear.

Sergeant Abby Cross, fearless female detective, cold-cocked by a scrawny stray cat.

SARA BETH AWAKENED to darkness. And to voices.

Her first thought was that her mama and daddy were fighting again, but then she remembered that she wasn't in her room or her bed. She wasn't exactly sure what this place was, but she knew it wasn't home. She knew her mama wasn't just down the hall.

Lying very still, she listened to the urgent murmurs in the darkness. She thought she knew one of the voices. The familiar sound should have made her feel better, but it didn't. Sara Beth couldn't understand why she'd been brought here. Why she wasn't allowed to go outside and play when it was daytime. Why there were dark curtains over the windows. Why she couldn't just go home.

She didn't understand, but she knew enough to be afraid.

Squeezing her eyes closed, she fought back tears as she strained to listen to those voices.

"...can't stay here. It isn't safe and you know it. Someone could stumble across this place."

"We have to stay," the voice that Sara Beth thought she knew said angrily. "It's too risky to move her."

"Then what," said the first voice, in a tone that sent a chill up Sara Beth's spine, "do you suggest we do with her?"

EMILY AWAKENED to darkness. And to silence.

But she wasn't alone. She could feel invisible eyes watching her from the deep shadows of the room, and she huddled more deeply under the cover. She was very frightened, even though she hadn't been hurt. She'd been given plenty of food and water. Dolls to play with. Pretty clothes to wear. But she wasn't allowed to watch TV or go outside, and she wasn't allowed to call her mama.

That frightened her most of all. If she couldn't call home, how would her mama know where to find her? How would she be able to come and get her?

And Emily desperately wanted her mama to come and get her. She didn't like it here. In spite of the pretty dresses and the dolls, she didn't like this place. She wanted her own toys and her favorite Pooh pajamas and the soft, pink quilt her Grandma JoJo had made for her. She wanted her own room and her own bed, but most of all, she wanted her mama.

She started to sob softly into her pillow, and a voice said from the shadows, "Hush, child. Hush, now. You'll be with your mama real soon."

Chapter Five

By the time Abby got to work the next morning, she was operating almost entirely on caffeine and sheer determination, chased with a large dose of desperation. Having to dodge reporters lying in wait outside the sheriff's station didn't improve her mood much, either.

Plopping her folders on the table in the small conference room off the sheriff's office, she settled in for the morning briefing, going over the remaining names she'd compiled from the printouts the night before while she waited for everyone else to arrive.

Of the ones she'd yet to check out, the most promising was a man named Bobby Lee Hatcher from Palisades, a tiny community near the Louisiana border. He'd been arrested for the aggravated assault and kidnapping of a local businessman's daughter nearly ten years ago, and had served nine years in Parchman. He'd gotten out of prison a month before Emily had gone missing.

Nine years, Abby thought, as she stared at his name. He'd been arrested for kidnapping in October after Sadie had disappeared in August. Could he be the one?

Unlike the other people whose names she'd taken from

the printouts, Bobby Lee Hatcher resided beyond the hundred-mile radius of Eden that Abby had set as a parameter. He was a long shot. A very long shot, but when children were missing, no stone could be left unturned.

After the morning briefing, Abby talked to Sheriff Mooney about making a trip down south to check him out.

"I called Sheriff McElroy down in Palisades this morning," she told him. "He's faxing me the guy's rap sheet. He said after Hatcher was released from prison, he came back to stay with his grandmother, but McElroy hasn't seen anything of him lately. He said Hatcher used to hang around with an older cousin. He didn't remember the guy's name or anything else about him except that he was one heck of an auto mechanic. But he thinks if we find the cousin, we may be able to find Bobby Lee. I'd like to drive down and talk to the grandmother, see what I can get from her."

"Think anything will come of it?" Sheriff Mooney asked her.

Abby shrugged. "I don't know. Palisades is a long way from Eden, but I'd like to go down there and check it out just the same. I thought I'd ask Special Agent Burke to ride along."

Sheriff Mooney sat down heavily behind his desk, his expression troubled. "Actually, I need to talk to you about Sam Burke."

"What about him?" Abby's heart skipped a beat at the sheriff's ominous tone, but she was careful to keep her expression neutral.

"You spent some time with him yesterday. What'd you think?"

Other than the fact that he had the coldest eyes she'd

ever looked into? Other than the fact that she'd felt an immediate attraction to him in spite of their animosity?

She shrugged. "I didn't think much about him one way or another. He seems to know his job. Anything else I *should* know?"

Sheriff Mooney picked up the phone and said something to his secretary. After a moment, the door to his office opened and a tall, blond man walked in. The guy was extremely easy on the eyes, the kind who would have set most female hearts a-flutter. But Abby didn't feel so much as a twinge when she looked up at him. He just wasn't her type.

And Sam Burke is? a little voice asked sarcastically.

Oh, what do you know? she countered.

That same little voice had steered her grandmother, her mother and her sister into relationships that had all ended disastrously. Those breathtakingly handsome men had all moved on to greener pastures, leaving the women in Abby's family behind with broken hearts and fatherless children. Abby's dad had stuck around longer than most. He'd sired two daughters before taking off to parts unknown.

"Abby, this is Special Agent Talbot Carter. He's the agent we were expecting from the field office in Jackson yesterday afternoon. This is Sergeant Abby Cross. She's working the Brodie investigation."

Carter's brows rose as he turned back to Sheriff Mooney, barely acknowledging Abby's presence. "I would have thought someone with more experience would be assigned to these cases."

"Sergeant Cross is a very able investigator," Sheriff Mooney assured him.

But the agent didn't seem convinced. He gave Abby a cool, dismissive look, one she'd seen too many times in the past. The fact that her age and gender, rather than her ability, were still issues rankled. But she knew enough to keep her mouth shut. Contrary to Carter's opinion of her, Abby had enough experience to know that some people's opinions regarding women in law enforcement were never going to change.

"Abby, Special Agent Carter here needs to ask you a few questions about Sam Burke."

Abby glanced at Talbot Carter in surprise. "What kind of questions?"

"Questions about his possible whereabouts. Sam Burke lied to you and Sheriff Mooney yesterday, Sergeant Cross. He's not assigned to this case. In fact, he's not assigned to any case. He resigned from the FBI a month ago."

A chill ran down Abby's spine. "Are you saying he's down here flashing around fake credentials?"

"Oh, his creds are authentic," Carter said. "He used to be a profiler with the Investigative Support Unit at Quantico. If you saw the movie *Silence of the Lambs* you got a somewhat glamorized version of what they do there. Burke still consults on cases, and he teaches criminal personality profiling at the Academy. But he's no longer a special agent."

The irony was more than a little unnerving to Abby. Profiling had been a dream of hers for years, a secret ambition that had been carefully tucked away long ago, just like the acceptance letter from the FBI Academy she'd received after completing her masters in criminology at Ole Miss. The letter now resided in the farthest corner of her top dresser drawer where Abby had put it the same day she'd received it, never to look at it again.

The ambition had been a little harder to ignore, but over the years, she'd come to terms with it. She'd come to accept the fact that she would never leave Eden. Not as long as her sister harbored the hope that Sadie could still be found, and that if anyone could find her, it was Abby.

"In the last ten years, Burke's worked nearly every major serial killer case in the country," Carter was saying.

"*Serial killer?* Is that why he's here?"

"To be honest, we don't know why he's here," Carter admitted grimly. "We know our office didn't contact him for assistance, and as far as I can determine, none of your people called Quantico for help. But the fact that he led you and Sheriff Mooney to believe he was officially investigating these abductions is…puzzling to say the least."

"Not to defend his action or anything," Abby said. "But a profiler might be able to fill in some of the blanks for us here. Give us a fresh perspective."

Carter scowled. "That's why I'm here, Sergeant Cross, to offer the expertise and the technical support of the FBI." He paused. "Do you have any idea where I can find Burke this morning?"

She shrugged, but her mind was spinning in a dozen different directions. Sam Burke was no longer with the FBI. He'd lied to her. But why? What was he up to?

Abby knew she should probably tell Carter about the episode on the playground last night, but she didn't much care for his attitude. Let him do his own legwork. "Sorry. I haven't seen him."

Carter didn't look at all happy with her answer. "If you do see him, I'd appreciate getting a heads-up. We need to know why he's down here. If someone, one of the families maybe, hired him as an outside consultant, we need to know that, too. The last thing we want is a loose cannon on these cases."

Translation: Carter had ridden into town to save the day. He didn't want some hotshot profiler stealing his thunder. He was so easy to read, Abby almost smiled. "If I see him, I'll let you know." To Sheriff Mooney, she said, "Is that all?"

"Let me have a word with you before you take off." He turned to Carter. "Won't take long."

Carter took the hint. "I'll wait for you outside, Sheriff." He nodded briefly to Abby. "Sergeant Cross."

Abby turned to Sheriff Mooney as the door closed behind the agent. "What's this all about?"

Sheriff Mooney shrugged. "Damned if I know, but that boy sure as hell got his Jockeys all in a wad when I mentioned Sam Burke. And the feds always think *we* have a thing about jurisdiction." He shook his head.

Abby sat down in the seat across from the sheriff's desk and leaned toward him. "Agent Carter doesn't seem to think too highly of the Investigative Support Unit, but they were instrumental in helping to capture the Atlanta child murderer. There's been a lot of publicity on these two cases. Do you think that could be why Sam Burke is here?"

"As a hired gun, you mean?" Sheriff Mooney pulled a hand through his already unkempt hair. "I don't know, Abby. He didn't strike me as the mercenary type."

Sam hadn't struck Abby that way, either, but he *had* lied to them. For all she knew, he'd resigned from the FBI to become a professional profiler, a man who sold his expertise to terrified and desperate families. But it left a hollow feeling in her stomach to think so.

The image of Sam standing on the street, gazing at the playground, materialized in her mind once again. She'd once read that to be a profiler, you had to be able to suspend disgust and outrage, even in the most gruesome crimes, in order to crawl inside the perpetrator's mind. To understand him. To even, at times, appreciate his cunning. What if that appreciation turned into something else?

Abby thought about Sam Burke's eyes, so cold and distant. So very dark.

And a chill, like nothing she'd ever known before, coursed through her.

AUGUST IN MISSISSIPPI was hell on earth.

Sam had been in some hot places before, but nothing like this. He'd run the air conditioner full blast in his rental car all morning, but by the time he pulled into Curtis Brodie's car dealership in downtown Eden, his cotton shirt was already sticking to his back.

He resisted the urge to take off his jacket and loosen his tie, but he'd learned a long time ago that the dark suit, white shirt and polished shoes projected a certain image, an image he hadn't been able to shed in the month since his resignation. Even though with the passing of J. Edgar Hoover the clothing regulations had been lifted—along with the ban on drinking coffee on the job—Sam never discounted the intimidation factor of the G-man uniform.

Getting out of the car, he shaded his eyes. The sunlight was almost blinding as it bounced off the rows of windshields on the new automobiles that sat baking in the morning heat. There were no customers around that he could see, and unlike most of the car lots he'd visited in his time, no salesman came rushing out to greet him. It was as if the soaring temperature had even managed to beat back ambition and avarice. At least temporarily.

Pulling open the glass door, he stepped into the showroom. Across the lobby, two men in short sleeves and khaki trousers stood talking and drinking sodas, and Sam started toward them. The chatter halted as soon as he was spotted, and one of the men broke away to saunter over.

"Morning," he drawled. "Interested in owning a Lincoln?" He patted the top of a dark blue Continental. "Not a finer car on the road, I can guarantee you that. And made right here in the good ol' U.S. of A."

"I'm not here to buy a car." Sam took out his credentials and flashed them—just long enough for the man to see the FBI emblem and not the status.

"Alton Clark." The salesman's expression grew wary as he stuck out his hand and his voice lowered. "You here about Curtis's little girl?"

"That's right."

Alton shook his head. He was a young man, but he had the hangdog expression of a guy who'd seen his share of bad luck. "Damn shame about Sara Beth. I still can't believe it. Hell, this is just a lil' ol' hick town. Stuff like that goes on in New York and L.A., places like that. Not here in Eden."

"From what I understand, it's happened here twice before."

"Yeah. That's the scary part. My wife won't let our two-year-old out of her sight since those little girls disappeared. Won't even leave him with my mother. Kid'll probably grow up warped or something, but what can you do?"

Sam heard the underlying frustration and fear in the man's words, and he sympathized. Every time Jonathan had left the house, Sam had been racked with images from the child-murder cases he'd worked. The innocent faces. The broken bodies.

In the end, it wasn't a monster that had taken Jonathan away, but the disease that had ravaged him had been no less brutal. Sam had been left with the same terrible question he'd seen in the eyes of all those tiny victims' parents. Why?

"Is your boss in?" he asked brusquely, shoving the memories to the far recesses of his mind.

"Curtis? Naw. He took off a little while ago. Don't know where he was going, but he was all dressed up, like maybe he had a meeting or something." Alton frowned almost imperceptibly. "You might think he'd be out looking for his little girl, but I guess he's got more important business to take care of."

"More important than his daughter's disappearance?"

Alton looked uncomfortable, as if he'd said too much already. He glanced down a hall lined with glassed-in cubicles before taking a few steps away. He nodded for Sam to follow him. Across the room, the second salesman watched them with avid curiosity. "Word around this place is that Curtis has got himself some pretty heavy-duty financial trouble."

"Such as?"

"I don't know the details, and even if I did, I wouldn't want to bad-mouth my boss. Curtis has his faults, but he's been decent enough to me." Alton paused for a long moment, as if searching his conscience. His gaze finally met Sam's. "But it bothers me that he's not out there. You know?"

Sam said noncommittally, "Different people react to stress in different ways."

"I guess." But Alton didn't look convinced. "You got kids, Agent Burke?"

"No." Sam felt a pang of guilt, as he always did, for not acknowledging his son. But he didn't want the questions. The pitying looks. He'd never talked about Jonathan's death with anyone, and he wasn't about to start now.

"Then maybe you can't understand this," Alton was saying. "But if it was my kid missing, I wouldn't care if the IRS, or the whole damn government for that matter, was breathing down my neck. I'd be out there looking for my boy, and I wouldn't give up until I found him. I wouldn't care how long it took."

His words touched a long-buried memory inside Sam. He remembered sitting in Jonathan's hospital room one afternoon toward the end. The sunshine streaming in through the window had highlighted the pallor of the boy's skin, the frailty of his nine-year-old body. He was bald by this time, his lashes and brows gone from the treatments. They both knew he was dying, and Sam didn't try to pretend otherwise. They'd talked about it quite a bit, but Norah would have no part of it. Sam didn't blame her. It was a hard thing, letting go.

"When you get to heaven some day, will you come and look for me?" Jonathan had asked.

Sam had to swallow hard before answering. "You know I will."

"But heaven's a big place, isn't it, Dad?"

"Doesn't matter. I'll keep looking until I find you. I don't care how long it takes."

The memory faded, and Sam pushed the remnants of pain away with practiced ease. He couldn't bring Jonathan back, but two little girls were missing who might still be saved. That was what he had to focus on. That was all he could afford to focus on.

Alton must have taken Sam's silence for impatience because he said quickly, "Hey, I didn't mean to bend your ear like that. You got better things to do than stand around here listening to me jaw. Luanne, Curtis's secretary, might be able to tell you where he was headed." He pointed toward the hallway. "It's the office at the far end there."

"Thanks."

"Agent Burke?"

Sam had started to walk away, but he glanced back over his shoulder.

Tears glittered in the man's eyes as he said softly, "I hope you find those little girls."

Sam nodded. "I'll do my best."

"Promise me you won't stop looking, Dad."

"I promise, son. I'll never stop looking."

UNLIKE THE TINY compartments used by the salesmen, the secretary's office was plush and spacious, suggesting that Curtis Brodie's private domain might border on opulent. Leather furniture. Hardwood floors. Fresh flowers. Sam took it all in with a glance, but his gaze lingered on the woman seated behind a large glass-block desk.

She was around thirty, attractive in a fine-tuned sort of way and stylishly attired in a light blue suit that had Designer Label written all over it.

Fancy duds for a secretary, Sam thought. But then, according to Abby, Luanne Plimpton was more than just Curtis Brodie's assistant.

"Yes? May I help you?" she asked impatiently.

"Luanne Plimpton?"

"And you are?"

He walked across the room and flashed his creds. "Sam Burke. FBI."

Her gaze didn't waver, her expression didn't so much as flicker, but Sam had the impression that it was a struggle for her to remain so placid. Before she had time to scrutinize his ID, he put it away.

"I'm sorry, but Curtis isn't in at the moment," she said.

"Actually, I'd like a few moments with you, Miss Plimpton. May I?" He sat down in the chair across from her desk before she could protest.

"I've already talked to the police," she said with a

scowl. "I spoke at length with Sheriff Mooney and What's-her-name. That woman deputy."

"Sergeant Cross?" An image of Abby immediately formed in Sam's head. Not that he had to work to conjure it. She hadn't been out of his mind for more than five minutes since he'd met her, and Sam didn't like being preoccupied with anything other than a case. Except for when his son was sick, he'd never let personal feelings interfere with his work—which was why he was divorced.

"Yes," Luanne Plimpton was saying. "Abby Cross. She's the one."

Something in her tone suggested that she and Abby hadn't exactly hit it off. Sam could see why. The two were polar opposites. Luanne Plimpton was the kind of woman who wouldn't set foot out of her house until she'd spent at least an hour and a half in front of a full-length mirror. The kind who probably drove all the way to Memphis or Jackson to do her shopping and had a standing appointment at the nail salon and beauty shop.

Sam knew because Norah had been just as fastidious about her appearance. There wasn't a thing wrong with that, but he couldn't help remembering the careless way Abby had pushed back her hair yesterday in the heat, or the faded T-shirt and jeans she'd worn to search for the two missing children.

It had been obvious that her appearance was the last thing on her mind, and yet Sam couldn't remember when he'd found a woman so attractive.

He glanced at Luanne Plimpton, finding her carefully cultivated facade not in the least appealing. "How long have you been working for Curtis Brodie?"

She shrugged. "A little more than two months."

"How long have you been seeing each other socially?"

When she didn't answer, Sam cocked a brow. "A little over two months?"

She gave him a cold appraisal. "I don't see where my personal life is any of your business."

"Anything or anyone connected to those missing children is my business." He was making it his business.

"All right," she said grudgingly. "Curtis and I have been seeing each other for a while. What of it?"

"Since before you moved to Eden?"

"My, my. You've been in town how long? And you're already up to speed on the latest gossip." She folded her arms on the desk and gazed at him dispassionately. "Look, there were problems in that marriage before I ever met Curtis. I'm not some home-wrecker, if that's what you're thinking."

"Are you and Curtis living together?"

"No. Who told you we were? His wife? Sounds like something she'd do," Luanne said bitterly. "I can't *believe* that woman."

Sam let that one pass. "Why did Curtis send you to pick up Sara Beth at school the day she disappeared? Why didn't he go himself?"

"He was busy, tied up in a meeting or something. It was no big deal. I'd picked her up before."

"You didn't notice anything unusual that day? No strange cars parked near the school? No strangers lurking about? You didn't see anyone follow you to the drugstore?"

"Of course not. If I had, I would have reported it immediately." A muscle had begun to twitch very faintly at the corner of her left eye.

"Were there any other customers in the drugstore that day?"

"None that I saw."

"You didn't hear anyone else come in after you were inside? There's a bell over the door, isn't there?"

She shrugged. "If there is, I didn't hear it. And neither did Gerald Ferguson."

"Gerald Ferguson is over sixty," Sam pointed out, remembering the details Abby had given him. "His hearing may not be what it used be."

"I wouldn't know about that. As I said, I didn't see anyone in the store when I got there, and I didn't hear anyone come in afterward. I didn't see any strange cars in the parking lot, no weirdoes hanging around the school or the drugstore, and if I was followed, I didn't know it. I didn't see anything." She looked almost smug after her long recitation, as if she dared him to find a flaw in her story.

Sam decided to change tactics. "Would you say you've spent a lot of time with Sara Beth during the last two months?"

"Some."

"Does she like you?"

She seemed surprised by the question, and for a split second, Sam actually thought he'd ruffled her. But Luanne Plimpton was a pro. She gathered her poise and smiled at him coolly. "You would have to ask Sara Beth that question. But, of course, that's impossible, isn't it?"

"For now," Sam agreed, but inside he was seething. The woman was *cold*. She showed not the slightest concern for the child's welfare, not the least bit of fear that Sara Beth might never return.

He stared at Luanne Plimpton for a long moment, until she finally glanced away. Her capitulation seemed to annoy her. "If I were you, I'd be talking to Sara Beth's mother. Parents are always the number-one suspects in cases like these, from what I've read. And I can tell you from experience that Karen Brodie is a real head case. She's the reason Sara Beth was such a little sh…brat.''

"What do you mean?''

"Karen has some real problems. Bad problems. She can be violent, if you want to know the truth. The way Sara Beth treated me…'' Luanne trailed off, shrugging. "She was only emulating her mother.''

"Are you suggesting Karen Brodie is behind Sara Beth's disappearance?''

Luanne pushed back her chair and stood. It was a tactic Sam had witnessed when he'd interviewed criminals in prison. The subject would stand, or in some cases even sit on the back of his chair, in order to elevate himself above his interrogator. It was a power thing. "I'm suggesting the woman is spiteful enough that I wouldn't put anything past her.''

"Has she ever threatened you?''

"Not directly, no. But she's threatened Curtis.''

"In what way?''

"She threatened to take Sara Beth away for one thing.''

"You heard her say that?''

The woman lifted her chin. The tic at her left eye became even more pronounced. "I didn't have to hear her. I know what she's like. Curtis has told me things you wouldn't believe, including the fact that she tried to kill him once. With a butcher knife. Did you know about that?'' Before Sam could answer, Luanne smiled. "I thought not. You've heard only Karen's side of things, haven't you? She's not the Goody Two-shoes people around here seem to think.''

"Has she ever taken Sara Beth away without Curtis knowing?''

"Not that I know of.'' But Luanne looked pained having to admit it. "Look, if you want to know about Karen

Brodie, I suggest you go talk to her yourself. I've got a lot of work to do.''

"Just one last question." Sam rose, putting himself once again in the position of power. "Why did you refer to Sara Beth in the past tense?"

Chapter Six

As it turned out, it was almost noon before Abby got away from the station. The amount of data coming in on both cases was staggering, and she'd taken the time to sort through it all. She didn't want any piece of information, no matter how trivial, to go unnoticed. No lead to go unchecked. She'd thought from the very beginning that Sara Beth's abduction was unrelated to the other two, except in the timing, and her gut feeling hadn't changed in that regard.

Now, as she drove toward Enchanted Hills, a posh subdivision on the north side of town near the lake, Abby tried to separate the two disappearances in her mind and concentrate on the Brodie case.

As in all child abductions, the parents were initially the chief suspects. Nine times out of ten, when a child disappeared, one or both of the parents was responsible. Abby had spoken to Karen Brodie twice before, once with Sheriff Mooney and once alone, and both times she'd come away from the interview with an unsettled feeling.

It wasn't that she thought Karen Brodie was lying, nor did she seem the type of woman who would hurt her child. Abby could hardly imagine any mother harming her own child, but it happened all too often. But there was something about Karen Brodie, something Abby couldn't quite put her finger on, that troubled her.

Curtis Brodie, however, was another matter altogether. He wasn't the least bit hard to figure out. The epitome of tall, dark and handsome, he exuded a kind of raw masculinity that some women found attractive, but that Abby found merely irritating.

He'd been cooperative, even charming, until the questions began to take a turn he hadn't cared for, and then he'd grown snide and belligerent, attacking the county sheriff's department for what he perceived as incompetence.

But even in the midst of his rant, Abby had seen him glance at his watch once, as if something more pressing than his daughter's disappearance was occupying his mind.

In short, Curtis Brodie had made a very unfavorable impression on Abby, and she secretly thought that both Karen and Sara Beth were better off without him. That opinion, however, she kept to herself.

She pulled to the curb in front of the Brodie residence, a beautiful two-story Mediterranean, one of the nicest and biggest houses in a subdivision that remained underdeveloped because few people in Eden could afford such luxury. Unlike Emily Campbell and Sadie, Sara Beth obviously came from an affluent family. But if money was the motive for the kidnapping, why had there been no ransom demand?

Abby got out of the car and glanced around. The neighborhood was somnolent in the heat. A lawn mower droned in the distance and somewhere down the street, a stereo played vintage Patsy Cline from someone's patio. But beneath the tranquillity of a lazy summer morning lay a profound darkness, a troubling cancer that had taken three of Eden's children.

Abby wanted to believe, *had* to believe, that Sara Beth and Emily would be found safe and unharmed. That unlike her sister, Naomi, Karen Brodie and Tess Campbell wouldn't be robbed of all those precious years with their children.

But an ex-FBI profiler had come to town. A profiler who'd worked serial-killer cases. A profiler who had glimpsed, perhaps, the existence of an evil in this town that no one here wanted to believe was real.

But it was. It was real.

Shivering in the heat, Abby headed up the walkway and rang the bell. After a moment, the housekeeper answered the door. Virginia Temple, middle-aged with graying hair and a sweet round face, caught her breath when she saw Abby. Her expression twisted in fear. "Sara Beth—"

"No, no, it's nothing like that," Abby said quickly. "I just need to speak with Mrs. Brodie for a moment. Is she in?"

The woman wiped her hands on the yellow gingham apron she wore tied around her waist. "Yes, of course. She hasn't gone out since it happened. She doesn't eat. She doesn't sleep. All she does is brood and worry. If she could just get out for a while—"

Abby nodded. "I know it's difficult. But believe it or not, she's doing the right thing. We need her here by the phone."

"But there's a deputy here around the clock. *I'm* here." A tear spilled over and ran down the woman's face. She wiped it away with the corner of her apron. "I just feel so helpless. Sara Beth is like my own granddaughter to me. If anything happens to that baby—"

"We're doing everything we can to find her," Abby

said. "In the meantime, there is something you can do. Something we can all do. Pray."

The woman nodded. "I keep telling myself it's all in His hands. He'll protect Sara Beth and Emily, but then I think about that other little girl. The one who disappeared all those years ago. She was never found, and God only knows what happened to her—" She broke off, as if realizing suddenly Abby's relationship to the missing child. She wiped her eyes again, and said softly, "I'll go find Mrs. Brodie and tell her you're here. Why don't you wait in the living room?" She gestured to a room to the right of the foyer.

After the housekeeper disappeared, Abby walked about the beautifully appointed room, wondering briefly what it would be like to live in such a place. For all its expensive furnishings and gleaming chandeliers, the house seemed cold. Sterile. Not at all like Abby's grandmother's house. It was hard to imagine a child feeling at home here.

A set of atrium doors looked out on a tropical landscape designed around a huge, grotto-like swimming pool. Near the waterfall, a man and woman stood talking.

The man had his back to Abby, but the woman was Karen Brodie. She appeared very distraught, and as Abby watched, the man took her in his arms and held her gently.

The action was tender and poignant, and Abby felt as if she were intruding on a very private moment. Then the couple moved slightly, and the man lifted his head. Abby could see his profile, and her breath caught in her throat.

Well, well, she thought with a sinking feeling in the pit of her stomach. Sam Burke was just full of surprises.

THE MOMENT he spotted Abby, Sam released Karen and took a step back from her.

Damn, he thought. This wasn't the way he'd wanted

Abby to find out about Karen. He braced himself as Abby opened the glass door and stepped out onto the patio.

Karen, still oblivious to Abby's presence, took a tissue from the pocket of her slacks and wiped her eyes. She was thinner than Sam remembered, but still just as pretty with her short, blond hair and cornflower eyes.

She'd grown into an elegant, sophisticated woman, with an expensive hairstyle that subdued the ringlets she'd always hated and makeup that gave color to her pale, fragile skin. But there was still a waif-like quality about her that tugged at Sam's guilt. He shouldn't have let her disappear from his life. He knew that now. He should never have walked away when she'd needed him the most.

"Sorry. I didn't mean to fall apart like that." She dabbed at her nose with the tissue. "I'm usually much stronger. I promise."

Her words seemed almost pitiful to Sam, as if she were trying very hard to convince him of her strength. As if she were trying to absolve him of his guilt.

"You're entitled," he said gruffly, his gaze on Abby as she walked across the flagstones toward them.

Karen opened her mouth to say something else, but then she noticed the direction of his attention and whirled. "What's *she* doing here?" she muttered, spotting Abby. Then, anxiously, "You have some news about my daughter?"

"I'm afraid not," Abby said. "I'm sorry if I alarmed you."

Her dark gaze collided with Sam's, and the impact jolted him. She wore jeans again today and a white T-shirt that did very little to disguise her feminine curves. Her dark hair was pulled back into a ponytail, her tanned face devoid of any makeup. But there were purple smudges beneath her eyes, as if, like Sam, she hadn't slept well last night.

She would have lain awake, obsessing about the disappearances, he thought. She would have tried to play out every scenario in her head, rack her brain for anything the investigation might have missed thus far. She would have tried to put herself in both the victims' and the perpetrators' shoes. Sam knew, because he'd done the same things himself.

But, once in awhile, images of Abby had intruded. He couldn't seem to separate her from these cases. Her determination, her *passion* made him at times feel old, all used up inside. She believed with all her heart they'd still find those little girls, safe and sound, because she hadn't been a cop long enough to be jaded. She hadn't yet seen what Sam had seen.

She was what he'd once been, and glancing at her now, Sam was reminded of a time when the world had seemed all black and white to him, too. Good against evil. But that was before he'd seen what human beings could do to each other. That was before Jonathan had died. Sam was still convinced of the existence of evil; he'd seen it. He just wasn't as certain of the other side anymore.

As if glimpsing something in his eyes she didn't want to see, Abby turned back to Karen. But her gaze strayed almost immediately back to Sam. "I'm surprised to see you here."

"You two know each other?" Karen asked, surprised.

"Perhaps I should be the one asking that question." Abby's tone held a note of accusation and something else Sam couldn't quite define.

"Karen is my sister, Abby."

"Your *sister?*" Shock flashed across her features, followed by a quick look of comprehension. "Your sister," she repeated. "Well, that certainly sheds new light on the matter. Why didn't you tell me this yesterday?"

"Because I didn't want that knowledge to limit the amount and quality of information you were willing to give me."

She gave him a cool smile. "At least you're being honest about that. It seems there are quite a few things you neglected to share with me yesterday, *Special Agent* Burke. You and I need to get a few things straight when I'm finished here."

Karen stared at Abby in confusion. "If there's some problem about Sam being here, maybe I can clear it up. I'm the one who called him," she said almost defensively. "Given his background, I thought he could help."

Abby shot Sam a glance. "Oh, I'm sure he can." Her tone bordered on sarcastic, and Sam knew that she was still thoroughly pissed. He couldn't blame her. But he'd had his reasons for withholding the information. Whether Abby would understand them or not was a different matter.

"Shall we sit down?" She motioned to a patio table in the shade, and once they were settled, she focused her attention on Karen, ignoring Sam as if he were nothing more than part of the scenery. "As you know, I've been assigned to your daughter's case, so you'll be seeing a lot of me," she said almost apologetically. "In fact, I'm sure you'll get sick of seeing me, and you'll get even more tired of all my questions. But everything I do is with one goal in mind, and that's finding your daughter. I'll give my heart and soul to this case, Mrs. Brodie. I won't rest until we find Sara Beth and bring her back home to you safely."

She was so certain, Sam thought. So sure that good and right would prevail. She leaned forward slightly, her brown eyes wide and earnest. It almost seemed as if she could somehow bolster Karen's courage by sheer force of will.

But his sister seemed to have grown paler since Abby arrived, as if her official presence here only reinforced the gravity of the situation and reminded Karen of the lessening odds of finding Sara Beth alive with each tick of the clock.

"I'll try to make this brief," Abby said. "We've talked to some witnesses who have placed a white, Chevrolet Caprice, possibly a '91 or '92 model, in the vicinity of Ferguson's Drugstore at the time Sara Beth was taken. Do you know anyone who drives a car matching that description?"

Karen shook her head. "Sam asked me the same question earlier. I've been racking my brain all morning, but I can't think of anyone who drives a car like that. I'm sorry."

Abby finally flashed Sam a glance, but it wasn't a pleasant one. She didn't like that he'd beat her to the punch. Well, too bad, he decided. Abby wasn't going to like a lot of things she found out about him, but it didn't matter. Nothing mattered except finding Sara Beth. His sister's daughter. A child Sam had never even set eyes on.

"Mrs. Brodie—"

"Call me Karen."

Abby smiled. "And I'm Abby." She paused. "We've been over some of the questions I'm about to ask you before, and I know they're a bit uncomfortable. But they are necessary."

Karen nodded, closing her eyes briefly.

"Why did you and your husband decide to separate?"

Karen stared at a spot on the patio table. "I'd like to

tell you it's a matter of irreconcilable differences, but...it's more that. Curtis is...very difficult to live with.''

''In what way?''

''He's very controlling.''

''Violent?'' Abby asked softly.

Karen hesitated. Sam saw that her hands, clasped in her lap, were still trembling.

''Did he ever hit you?'' Abby persisted.

''Once. He never did it again.'' Karen kept her gaze on the table, as if she was too ashamed to look up.

''Did he ever hit Sara Beth?''

Karen flinched. ''No.''

''Is she afraid of him?''

''I don't know. She doesn't like to go to his house. She says he gets mad at her a lot and yells at her, and that his new girlfriend doesn't like having her around.''

''Are you referring to Luanne Plimpton?''

Karen's face remained placid, but her hands curled into fists in her lap. ''Yes. The one who picked Sara Beth up at school the day she disappeared.''

Abby leaned slightly toward her. ''As I understand it, you and your husband are each trying to get full custody of Sara Beth. Do you believe he could have had anything to do with her disappearance?''

Sam didn't think his sister was going to answer at first. For the longest time, she seemed to cling to the last vestiges of her self-control. Then her expression crumpled. She put her hands to her face and said in a near whisper, ''I think Curtis is capable of almost anything. The separation was my idea. I kicked him out. I told him I never wanted to see him again. You don't turn on Curtis like that. You don't cross him.'' She drew a tremulous breath. Her hands fluttered back to her lap. ''He knows the only thing I care about in this world is Sara Beth. I think he would do just about anything to keep me away from her.''

ABBY TALKED to Karen for several more minutes, and when her interview was concluded, she stood and asked Sam to meet her out front.

"Just give me a minute here."

Her gaze was still cool as she nodded.

After Abby left, he turned back to his sister. "Are you okay?"

"Oh, God." Her face had grown deathly white. She put a trembling hand to her mouth. "I...think I'm going to be sick."

Sam was instantly at her side. "Here. Put your head down between your knees. That's it. Take deep breaths. Just relax."

"I'm so sorry," Karen murmured, over and over, her voice a broken whisper.

"Don't be." Sam took her hand in his. Her skin was ice cold.

After a few moments, she sat up, still looking unnaturally pale, but there was a hard gleam in her eyes now. She backed her shoulders, as if summoning every last scrap of courage and determination from some secret place inside her.

The same courage and determination that had sustained her after he'd left home, Sam thought. After he'd abandoned her to their father's tyranny.

"I'm okay now."

But Sam thought the declaration was meant to convince herself more than him.

He wanted to touch her hand again, put his arm around her, offer her some bit of comfort, but in spite of the circumstances, their relationship remained awkward and strained.

Until he'd arrived in Eden, Sam hadn't seen his sister in years, and it struck him as he gazed down at her that this pale, fragile woman was hardly more than a stranger to him. He knew very little about her life, only that she was separated from her husband and that her child was missing.

She can be violent, if you want to know the truth.

Luanne Plimpton had told a very different story than the one his sister had related to Abby, but that wasn't unusual in messy divorce cases. Emotions ran rampant. Feelings got out of hand. But how had all that animosity affected Sara Beth? What—if anything—did the bitterness between Karen and her husband have to do with their daughter's disappearance?

As if reading his mind, Karen managed to muster a wan smile. "You must not know what to make of all this. You don't know Curtis. You've heard only my side of things. And you didn't come all the way down here to get dragged into my divorce."

Sam shrugged. "I've been through a divorce myself, remember?"

"I'm sorry."

"Don't be. It's over and done with. And I told you before, I'm here because I want to be."

"I know. And I know you'll do everything you can to help, but…" Karen trailed off, turning to gaze at the pool. After a moment, she said softly, "Not that you owe me anything. I'm sorry I didn't come to Jonathan's funeral. I've always regretted that I wasn't there for you."

Sam shrugged, but he felt that same aching emptiness he always experienced at the mention of his son. "It's okay."

"No, it's not. I wanted to come. There were…reasons why I didn't." She looked very tired and very sad. "I've made such a mess of my life, Sam."

"You're going through a rough time, but you'll get through it."

"You're lucky you got out when you did," she said almost fiercely.

He knew what she meant. He'd escaped home at seventeen and by the time he'd come back, Karen had grown into a very troubled teenager. A girl who'd had a penchant for dangerous relationships. A young woman who had already been lost to a big brother who'd wanted to help her.

"I never should have left without you," he said with deep regret.

She made a helpless gesture with her hand. "You were young. What would you have done with a ten-year-old kid? Besides, it wasn't as bad for me. He didn't hit me. Not like he did you."

Their father might not have beat her, but Sam knew that men like Kenneth Burke had other ways of imposing their will, of instilling fear. The threats, the constant degradation, the steady erosion of confidence and self-esteem were sometimes more damaging than fists. Sam knew the lengths someone like that would go to for control. He'd witnessed firsthand the battered bodies men like their father had left in their wakes.

And from everything he'd seen and heard, Sam suspected Karen had married someone very much like their father, very much like the man she'd been trying all her life to escape.

Sam's hands balled into fists at his sides. "I should have done something."

"What could you have done?" Karen's gaze looked haunted. "And besides, he was harder on you than any of us. Back then, I couldn't understand why Mother wouldn't make him stop when he started in on you. Now I understand it was because she was afraid of making him worse. Of pushing him into doing something even more savage.'' For the first time since he'd arrived, Karen reached out and placed her hand over Sam's. Her gaze met his, and it seemed to him that there was a message buried in the depths of her blue eyes. A subtle entreaty that he couldn't quite decipher. ''Mother tried to protect you in the only way she knew how. Don't think too badly of her.''

''I don't,'' Sam said. ''It's all in the past. They're both dead now, and there's nothing we can do to help either one of them. What you and I have to concentrate on is your daughter.''

Karen nodded, her expression grave. ''She's all I ever think about.''

ABBY WAS WAITING for Sam by her car. Leaning against the fender, she watched the street, her gaze tracking a kid who rode by on a bicycle. It was such a normal activity. Such a normal scene. And yet Sam and Abby both knew there was nothing normal about this morning. About this neighborhood. About this family.

''All right,'' she said when he walked up to join her. ''Let's have it. Why didn't you tell me Karen Brodie is your sister? Why did you deliberately lead Sheriff Mooney and me to believe you'd been sent down here from Washington? That you'd been assigned to this case? You're not even a federal agent anymore. What am I suppose to call you? *Mr.* Burke?''

''How about Sam?''

She folded her arms. ''I don't know that I want to be on a first-name basis with a man I can't trust.''

He sighed. "I didn't deliberately set out to deceive anyone. When I showed up at Fred Mooney's office, he assumed I was the agent you guys had been waiting for."

"And you didn't bother telling him the truth."

"If I'd told him I was Karen's brother, let alone that I was no longer with the FBI, I wouldn't have gotten a damn thing from him, and you know it. I seized an opportunity. You would have done the same thing."

Abby frowned, her gaze watching the slow rotation of the sprinkler next door. She seemed almost mesmerized by the action, but Sam knew that inside her head, the wheels were turning. His best bet was to tell her everything, throw himself on her mercy, but that went against his grain. Went against the code of silence he'd lived by since he was a kid.

"The FBI is looking for you," she finally said. "Special Agent Talbot Carter, to be precise. He was in the sheriff's office this morning, asking questions about you. Wanting to know if I could help him locate you. He wasn't too pleased to hear you've been passing yourself off as a federal agent. I believe that's a felony, isn't it, Sam?"

He ignored her last comment. "What'd you tell him?"

"The truth. I told him I didn't know where you were at the moment, but I'd let him know if I saw you. Any reason why I shouldn't give him a call right this very minute?" she challenged.

"Just one. Because I'm asking you not to."

Her expression hardened. "Not good enough."

She started to turn away, but Sam caught her arm. "Abby—"

The gesture was out of character for him, and he pulled back the moment his hand made contact with her arm. But they'd both felt the touch, light as it was, and he could see Abby's response in the softening of her eyes, in the slight intake of her breath, in the prickle of chill bumps along her skin.

And suddenly, all Sam could think about was touching her again. Moving his hands over her skin. It would be silky smooth—he just knew it—and warm from the sun. Hot, supple...

Beneath her T-shirt, the slight rise and fall of her breasts drew his gaze in spite of his best effort to control the direction of his thoughts.

"My reputation is at stake here," she said angrily. "I could be risking my job if I don't tell them what I know. Come to think of it..." She gazed up at him accusingly. "Why don't they already know? About Karen, I mean? I thought the feds kept files on everyone, especially their own agents. Or in your case, former agent."

"They do. When you're under consideration by the Bureau, they interview practically anyone that ever crossed paths with you. They talked to my family, but that was a long time ago. Karen was just a kid then and her name was still Burke. After she married and moved away, we lost touch. Until she called, I hadn't seen her in years."

"Are you saying the Bureau doesn't know about her?"

"I'm saying they haven't made the connection yet." But they would, of course. It was only a matter of time, and now that Abby knew, it didn't much matter. If she wasn't willing to help him, Sam would be shut out of the investigation.

"So you've never even met your own niece?"

He could see the disbelief in Abby's eyes, the mounting doubt about his character. In a small town, everyone knew everyone else. Turning your back on your family would be unthinkable. Leaving a kid to be raised by a man like Kenneth Burke would be unforgivable, and yet at the time, Sam hadn't had a choice. At seventeen, he'd grown into a physical match for his father, but he hadn't known how to control the rage. He'd had to leave…or risk doing something that could have ruined a lot of lives.

"My family was complicated, to say the least," he said. "But none of that's important now. Saving Sara Beth is all that matters."

"That's something we can agree on." Abby glanced up at him. "Just one more question."

"What?"

"Why did you resign from the FBI?"

Sam thought about that for a moment, wondering how to explain. Wondering how much he should tell her. Abby was a cop, but she was young. She was just starting out, and his career was over. Would she be able to understand his loss of faith? His loss of hope for mankind?

Would she understand that when you crawled around in a cesspool for years, some of the muck was bound to rub off on you?

He ran a hand through his hair. "Look, can we go somewhere and talk?"

"You mean someplace where Agent Carter isn't likely to see us?" Abby shrugged. "Sure. We can talk, but I don't know what good it will do."

"Just hear me out. That's all I ask."

"I wish I could believe that," she said softly, suspiciously. "I wish I could believe that all you want from me is a conversation. But that's not the case, is it, Sam?"

Whether the use of his first name had been intentional or not, Sam had no idea. But it served to create a familiarity between them, an intimacy. It opened a door that Sam walked through with no small measure of trepidation.

Chapter Seven

Sam followed Abby to a little hole-in-the-wall barbecue joint in the area of town known as Mount Ida. The depressed neighborhood was a far cry from the one they'd just left, but Abby thought it unlikely they'd run into Special Agent Carter or anyone from the sheriff's department there. Not many people outside of Mount Ida knew of Evie's Sweet and Spicy Ribs, but the owner, Evie Mae Sweet—known to kinfolk and stranger alike as Mama Evie—had been a childhood friend of Abby's grandmother. The two had been like sisters back when socializing between blacks and whites had sometimes produced dire consequences in Jefferson County.

When she was little, Abby had sat enthralled at the feet of the two old women as they'd rocked on the front porch of Grandma Eulalia's house, shelling peas and reminiscing about the hardships of growing up poor in rural Mississippi.

Both Eulalia and Evie Mae had worked in the cotton fields for years, but with the advent of herbicides and the cotton-picker, the need for field hands had all but been eliminated. Eulalia had turned to dressmaking and Evie Mae had opened her rib joint, where people in the know could get the best pork barbecue in the county.

In her seventies now, Evie Mae still opened and closed the place every day, but she'd finally allowed one of her grandsons to take over the cooking while a couple of her granddaughters waited tables. One of them, a pretty girl named Shani, seated Abby and Sam and placed plastic menus on the table before them.

"Shani!" Evie Mae bellowed from behind the counter. Her dark skin, still amazingly unlined, gleamed like ebony in the heat. A woman of ample proportions, she wore a red bandanna tied around her gray hair and a spotless white apron tied around her neck. Waddling from behind the counter, she swatted her granddaughter's backside with a dishtowel. "What you mean, givin' Abigail a menu like she's some kind of stranger comin' in here? That girl knows what she wants. Always did."

As she lumbered toward the booth, Abby grinned and stood. "How are you, Mama Evie?"

"Oh, fair to middlin', I reckon. My rheumatism's been acting up something terrible lately, and Doc Greene says I done got the arthritis in one of my legs." She shifted her weight in the house slippers she always wore. "But I'm not complaining."

"Mama Evie, you're always complaining about something," Shani teased, then grinned and darted out of the way of her grandmother's dishtowel.

"I surely don't know where that young'un gets that smart mouth from." Evie Mae heaved a weary sigh, and Abby couldn't help but smile. From the tales she'd heard on Grandma Eulalia's front porch, Evie Mae Sweet had been a pistol in her day.

"Well, don't just stand there," she grumbled. "Get yourself over here and give me a hug."

Abby put her arms gently around the woman, who had seemed a bit frail lately, but Evie Mae would have none of that. She squeezed Abby as if she hadn't seen her in years when, in fact, Abby had been in only last week.

For a moment, Abby drank in the scent of line-dried cotton clothing tinged with the spices—the secret ingredients—Evie Mae put in her barbecue sauce. Underlying both was the flowery cologne she mixed and bottled herself. Chances were, she could probably have profited more from her potions and perfumes than from her barbecue, but Evie Mae swore her alchemy was just a sideline. She dabbled just enough to keep the old family recipes from becoming lost.

After several long seconds, she pushed Abby away and held her at arms' length. "Them dark circles under your eyes tell me you're not getting enough sleep." Her sly gaze stole to Sam, who had stood when she'd approached the table. "Don't tell me you done got yourself a new man."

Abby felt herself blushing all the way to the roots of her hair, and she rarely blushed. Not after five years of the kind of bathroom humor that was rampant in the sheriff's department. But she was blushing now. Furiously. "Mama Evie, I'd like you to meet Sam Burke. He's consulting with me on a case."

"Consulting, huh?" She nodded toward his dark suit. "You a government man or an undertaker?" She left out the middle syllable in *government,* pronouncing it "gov-ment."

"Actually, neither."

"Well, whatever you are, you gone smother in that suit less you're careful." Evie Mae put her hands on her hips and looked him up and down. "He looks a mite ragged around the edges, if you ask me, but nothing one of my potency potions won't fix right up." She winked at Abby, and then, seeing the look on Abby's face, cackled with laughter.

Abby didn't think her face could get any hotter, but she felt as if flames must be dancing on her forehead. She wished the floor would open up and swallow her, but no such luck. When she glanced in Sam's direction, he was smiling wryly, which only made things worse somehow.

Finally, Evie Mae plodded off to see to their lunches and drinks, and Shani, grinning first at Abby and then at Sam, placed silverware and napkins before them. She leaned over and whispered to Abby, "Don't pay Mama Evie any mind. All those potions have addled her brain, if you ask me." She glanced over at Sam and giggled. "He looks like he's got plenty of life left in him to me." She was still giggling when she sauntered off.

Abby propped her elbows on the table and put her face in her hands, trying to cool her heated cheeks. "Lord help me," she muttered.

"Friends of yours?" Sam asked.

"More like family. Mama Evie has known me since I was born. She and my grandmother were best friends. I love her to death, but she does have a tendency toward...indiscretion."

"I think she's great."

Abby couldn't tell if he was serious or not. She glanced up, not wanting to find a smirk on his features. Not wanting to see the condescension in his eyes that she'd seen before in outsiders who'd spent some time in their town.

"I mean it," he said. "She's quite a character."

"That's putting it mildly."

He leaned toward her suddenly, causing Abby's breath to catch in her throat. "Tell me something, Abby." The way he said her name...the way he stared at her so intently...

Abby had to fight the urge to fan her face. Between Sam and Evie Mae, her blood pressure had risen to dangerous levels in the short time they'd been inside the restaurant.

"Do you know everyone in town?" he asked.

"Eden's a small place. Everyone knows everyone. Plus, before I made detective, I used to be on patrol. You really get to know people that way."

"It's more than that." Sam studied her for a moment. "You have a rapport with these people."

"That's because *these* people are my people," she said a little defensively. "I'm one of them."

"Is that why you've never left Eden? I've seen you work. You're a good investigator. You could go anywhere you wanted and get a job."

Even with the FBI? she wanted to ask him. "I've got a lot of reasons for staying in Eden. My family's here, for one thing."

"Family's important," Sam conceded, but there was a flicker in his gray eyes Abby couldn't quite discern.

They chatted on for several minutes, until Shani brought out their plates—pork barbecue sandwiches with side orders of baked beans and potato salad. There was cole slaw as well, but instead of being served as a side, it was slathered on top of the pork as a condiment.

After Shani had served the meals, Evie Mae brought over two frosty glasses of her special sun tea. Then she stood back and waited for them to eat.

When Abby hesitated, she said, "Well, what you waiting for, girl? Eat up. You could use a little more meat on them skinny bones of yours."

Abby refrained from telling the older woman that she'd been trying for months to lose a few pounds, but it wouldn't matter. Food was almost a religion to Evie Mae and waste a very grievous sin.

Sam took a bite of his sandwich, paused, then took another bite. "Damn, that's good."

Evie Mae beamed and gave him a wink. "I put a little something extra on there for you. You struck me right off as the kind of man who'd like it a little spicy."

Sam almost choked at the innuendo, and Abby wanted to sink under the table. Evie Mae always had a colorful way with words, but more so today than usual. For some reason, Sam brought out the devil in her.

Abby eyed her plate for a moment, thought about all the miles she'd have to run to burn even a fraction of the calories, then shrugged. She'd never met a barbecue sandwich she didn't like, and Evie Mae's were particularly savory. Abby dug into the food with gusto.

She and Sam ate in silence for several minutes, and then, appetite sated, Abby pushed back her plate and excused herself to go wash her hands. Evie Mae's sandwiches were delectable, but messy. When she came back, she slid into her chair and folded her arms on the table.

"Okay," she said. "Where did we leave off earlier? Oh, yes. You were going to tell me why you resigned from the FBI."

Sam, finishing his sandwich, shrugged. "After twenty years, it was time for a change."

"Twenty years?" Abby hadn't meant to sound so incredulous, but it just slipped out.

Sam looked up and grimaced. "Yeah. I'm an old man, Abby. Past my prime."

He looks like he's got plenty of life left in him to me.

Abby secretly agreed with Shani's assessment, although she had a feeling Sam still wasn't telling her the truth.

Not the whole of it anyway. Something other than the desire for a change had prompted him to leave the FBI.

"And tell me again why I shouldn't call Special Agent Carter and have him join us."

Sam pushed his plate aside and toyed with his glass. "It's simple. I don't want to be frozen out of this investigation. You, of all people, should understand that."

Abby did understand. She remembered all too well the frustration of being on the outside when Sadie had disappeared. Of knowing that she and Naomi were only getting the information the police wanted them to have. She understood, but she didn't see how she could help him.

"By letting Sheriff Mooney and me think you were the FBI agent assigned to this case, you gained access to information you weren't entitled to," she said in frustration. "You interfered with an ongoing investigation. That's serious business, Sam."

"I know that, and I'm prepared to deal with the consequences. But right now, my only concern is finding Sara Beth. And Emily, too, if I can. Don't shut me out of this, Abby."

She gave a helpless shrug. "It's not up to me. And besides that, you're already shut out. Why can't you get that through your thick skull? You are no longer with the FBI. You're retired, resigned, whatever. You can't be privy to this investigation." Abby pronounced the words slowly, succinctly, as if his problem was one of comprehension.

His gaze on her darkened. "I could be, if you'd agree to help me."

"Help you, how?"

He studied her for a moment, as if calculating his chances. "You could convince Sheriff Mooney to use me as a consultant on the case. Police departments use outside experts all the time.''

She gave him a doubtful glance. ''Not down here we don't. We're a small county with a very small budget. We don't have funds for outside consultants.''

''I'm volunteering my services.''

Abby sighed. ''You're also too closely tied to this case. Karen Brodie is your sister.''

''Until I arrived in town, I hadn't seen her in years. We aren't close.''

''That's a weak argument and you know it. And I doubt very seriously it would wash with Sheriff Mooney.''

He sat forward, gazing at her earnestly. ''I let her down once, Abby. I can't let her down again.''

Abby saw the guilt in his eyes, and the torment, but she was at a loss as to how to help him. Her hands were tied. She couldn't risk her own career, could she? ''I don't know what I can do,'' she said helplessly.

''This could just be between you and me. No one else has to know.''

Abby glanced up in alarm. She felt almost breathless by what he was asking her to do, and not a little angry. ''You mean go behind the sheriff's back? I can't do that. You're asking me to risk my job for you.''

''Not for me. For Sara Beth. For Emily.''

He knew exactly the right buttons to push, Abby thought bitterly. All the right bells to ring. He knew exactly how to get to her.

As if sensing her weakness, he pressed his point. ''I was with the FBI for twenty years. I've been a profiler for ten. There's no one on these cases more experienced than I am. I can help you find those children. I know I can.''

The problem was, Abby knew it, too. She'd known it

from the first. She'd also known that Sam Burke was going to be a dangerous man. Dangerous to her career. Dangerous to her peace of mind. Maybe even dangerous to her heart.

"Come on, Abby. You need my help. You know you do."

"You have no right asking me to do this," she said angrily.

"I know I don't. But I'm asking anyway. Abby—"

"Oh, just shut up for a minute and let me think," she snapped.

All right, here's the deal, she told herself. She could make a phone call, get Agent Carter over here, and let him handle the situation. She could get up from this table, leave, and forget she'd ever met an ex-profiler named Sam Burke. She could discount the very real possibility that his experience and expertise might be invaluable in solving these cases. Might help lead them to those missing children before it was too late.

She could wash her hands of the whole mess and just walk away.

But the trouble was, she couldn't walk way. Her conscience was even now flailing her that she would consider for one moment putting her own career needs before the welfare of those children.

Would it hurt to at least ask Sheriff Mooney about the possibility of Sam consulting on the cases? The sheriff wasn't an unreasonable man, and he had no particular fear of or affinity for the FBI. Just because Sam had apparently fallen from the Bureau's good graces didn't mean his services wouldn't still be valued by the Jefferson County Sheriff's Department.

But what if Sheriff Mooney said no? What then? Would

Abby really have the guts to go behind his back and keep Sam active in the investigation?

Yes, she thought. She would do anything to find Sara Beth and Emily, even risk her own career. Because if she didn't use every tool available to her to bring those children home, how would she be able to live with herself?

"I'll do what I can," she said reluctantly, "On one condition."

"Name it."

She gave him a warning look. "The knife cuts both ways. You find out anything, you let me know ASAP."

"That goes without saying."

"No," she said. "It doesn't. I want to hear that you agree."

He gave her an exasperated look. "Anyone ever tell you you're a real hard-ass, Sergeant Cross?"

"Every single day. So, do we have a deal or don't we?"

"We have a deal. And now if you'll excuse me, I'd like to go wash Mama Evie's barbecue sauce off my hands."

"You might want to hit that spot on your tie a lick, too, while you're at it," Abby said dryly.

She watched him walk away, feeling a quiver of excitement in her stomach and a sense of dread in her gut.

With or without the sheriff's blessing, Abby and Sam were going to be working together on this case. Day in and day out. Far into the night. Familiarity bred contempt, she'd always heard, but it could also nurture intimacy.

The kind that almost always spelled trouble.

As SAM HEADED toward the back, Abby got up and walked over to the cash register to settle the bill. Shani rang her up, but before Abby could leave, Evie Mae came bustling out of the kitchen and thrust a tiny glass vial into her hand.

"What's this?" Abby asked, glancing at the contents with a fair amount of suspicion.

"A little of this, a little of that." Evie Mae smiled mysteriously. "Use it sparingly."

Abby narrowed her eyes. "This isn't some kind of love potion, is it?"

Evie Mae grinned. "You don't need no love potion. I done seen them looks you two been giving each other. I know a dog in heat when I see one."

Abby didn't think she could possibly be any more mortified, but then she turned and saw that Sam had come out of the rest room. He was standing behind her, and he couldn't have missed the comment unless he was deaf as a fence post. Which Abby knew he wasn't.

She stuffed the vial into her purse and strode out of the restaurant before Evie Mae could do any further damage to her poise.

"Sorry about that," she muttered as they stood outside in the heat.

Sam shrugged. "Don't be. I told you, I think Evie Mae's great."

"I don't think I've ever blushed so much in my life."

"Looks good on you." It did. Sam glanced down at her, noting the high color beneath her tan. It brought out the warmth of her brown eyes. The softness of her features. "Besides," he said softly. "She's right."

Abby's gaze shot to his. "What do you mean?"

"I *am* attracted to you."

"Sam—"

"If we're going to be working together, I just thought we should lay all our cards on the table."

"Oh, now you want to be honest?" She gave him a

long, hard look. "Well, forget about it. It's not going to happen. A male officer goes out with one of his colleagues, everyone just shrugs and says 'boys will be boys.' You know what they call a female officer who dates an associate?"

Sam knew all right. The euphemisms changed depending on the law-enforcement body and the area of the country, but they all meant the same thing, and none of them were flattering. "I'm not a cop," he pointed out. "I'm not even FBI."

"Maybe not, but if you're going to be involved in these cases, any kind of personal relationship between us is strictly taboo. You got that?" She pushed back a strand of hair that had fallen loose from her ponytail.

"Loud and clear," Sam said with a shrug, but he was a little put off by her attitude. "We're not going to sleep together. Okay. Got it."

"Good." She turned and started toward her car. "Just so you know."

Sam said to her retreating back, "Do you always have to have the last word?"

"You don't know Southern women very well or you wouldn't have to ask that question." Pausing at her car door, she glanced back at him. "This is against my better judgment, but do you want to take a ride with me this afternoon?"

"Where to?"

She jerked a thumb over her shoulder. "South. We won't be back until late."

He gave her a skeptical look. "Care to elaborate?"

"No. So, you coming or not?"

"Yeah," he said. "I think I will."

His chest tightened as he walked toward her. She was right, of course. A personal involvement, even a one-night stand, was out of the question, and not just because of the ethics. He and Abby were worlds apart in their thinking, in their experience and especially in their ages. She was not the kind of woman he wanted to take any chances with.

But his resolution did little to lessen his attraction for her. He was in Eden after all, and the forbidden fruit was always the most tempting.

Chapter Eight

As they drove south toward Crawford County, Abby explained to Sam about the printouts she'd received from the state crime center and how she'd been searching the lists for viable suspects.

"I admire your tenacity," he said. "But it must be a little like looking for the proverbial needle in a haystack."

"Except a lot more depressing." She watched the road for a moment. "All those names. All those child molesters that we know about. And then the ones we don't—" She broke off, shuddering. "They're out there watching and waiting for their innocent little victims."

"It's disturbing," he agreed. "To say the least."

Abby shot him a glance. "I guess no one would know that better than you. I can't imagine the cases you must have seen in the ten years you were a profiler."

He frowned at the passing scenery. "Believe me, you don't want to imagine them."

"Is that why you left?"

He shrugged. "I left the FBI for a lot of reasons, none of which are relevant to these cases."

Meaning he had no intention of telling her the full truth of his resignation from the Bureau. Fair enough, Abby guessed. She had things in her life she didn't like to talk about. Her ambition, for one thing. Her dream of being an FBI profiler. What would Sam say if he knew about that? About the acceptance letter from the Academy in her bureau drawer?

Maybe that was why she couldn't leave his retirement alone. He'd had what she'd always wanted, and he'd walked away from it. Abby couldn't help wondering why.

Still, he was entitled to his privacy, so, for the time being, she let the matter drop.

He was studying the rap sheet Sheriff McElroy in Palisades had faxed Abby earlier that day. "What is it about this guy that warrants a road trip?" he asked.

Abby shrugged. "He's not the only name I pulled from the list, but he's the only one I couldn't resolve to my satisfaction over the phone. Most of the others are either dead or back in prison. But Hatcher is still out there somewhere. He spent nine years in Parchman for aggravated assault and kidnapping. He went in after Sadie disappeared, and he got out a month before Emily and Sara Beth were abducted. The length of his sentence caught my attention as much as the crime."

"What did the local authorities have to say about him?"

"Not much," Abby admitted. "A man named Wayne McElroy is the sheriff down there. I'm hoping he'll be a little more cooperative when we show up in person."

But McElroy was just leaving his office when Abby and Sam arrived shortly after five o'clock. She'd hoped to get there earlier, but traffic on the Interstate had slowed them down.

McElroy was around fifty, with grizzled hair and a jagged scar over his left eye that gave his appearance a sinister quality. The image was further enhanced by his sidearm, a wicked-looking Colt Python he'd strapped to his lean hips. A cigarette dangled from the corner of his mouth as he shoved back his Stetson and gave them an unfriendly perusal.

"You folks caught me at a bad time," he said as he grudgingly led them back to his office. "I was leaving a little early today. Hoping to get an hour or so of fishing in before dark."

"This won't take long," Abby said. "I need to follow up on our phone conversation this morning."

"You get the fax?"

"Yes, thank you."

He shrugged off her gratitude. "Don't know what else there is to say. It was all in the report."

Abby hesitated. "I had a feeling there were some things you weren't telling me about Bobby Lee Hatcher."

"Like what?" The cigarette moved up and down as he talked, loosening ashes that drifted to the surface of his desk. He swiped the mess to the floor with the back of his hand.

"What can you tell us about the kidnapping?" she asked.

McElroy frowned. "It was in the fax I sent you. Didn't you read it?"

"Yes, of course, I read it," Abby said impatiently. "But you were there when Hatcher was arrested. You know as well as I do that not everything goes into the official report."

He shrugged. "Maybe it did, and maybe it didn't."

"Meaning?"

McElroy turned to Sam in disapproval. "You always let her do all the talking?"

"It's her case," Sam said. "I'm just along for the ride."

McElroy's gaze narrowed shrewdly. "Never met a fed who was just along for the ride."

"All right," Sam said. "I do have a question for you. What is it you're not telling us about Bobby Lee Hatcher? Is he a relative of yours?"

McElroy gave a short grunt of laughter. "The Hatchers are no kin of mine, that's for damn sure. But the boy did his time, and that's a fact."

"We still need to talk to him," Abby said.

"If it's about those kidnappings up in Jefferson County, I think you're barking up the wrong tree. Bobby Lee's victim wasn't a five-year-old. The girl was seventeen, and Bobby Lee knew her. He didn't just grab her off the street."

"He may not have grabbed her off the street, but he did assault her," Abby said. "He did use violence."

The sheriff shrugged. "He roughed her up a little, but I reckon nothing more than he did to his own wife."

"Bobby Lee is married?"

"Was. I expect they're divorced by now." McElroy flicked ashes toward a glass ashtray as he stared at the ceiling for a moment. "Damned if I can remember what they called that ol' gal." He shook his head. "I never was any good with names."

"Then I guess you haven't remembered the cousin's name, either," Abby said.

"No," he admitted. "But I asked around after you called. One of my deputies remembered him. Name was Marvin. Not much of a looker, but he was the best damn auto mechanic I ever saw in my life. Hated to see him leave these parts, even if he was a Hatcher."

"What about Bobby Lee's wife? What can you tell us about her?"

"Not much. She didn't hang around long after Bobby

Lee got sent up. She was from New Orleans, best I remember. I heard tell she used to dance in one of those nightclubs down on Bourbon Street. That's where she met Bobby Lee, and then she followed him up here. They stayed out there with his grandma for awhile after they went and got themselves hitched. I figure the girl hightailed it back down to New Orleans because she was afraid to live with the old woman once Bobby Lee wasn't around to referee."

"By old woman, you mean the grandmother?"

McElroy nodded. "There wasn't any love lost between those two. Nellie Hatcher claimed the kidnapping was the girl's idea, that she used drugs or voodoo or some damned thing to get Bobby Lee to go along with her."

"What did you think?" Sam asked.

"I don't believe in voodoo, but I always figured there was some truth in what Nellie said. You could tell that girl was bad news just by looking at her." He struck a match and lit up another cigarette, blowing a stream of smoke from the corner of his mouth as he shook out the flame. "I never could prove it, though."

"Where can we find Nellie Hatcher?" Abby asked.

"The old Hatcher place is out near the swamp. You take Highway 7 east out of town, and about five miles down the road, you'll see a catfish house on the left. There's a gravel road that leads back to the swamp." The cigarette flopped at the corner of his mouth, like some forgotten appendage. "The house is at the end of the road, but if you're going, you best get on out there now. You don't want to be near that swamp after dark. The place is crawling with gators and moccasins."

Abby suppressed a shudder. "Thanks for the warning."

McElroy took the cigarette out of his mouth and aimed the tip in their direction. "Another thing you got to watch out for—Bobby Lee's younger brother still lives with the old lady. She and Ray Dean are both a little prickly about the law, especially since what happened with Bobby Lee. The boy likes to carry around a twelve-gauge shotgun that he says he uses for protection out in the swamp when he's hunting.''

"Sounds reasonable enough," Abby said doubtfully.

"Yeah," McElroy agreed ominously. "'Cept what he hunts are cottonmouths, the bigger and meaner the better. Sells 'em to one of those snake-handling preachers over in Mason County. Sometimes he'll have thirty or forty of those damn things crawling all over each other in a cage he keeps out back somewhere. I wouldn't want to be around if he ever turns 'em loose."

Great, Abby thought. This just kept getting better and better.

THE GRAVEL ROAD narrowed as they neared the swamp. Huge cypress trees grew in profusion, their lacy fronds creating a delicate green parasol that blocked the late sunlight. Even in the car with the windows up, Sam could feel the thick humidity seeping through the air-conditioner vents, but he didn't remove his jacket because he didn't want to reveal the 9mm SIG Sauer he wore in a shoulder holster beneath. He didn't want to inspire Ray Dean Hatcher's itchy trigger finger.

He glanced out the window. Ahead of them, something slithered in the underbrush. A huge tail whipped, then disappeared. "Did you see that?"

Abby stared grimly at the road. "Yeah. One of the gators McElroy warned us about?"

"Or one hell of a big moccasin."

She glanced at him. "You're not afraid of snakes, are you?"

He shrugged. "I don't have a phobia, if that's what you mean, but I wouldn't want to be around if thirty or forty cottonmouths were turned loose in the same place."

Abby shivered. "Me, either."

"Look." He pointed ahead to where the house had come into view fifty yards or so in front of them. It was bigger than Sam had imagined, a two-story farmhouse with fading wood and a wide porch that sagged slightly at one end. An old red truck sat on blocks at the corner of the yard, keeping company with a banged-up aluminum fishing boat and two small tractors that had been stripped of various parts. Toward the back of the house, more abandoned vehicles littered the property. Sam remembered that Sheriff McElroy had told them Bobby Lee's older cousin was an auto mechanic. He wondered if the junked cars in the back were Marvin Hatcher's handiwork.

As Abby pulled into the shale driveway, startled chickens scattered for cover.

She and Sam got out of the car and approached the porch with caution. Glancing over her shoulder toward the woods, Abby said, "Someone's out there, just beyond those tractors."

"I saw him." Sam kept his gaze straight ahead as he and Abby started up the steps. It was so dark inside the house, they could barely see through the screen. Sam knocked on the rickety frame. "Hello! Anyone home?"

A shadow appeared in the doorway. For a moment, Sam thought the woman a figment of his imagination. From McElroy's description, he'd pictured Bobby Lee Hatcher's grandmother as Ma Barker, looking a lot like Shelly Winters in the role. But this woman was tiny. She couldn't have been five feet tall or weighed more than a hundred pounds soaking wet. Her white hair was pulled back into an old-fashioned bun, and a gingham apron covered her long-sleeved, high-collared dress. She looked as old as the hills with her wizened face and crinkled eyes, and as harmless as the chickens who'd run for cover at the first sight of a stranger.

But Bobby Lee Hatcher's grandmother didn't run. Nor did she seem all that harmless when she spoke. Her voice was coarse, her tone rigid, stern. A voice used to barking orders at errant grandsons. "Are you lost?"

"No, we came here to see you, Mrs. Hatcher. My name is Sam Burke. FBI." He kept his introduction purposefully vague, not outright lying about his affiliation with the Bureau. He could feel Abby's gaze on him. He couldn't tell whether she approved or not, but the fact was, FBI credentials opened doors.

Not in this case, however.

"The Eff-Bee-Eye?" Nellie Hatcher growled in a thick, country drawl that gave each letter two syllables. "A revenue man, as my pappy used to call 'em. He didn't have no use for 'em, and neither do I."

When she started to back away from the door, Sam said quickly, "We'd like to ask you a few questions about your grandson."

She hesitated. "I got a whole mess of grandsons, boy, and I pert near raised ever dang one of 'em myself."

"We want to talk to you about Bobby Lee," Abby said.

The old woman glared at Sam. "She the Eff-Bee-Eye, too?"

"My name is Abby Cross. I'm a detective with the Jefferson County Sheriff's Department." She showed the woman her ID and badge.

Mrs. Hatcher shrugged. "Don't mean nuthin' to me. This is Crawford County."

"May we come in and talk to you? It won't take long," Abby said.

The old lady paused again, then shoved open the screen door so quickly, it almost caught Abby in the face. Sam grabbed her arm and pulled her back, and for a moment, the feel of his skin against hers spurred his pulse. *You're not going to sleep with me. Okay. I got it.*

Nellie Hatcher's heavy cane thudded against the bare wood floor as she ushered them into the living room. The front room, she called it. Dust motes danced in a beam of light from a high window, but other than that, the area was dark and cheerless. There was no air conditioner so the room was hot and fetid with the smell of cooking meat.

The old lady plopped down in a wooden rocker and cradled her cane in her lap. She didn't invite Sam and Abby to sit, so they both remained standing.

"So," she said, glaring up at them. "You think my boy's got something to do with those kidnappings up in Jefferson County, do you?" When she saw their surprised expressions, she gave a satisfied snort. "McElroy's done been out here asking questions."

Figures, Sam thought. That was why the sheriff hadn't been overly helpful. He'd started his own investigation, hoping, no doubt, to garner himself a little publicity.

"We just want to talk to Bobby Lee," Abby said. "Do you have any idea where we can find him?"

"No, I don't. But I wouldn't tell you if I did. The boy did his time. He did his time, and hers. Just leave him be, you hear me?"

The screen door creaked open and a young man of about twenty came into the room. He wore a pair of muddy rubber boots, filthy jeans, and a plaid shirt with the sleeves cut out to reveal a series of tattoos all up and down his arms. He carried a burlap sack in one hand and a twelve-gauge shotgun in the other.

He glared at Sam. "What's going on, Grandma?"

"The Eff-Bee-Eye is a-looking for Bobby Lee."

"What the hell for?"

"We'd like to talk to him," Sam said. "Do you know where we can find him?"

"He's probably down in New Orleans by now."

The rap of the old woman's cane against the wood floor was like the sound of a shotgun blast and had Sam reaching for his weapon before he realized what had happened.

"Now, you listen to me, boy," the old woman thundered. "Bobby Lee ain't down in New Orleans. He got that she-devil out of his system a long time ago."

"I don't know, Grandma. I bet he went down there to try and find—"

The cane crashed against the floor again. "Don't ever speak that woman's name in this house. You know better than that, Ray Dean Hatcher. Now you get on into town and get me that chicken feed before the store closes."

"Yes'm." The boy looked properly chastised except for his eyes. They gleamed with some secret satisfaction. He turned and ambled back outside, casually resting the shotgun over his shoulder as he went out the screen door. After a moment, a car engine started up.

Mrs. Hatcher trained her gaze back on Sam and Abby. "Light'll be gone soon. You two best head on back to town, too. You don't want to be caught out here after dark. Folks get lost in that swamp, they never come out again."

"I THOUGHT that went rather well," Abby said dryly as she and Sam started across the yard toward the car.

"We're both still in one piece," he said. "That's something, I guess."

"Yeah, well, we're not out of here yet." Abby glanced

around. Here in the yard, the sun was still shining, but a few feet away, the woods, and presumably the swamp beyond lay in deep shadows. A couple of outbuildings were almost hidden by the graveyard of rusty, abandoned cars and boats at the back of the house.

A chill went up her spine. What if Bobby Lee Hatcher was the one? What if he'd taken Sara Beth and Emily and brought them down here to this godforsaken place? What if they were hidden even now in one of those old sheds? What if they were hurt, sick, frightened that no one would come and find them?

Okay, it was a long shot, Abby thought. They were over two hundred miles from Eden. Why would Bobby Lee have driven north for four hours to seek out his prey? Why not go on the prowl closer to home?

Fear of being apprehended?

Abby tried to turn back to the car, but she couldn't make herself. Her gaze kept straying to those buildings.

"What is it?" Sam asked.

She nodded toward the junkyard. "Those buildings," she said. "I keep imagining those little girls inside."

"We've found no evidence to suggest that."

"I know. But I don't think I can leave without checking. I'd keep seeing them in there, so close, so helpless, and I didn't do anything to save them."

Sam frowned. "We're on shaky legal ground here, Abby. We've been ordered off the property, and I doubt we can find a local judge who'd issue us a search warrant because of a gut feeling."

He was right, of course. And Abby had always played by the book. She'd always been a stickler for the rules because she knew she had to be. There were those, even in her own department, always looking to trip her up.

Always looking for an excuse to point out why women shouldn't be allowed in law enforcement.

But the abductions had changed all of that. All Abby cared about was finding those children, no matter what it took.

"You can turn your head and pretend you don't know what I'm doing if it'll make you feel better," she told Sam. "But I'm checking out those buildings."

"I'm not worried about covering my own butt," he said almost angrily. "I was thinking of your career."

"My career won't mean much if we don't find those children."

"All right," Sam said grimly. "Then we do this fast. You take one building and I'll take the other. Let's get this done before Ray Dean gets back with that shotgun. And for God's sake, be careful."

They skirted the house, taking cover among the junked cars and boats as they made their way toward the outbuildings. Abby moved toward the first shed, and Sam took the second. She had no idea what the buildings were used for, but as she opened the door, a dank, musty smell arose from the shadowy interior. The floor was concrete, and a garden hose ran through an open window to a sink beneath.

As Abby moved toward the basin, cold fingers moved up and down her spine. The porcelain was badly chipped and discolored, and as water dripped slowly from the hose, part of the stain became dislodged and washed in a pinkish trail down the drain.

Abby's heart slammed against her chest. Oh, God, oh, God, oh, God, she thought, reaching for her weapon. Please no. Please don't let it be—

She clutched the gun in her hand as she tried to calm

her panic. *Stay calm. Stay focused. Don't forget what you know.*

Fish scales shimmered on the concrete floor, and Abby told herself the sink was used for cleaning fish. Nothing more sinister than that.

But a deep premonition had taken hold, and the blood in her veins ran cold. Keeping a cautious eye on the open doorway, she walked deeper into the room. It was larger that she'd thought, narrow but long, and so jumbled with debris, she had to move slowly in order to search all the shadows, probe all the corners. Near the back, her heart stopped again as she spotted a large, boxy structure covered with a tarp. Large enough to hide a child?

Abby glanced back at the door. The late-afternoon sunlight streaming in didn't quite reach the back of the shed, and she hadn't brought her flashlight. She wished she had. She wished she and Sam had stayed together. She wished—

Something moved beneath the tarp, and Abby's pulse went wild. She reached down, grabbed a corner, and threw it back. At first, she thought the cage was empty, but then a movement drew her gaze to the bottom. To a writhing mass of sleek, intertwined ribbons. Snakes.

Abby gasped and stepped back. Into a hard body.

Before she could react, an arm came around her neck and a strong hand closed over her wrist, squeezing so hard the gun fell to the floor with a clatter. Abby was shoved forward, toward the cage.

She tried to struggle, but her captor was strong and he'd taken her by surprise. She'd done the one thing she'd been trained not to do. She'd left herself vulnerable.

Releasing her wrist, he unfastened the top of the cage. Abby tore at the arm cutting off her wind, but he grabbed her again and thrust her hand into the top of the cage, inching her fingers toward those writhing bodies, those deadly fangs—

"Let her go!" a voice said from the doorway.

For one heart-stopping moment, her hand remained poised over the snakes, within striking range. Then her captor released her, and she struggled away from the cage, her hand massaging her bruised throat. She leaned down and picked up her gun.

Sam moved slowly into the room, weapon drawn. "You okay?" he said to Abby.

"I'm fine," she said hoarsely. "Thanks."

Ray Dean Hatcher watched them through hooded eyes. He made no move to escape. He didn't have to. Sam and Abby were trespassing, and all Ray Dean had to do was claim he'd been threatened. Swear he was protecting his property. It was like Sam had said earlier. They were on shaky legal ground, and they all three knew it.

"Let's get the hell out of here," she muttered.

THEY RETRACED their route, traveling north toward Eden. Traffic was thin, and the weather was still clear. They made good time. Sam was driving. He'd offered after their run-in with Ray Dean, and Abby had resisted at first. "This is a sheriff's department car. You aren't authorized to drive it."

"We weren't authorized to search private property, either, but I didn't see that stopping you."

"Point taken." Abby had acquiesced. She supposed it was a testament to her growing comfort level with Sam that she'd given in so easily. That she could close her eyes and drift off to sleep if she wasn't careful.

She jerked her eyes open and glanced around at the darkened countryside. It had still been daylight when they'd left Palisades. "Where are we?"

Sam glanced at her. "Almost home."

"You mean I've been asleep for over three hours?" she said in amazement. "I can't believe it."

"Obviously, you needed the rest. How many hours have you slept since Emily disappeared?"

Not many, Abby thought. Not enough. She'd drag herself home when exhaustion threatened to drop her, only to lie awake, thinking about the horrors that might have been inflicted on those little girls. Having nightmares about it if she dared let herself doze off.

She sat up, trying to shake off the lingering inertia. "What did you make of the Hatchers?"

"My first impression is that they take the fun out of dysfunctional," he said dryly. "But I wouldn't want to make any snap judgments."

"Dysfunctional, or just plain weird, given Ray Dean's penchant for shotguns and snakes." Abby shuddered, remembering her close call. "It was pretty obvious he and his grandmother don't have much regard for the law. I'd say that goes for Bobby Lee as well, unless he learned his lesson behind bars."

"I wouldn't want to put money on it," Sam said.

"Or stake two little girls' lives on it." Abby paused. "That trip left me with more questions than answers. Bobby Lee was married before he went to prison, but we don't know to whom. He may be with his cousin, Marvin, but we don't know where. And we didn't connect any of the Hatchers to Eden, much less to the kidnappings. You must feel like I took you on a wild goose chase today."

"Not necessarily." Sam glanced her way. The dash lights illuminated his face, making his eyes seem darker than ever. "Actually, we know quite a bit more about Bobby Lee Hatcher than we did. All we have to do is find out his wife's name and/or where his cousin lives. One of them may give you your connection to Eden.''

She shook her head. "I'm afraid we're grasping at straws.''

He stared at road, saying nothing.

Abby closed her eyes for a moment. His silence seemed to speak volumes. "You don't think we're going to find them in time, do you? You think it's already too late.''

"I didn't say that.''

"You didn't have to. I can see it in your eyes.'' Abby felt almost overwhelmed by despair, but she fought it off. She wouldn't succumb to those terrible doubts, but it was hard to stay positive in the face of reality. Emily had now been missing more than five days. Sara Beth, three. The likelihood of finding either child alive and well grew dimmer with each passing hour.

"I'm not giving up, Abby,'' Sam said.

She lifted her chin. "I'm not, either. Those little girls are alive to me until I find out differently,'' she said with fierce determination.

THE PARKING LOT next to Evie Mae's Sweet and Spicy Ribs was deserted except for Sam's rental car. He pulled up beside it and parked. It was only a little after ten, but the restaurant was already closed.

He turned to Abby, his expression unfathomable in the sudden darkness. "I'm glad you asked me to ride along with you today.''

"Good thing I did, considering.''

For one brief moment, he put a finger to her bruised throat. "Are you sure you're okay?''

"I'm fine,'' Abby said, trying to hide her surprise, her reaction to his touch. She couldn't see his eyes, but she knew they were deep and dark. Mesmerizing. She tried to look away, but she couldn't.

"Abby—"

The way he said her name caused panic to bubble inside her. "It's late, Sam. I need to go home and get some rest."

He nodded, and reached for his door handle. Instead of sliding across the console, Abby got out to go around to the driver's side. Sam's car was parked on the passenger side. They met each other, sidestepped the same way, then back again. Sam took her arms. Abby thought he meant to guide her out of the way, but instead, he held her still. Her heart thundered in her ears as she gazed up at him.

He wanted to kiss her, she thought. But she remembered last night and how wrong her assumption had been then. How close she'd come to embarrassing herself. So, even when she perceived his head lowering toward hers, she did nothing for fear she was misjudging his actions again. And then, when his lips touched hers, she did nothing for a moment because she still couldn't believe it was actually happening.

But it *was* happening, fast and furious, giving Abby a glimpse at the dark passions beneath Sam's rigid facade. Giving her a hint of her own secret desires. The forcefulness of her feelings left her stunned. She wanted to wrap her arms around his neck and flatten her body against his. She wanted to run her hands over his shoulders, down his chest, lower and lower until she knew without a doubt he wanted her as much as she wanted him.

But the shock of his tongue against hers finally brought her back to her senses. She stepped back, putting up her hands in front of her like a wall. "Whoa," she said shakily. "Not a good idea."

"It seemed like one at the time," he said with a touch of irony.

"I meant what I said earlier, Sam. I can't get involved with you."

"One kiss hardly constitutes an involvement."

"No," she agreed. "But it's a step in the wrong direction. I won't go there."

He stared down at her in the darkness. "You keep telling me that and I might start to wonder who you're trying to convince."

Chapter Nine

Saturday

"Three words," Sheriff Mooney said the next morning when Abby had brought up the subject of using Sam as a consultant. "Conflict of interest."

"I'm a little concerned about that, too," she admitted. "But I've spent a lot of time with him, Sheriff. I know he wants to find those children as much as we do. And you can't deny his credentials. I even checked them out myself. His old boss at Quantico credits him with almost being able to walk on water. There's no one working these cases who even comes close to his experience. If we pass up his offer of help and this thing turns out tragic—" She broke off, not wanting to put into words everyone's secret fear. "We were willing to use a psychic, for God's sake. How can we not use a profiler?"

"Yeah, but he's not just any profiler. He's the uncle of one of the victims. Aside from the fact that he may have a hard time remaining objective, have you considered there may be another problem with using him?"

Abby frowned. She'd considered a lot of problems relating to Sam, not the least of which was her attraction to him. But she wasn't about to admit that to the sheriff. "What do you mean?"

Mooney leaned forward, resting his forearms on his desk. "He could be using his expertise to try and steer the investigation in the wrong direction."

His suggestion rumbled through Abby like an aftershock, but she couldn't say the possibility had taken her completely by surprise. Karen Brodie was still very much a suspect, just as her estranged husband was. Yesterday Sam had indicated that he and his sister weren't close, that he'd let her down once when she'd needed him. Was he trying to make it up to her now?

He'd misled Abby about his FBI credentials and about his relationship to Karen Brodie. Was he lying to her about his motives?

But Abby had seen the concern in his eyes, and she knew that his desire to find the missing children was as great as her own. Sam Burke, for all his secrets, was an honorable man. She had to believe that.

"It's a risk either way," Mooney said pensively. "If the media gets hold of this, we're damned if we do and we're damned if we don't. But the idea of a man with his expertise out there on his own, finding evidence and maybe destroying it—that troubles me."

"You really don't trust him, do you?" Abby said, a sinking sensation in her stomach.

"Let's just say, after the shenanigans he pulled that first day, I've got mixed feelings."

Abby understood his conflict only too well. "So what do you want me to do?"

"If we bring him into the investigation, we'll have to keep it under control. We restrict his access to information on a need-to-know basis only." Sheriff Mooney pointed a finger in Abby's direction. "But if he says or does one thing that raises your suspicions, you come straight to me. You got that?''

"Yes, sir."

"And another thing. We keep his involvement under wraps, just like we did the psychic. Make sure he knows we don't want him talking to the media. He leaks anything to the press, he's out. For good.''

"I understand.''

"I hope you do," Mooney said grimly. "Because if this thing goes south, you'll have to live with the consequences same as I will. Are you willing to risk it?''

Abby nodded, but her heart was knocking against her chest painfully. *Are you sure you know what you're doing?* a little voice asked her.

Yes, Abby thought. She knew what she was doing. She was playing with fire, that's what she was doing.

"Now," Sheriff Mooney said. "What'd you find out in Palisades?''

Abby filled him in on the pertinent details, leaving out the incident with Ray Dean Hatcher and the snakes. And Sam's kiss. Neither event presented her in a particularly favorable light. "I'm trying to track down Marvin Hatcher, the cousin," she said. "But it'll be hard to get anything done over the weekend. Most government offices are closed.''

"Lean on them if you have to.''

"I've asked Sheriff McElroy to try and get someone to go over to the Crawford County Clerk's office and look up Bobby Lee's marriage license. If we can track down the woman he married, it's possible she could shed some light on his whereabouts. The kid brother seemed to think Bobby Lee might have gone off to try and find her.''

"That's all well and good," Sheriff Mooney said. "But Bobby Lee Hatcher is a long shot, and you know it, Abby.

As far as we know, he has no connection whatsoever to Eden, much less to those children.''

"As far as we know," Abby agreed. But it was the unknown regarding Bobby Lee Hatcher that still nagged at her.

SHE FOUND SAM at the community center a little while later, working with the volunteers. When he saw her come in, he rose and strode across the room toward her. "You talked to the sheriff?"

Abby nodded. "Yeah. You're in. For the time being, at least. You'll be working with me while you formulate profiles on both cases. But, Sam—" She put a hand on his arm, then immediately removed it, realizing the intimacy of the action. Remembering the even more intimate feel of his lips on hers. "You have to keep a low profile. No talking to the press."

"Not a problem," he said. "But I don't think I'm the one you need to worry about." He nodded toward the front of the community center, where a buzz had started up among the few reporters milling about. Curtis Brodie had just come in, and the group descended on him like a swarm of hungry locusts.

"Mr. Brodie, has there been any word about your daughter?"

"Mr. Brodie, are the police keeping you informed about the investigation?"

"How do you feel about the fact that the task force seems to have no real suspects?"

Undaunted by the barrage of questions, Curtis Brodie seemed in no hurry to move away from the reporters. "They have no real suspects because they're incompetent," he said bluntly.

"How do you think the FBI's involvement will affect the investigation?"

"Unfortunately, their involvement is a matter of offering too little too late. They should have been brought in immediately, the moment the first little girl was taken. Sara Beth might be with us now. But Sheriff Mooney put his ego before our children's safety, and now my daughter is paying the price. And your child might be next," he said to the enthralled throng. He had a way of speaking that made everyone listen whether they agreed with what he was saying or not. As much as she disliked him, Abby couldn't deny the man's personal charisma. He was like a Svengali, she thought. Or a very slick politician.

His appearance certainly didn't work against him. He was tall, fit, his skin tanned to a deep bronze. But even apart from his good looks, he had a presence about him, an almost obscene vitality that seemed to suck the air out of any room he entered.

Two of the reporters were women, and he had them eating out of his hand. They hung on his every word, leaving the tougher questioning to their male counterparts.

"Sheriff Mooney has put a detective in charge of my daughter's case who has no experience in crimes of this nature," he said scathingly. "Sergeant Cross has already made one very serious mistake. Let's hope it wasn't a fatal one."

Abby started when she heard her name. She took a step toward the man, but Sam grabbed her arm, holding her back. "He wants a showdown. Don't give him the satisfaction."

It was sound advice, but Abby had a hard time standing silently by while Curtis Brodie maligned her reputation. She reminded herself that he was a very frightened parent and entitled to some slack. But Curtis Brodie didn't appear to be suffering at the moment. If anything, he loved the limelight.

"A car carrying a small child, a girl, was seen in the vicinity by several witnesses at the time of my daughter's disappearance. Sergeant Cross didn't bother interviewing these witnesses until the next day. Everyone knows that the first twenty-four hours following an abduction is critical. Everyone, that is, except Sergeant Cross."

Abby spun on Sam. "How did he find out about that car?"

Sam's eyes narrowed on her. "What are you implying, Abby?"

"Nothing," she muttered, backing down. Not willing to admit that Sheriff Mooney had put reservations about Sam's motives in her head. "I don't like leaks, that's all."

"It's not a leak. Curtis and Karen were both questioned about that car."

"Not about the child in the back seat. We purposely held that back."

"Then maybe one of the Pratt boys talked. Or Fayetta Gibbons. You can't keep every detail a secret. Not in a high-profile case like this."

Maybe not, but Abby knew she'd better figure out a way to keep Sam's involvement under wraps, or her career, what was left of it when Curtis Brodie got through, was toast.

SAM STARED out the window as Abby headed north, taking them along a stretch of road that afforded an occasional glimpse of the lake. The day had turned out to be hot and dry. The thunderclouds of early morning had dissolved into a crystalline blue sky, and across the water, white, palatial houses gleamed in the early-afternoon sunlight.

"Who lives over there?" He nodded across the lake,

trying to find a topic of conversation that might lessen the tension between them. Abby had been wound up tighter than a trip wire ever since Curtis's performance for the reporters, but Sam wasn't convinced the assault on her competence was the only thing bothering her. She was still ticked off about that kiss last night. Annoyed with herself, maybe, because she'd responded.

It probably hadn't been a great idea, Sam reflected, but he wasn't sorry it had happened, because the moment his mouth had touched Abby's, he'd felt alive again, after so many years of being dead inside.

Whatever emotions had been left after coping with Jonathan's death had slowly been eaten away by his job. When he got home most nights, he didn't think too much about relationships, or even one-night stands for that matter. Mostly what he felt was old and tired.

But last night, Abby had changed all that—with just a kiss.

He heard her speak, and with an effort, he pulled himself out of his reverie. He glanced at her profile as she sat behind the wheel, and he thought again what an attractive woman she was. In so many ways.

"...most of the houses on the other side of the lake are vacation homes. They're usually only occupied in the summer months."

"Does anyone local live over there?"

"A few. In fact, Curtis Brodie just bought a big place on the water." She waited a beat, then said, "You realize, of course, that both Karen and Curtis are still suspects in Sara Beth's disappearance? They have to be, especially considering the bitter nature of their separation."

"I understand that."

Abby lifted a hand and pushed back her hair. "What you also need to understand is that I'm going to go wherever this investigation leads me. I don't care whose toes I step on.''

''I wouldn't have it any other way.''

She nodded.

He said almost matter-of-factly, ''Did you know that Curtis is having some serious financial problems?''

''What kind of problems?''

''I think he may be in trouble with the IRS.''

Abby glanced at him in surprise. ''Who told you that? Karen?''

''No. Someone who works for Curtis. I think it bears a closer scrutiny.''

''Yes, but even if it's true, what would his finances have to do with his daughter's kidnapping—'' Abby stopped herself almost as soon as the words were out. She glanced at him, horrified. ''Insurance?''

''I'm not accusing him of anything,'' Sam said, but his stomach knotted at the very idea. He'd seen it all, even the bloody aftermath of a parent's rage against a child, but this was his sister's daughter. The fact that Sam had never laid eyes on her didn't matter. All his protective instincts rose to the surface with a vengeance. God help Curtis Brodie if he'd laid one finger on that child.

''You're okay with this?'' Abby asked doubtfully. ''I mean, this is your family we're talking about.''

''Curtis Brodie isn't part of my family. And believe me, if he had any part in Sara Beth's disappearance, I have no problem taking him down.''

''I understand.''

Their gazes met, and Sam thought, *she does understand, because she'd do the same if it were Sadie.*

But her motives would be far different from his. Abby's ten-year hunt for her niece was a labor of love. A search kept alive by devotion and family loyalty. Sam was here in large part out of guilt. He'd once let his sister down very badly. He couldn't do the same to Sara Beth.

"You're willing to take down Curtis Brodie," Abby said slowly, "But what about your sister?"

"What about her?"

"Curtis has made some pretty serious accusations against her. He said she came at him once with a knife."

Sam had heard that same allegation from Luanne Plimpton. Having Abby repeat it didn't make it any truer, or any less disturbing. "Have you asked Karen about it?"

"She denied it," Abby said grimly. "She said Curtis was the one who threatened her. There's no love lost between those two, that much is obvious. But what I want to know is where Sara Beth fits into the equation."

"I believe Karen loves her," Sam said.

Abby nodded. "I believe that, too. But you and I both know that people do terrible things in the name of love."

THEY WERE NEARING Fairhaven Academy. Although it was a Saturday, Abby had arranged for Lois Sheridan, the director, to assemble the teachers and support staff so that she and Sam could speak with them again. She wanted to get his impression of the people who had come into contact with both Sara Beth and Emily on a daily basis.

But he'd been so silent for the last several minutes that Abby wondered if she'd been wrong to voice her doubts about his sister. Her suspicions were nothing concrete. Nothing but a nagging intuition that something wasn't right in the Brodie household.

But family was family. Abby understood that, too. Sam had a right to be protective of his sister, so long as his loyalty didn't interfere with the investigation. So long as he meant what he said—that he was willing to follow the investigation no matter where it led them.

He could be using his expertise to try and steer the investigation in the wrong direction.

She shoved her doubts aside. "So how did you become a profiler?"

Sam had been gazing out the window, but he turned to face her now, his gray eyes deeply intense. "I was working out of the field office in Denver, and we had a serial killer who was preying on elderly women. He was as meticulous in his arrangement of the bodies and the cleanup of the crime scenes as he was vicious in his killings. Those of us working the case had never seen anything like it. We contacted Quantico and requested assistance from the Behavioral Science Unit. Back then profiling was still considered something akin to palm reading by a lot of people in the Bureau. Those guys didn't get a lot of respect, and the special agent in charge of the Denver office had reservations about bringing one in. But the profiler nailed the UNSUB cold."

"And you were impressed."

"Yeah. I was. I'd worked with him pretty closely on the case, picked his brain all I could, and before he went back to Quantico I told him I was interested in profiling. He gave me a recommendation, and within six months, I'd moved back east."

"Any regrets?"

"Sure. Everyone has regrets."

Abby wanted to ask him what those regrets were. Why he'd been compelled to resign after so many years. She remembered what his boss had said about him when Abby had called him. *Sam Burke? One of the best profilers I've ever seen. Damned uncanny at times.*

Abby found herself shivering. "I've always been interested in profiling."

"You don't want to be a profiler, Abby. Trust me."

"Why not? The work has to be rewarding." She tried to hide the stab of disappointment inflicted by Sam's casual dismissal of her dream.

"It is. But it's also grueling. You work in cramped quarters six stories underground. That alone can be stressful, but the work load is almost impossible. Twelve profilers handling hundreds, sometimes thousands of the most depressing and disturbing cases you can imagine. Burnout is not uncommon."

"I think what you're trying to tell me is that you don't think I could cut it," she said with a frown.

"Maybe," he conceded. "But not in the way you think. You're talented enough. You've got great instincts. But Eden isn't like the rest of the world. In a lot of ways, it's like stepping into a time warp. Oh, you have your computers and cell phones and twenty-first-century technology, but it's not like the outside world. Here, even the crime scenes are pristine. No blood. No bodies—"

"You think a child abduction is clean?" Abby asked in disgust.

"All I'm saying is that until you've seen firsthand what a truly sick mind can do, you have no concept of what it's like to work day in and day out on cases so gruesome your mind has a hard time comprehending such brutality. You can't believe what human beings can do to one another. And after you've spent fourteen or fifteen hours a day with such horror, you get to go home and dream about it."

"Is that why you quit?"

"No." He turned to stare out the window. "I quit because I *didn't* dream about it anymore."

Chapter Ten

Tall, thin, and impeccably groomed, Lois Sheridan seemed to personify the attributes one would associate with the director of a private school that catered mainly to the children of the upper crust. There had been exceptions over the years, of course, like Emily and Sadie. Neither child came from an affluent background, and as Abby studied the woman surreptitiously, she couldn't help wondering if Lois Sheridan had perhaps been galled by the fact that, due to unforeseen openings in her enrollment in those years, she'd been forced to accept children who would have normally been turned away from Fairhaven, albeit discreetly.

She was an imposing woman, Abby had to admit, with her ramrod posture and imperious, almost despotic, comportment. The students at Fairhaven were probably terrified of her. Looking down her nose, she gave Abby's own posture a reproving glance that made Abby immediately sit up straight, back her shoulders, and press her knees together like a propositioned virgin.

Sam, on the other hand, didn't seem in the least affected by the woman's arrogant demeanor, but then, he was a lot longer out of school than Abby was. And besides, she thought, if his posture was any more rigid, he might have to worry about rigor mortis.

"I've assembled everyone you asked to speak with," Lois Sheridan was saying. "Except for Miss Wilder. She left school yesterday before you called, and I haven't been able to reach her by telephone this morning. It is Saturday, after all," she said disapprovingly. "People have things to do. But I did leave a message, so perhaps she'll arrive before you finish."

Abby nodded. "We appreciate your cooperation."

"Yes, well, I don't really see the necessity of all this. We've all been interviewed by the police. I've even spoken with the FBI." Her gaze swept over Sam, but she seemed to sense that here was a man not easily subjugated by her commanding personality. She turned her attention to Abby who, for the life of her, couldn't help squirming a bit in her seat.

"Mrs. Sheridan—" Sam began, but she cut him off.

"I prefer Ms."

"We'd like to ask you some questions about Sara Beth Brodie."

The woman's brows arched slightly. "Well, then I'm afraid I really don't have anything to add to what I've already told the authorities. Sara Beth wasn't taken from school premises. Fairhaven can't be held responsible for her disappearance."

"We're not here to assess blame," Abby said, slightly taken aback by the woman's attitude. "We're here to try and find some answers."

"I understand that, but the more you people keep coming back here, the more the parents of my students are going to question their children's safety at Fairhaven. I've already had three students pulled from the roster, and a plethora of telephone calls and visits from other concerned parents. Fairhaven's reputation is at stake here."

"Surely you're not putting the school's reputation above the welfare of two missing children," Abby said.

Lois Sheridan stared at her with ill-concealed disdain. "Of course not. But I'm concerned about the welfare of all the children, not just the two who are missing. If that sounds heartless to you, then I'm sorry."

She didn't sound in the least sorry to Abby. She glanced at Sam, but other than a slight scowl, he displayed no reaction whatsoever to the woman's attitude.

"Would you consider Sara Beth a good student?" he asked.

Lois Sheridan smiled, but the humor didn't reach her eyes. "As I've told the other investigators, Sara Beth did not apply herself. Even at her young age, she displayed an alarming disregard for authority. Once she discovered she could attract attention by acting up in class, she became very disruptive, often impossible to deal with. To tell you the truth, I've regretted more than once my decision to accept her application. Unfortunately, she just isn't Fairhaven material."

And what about Emily and Sadie? Abby thought.

"Then why didn't you ask her parents to remove her from the school?" Sam asked.

She paused, straightening papers on her desk that were already in a neat pile. "I'm nothing if not a realist. Fairhaven relies heavily on private contributions for our funding, above and beyond the tuition payments. And Sara Beth's father made a very generous donation."

The child had been kept on at Fairhaven because of her father's money, but it was painfully obvious that Lois Sheridan despised the crass realities of economics. In a perfect world, her student body would be made up of per-

fect little Stepford children, and the ones like Sara Beth
Brodie would be banished back to the public school system, where they belonged.

And what about Emily Campbell? Like Abby's sister,
Tess was a single mother who struggled even to meet the
steep tuition requirements at Fairhaven. Donations to the
school would be out of the question. What if a child from
a well-to-do family wanted in after someone like Emily
and Sadie or even Sara Beth had been accepted? Lois
Sheridan couldn't banish them legally to make room for
the more desirable student. So what would she do?

She would resent them, Abby thought.

But had she resented Sara Beth and Emily enough to
get rid of them? Was maintaining the high standards she'd
set for Fairhaven that important to her?

It might be, if she had nothing else in her life. If the
school had become synonymous with her own identity.
Her own personality.

A personality that could tolerate not one single imper-
fection.

ABBY AND SAM spoke with Lois Sheridan at length about
Sara Beth and Emily Campbell, and although the woman
remained coolly detached from the children's plight,
sometimes downright cold, she didn't say anything that
could be considered remotely incriminating.

Neither did any of the teachers or support staff they
interviewed. With the exception of Lois Sheridan, Fairhaven's personnel were all extremely distressed over the
disappearances, and offered their unflagging cooperation.

After an hour or so, they'd talked to almost everyone
and hadn't come up with any new information. Abby was
exhausted by the monotony of the questions, but Sam
seemed to gather strength with each new interview. He

was a natural, but Abby supposed that came from his expertise in profiling. He knew how to read people. He knew when to press and when to pull back. When to flatter and when to intimidate. Abby found herself hanging back and letting him take over the questioning, a decision that would have been foreign to her a day ago.

Sam knew how to work her, too. He'd wormed his way into the investigation by playing on her conscience, her concern for the missing children, but he'd gotten under her skin in a personal way, too. Abby realized as the day wore on that not only was her respect and admiration for him growing, so were her feelings.

She studied him covertly as one of the last interviewees walked into the teachers' conference room Lois Sheridan had allowed them to use. Willa Banks, the school nurse, was a short, plump, motherly type who looked to be nearing retirement age, although her step was still quite spry.

Her green pants outfit was adorned with a large, yellow smiley-face button that was undoubtedly worn to calm apprehension in the children who came to see her. With her flat, ugly shoes and unpainted, careworn face, she appeared the antithesis of Lois Sheridan.

She seemed a little anxious when she first entered the room. "I hope this won't take much longer." She paused as if realizing how her words might have sounded. "I'll do everything I can, of course. I'm worried sick about those children. It's just that I have people visiting, and I need to get back to them."

"We'll try to make this fast then." Sam smiled to put the woman at ease.

"You do think you'll find them, don't you? I know it's been days, but I refuse to believe that any harm has come to them. How could anyone hurt such innocent children?"

Abby knew exactly what Sam was thinking. Children were hurt everyday, but he merely nodded sympathetically at the nurse. "We're doing everything we can to find them and bring them home safely. That's why we keep coming back, asking more questions. We can't afford to leave any stone unturned."

Willa Banks nodded almost eagerly. "I understand. How can I help?"

"What can you tell us about the girls? Did you have much contact with them?"

She seemed to consider the question for a moment. "Not really. Neither one of them was prone to accidents as some of the children seem to be. But my office faces the playground, and if I'm not busy, I like to watch the children at recess. I know almost all of them by name. They're so sweet and innocent at this age. Emily is a quiet child. Timid and a bit of a loner. She could swing by herself for hours and be content, but Sara Beth is more rambunctious. She spends most of her time on the jungle gym, climbing like a little monkey." The women hesitated. "Is that the sort of thing you want to know?"

"We want to know whatever you can tell us about either child," Sam said.

For several minutes, he guided her through a series of questions, then thanked her for her cooperation. At the door, she turned, her expression worried. "I wonder if I could ask *you* a question?"

"Certainly," Sam said.

"Have you spoken with Miss Wilder?"

"Not today, no."

Willa sighed. "I'm very worried about her. She's such a young thing to have something like this happen. She was the one in charge of the playground the day Emily

disappeared. She felt so guilty, especially considering—''
She broke off, pursing her lips together as if she were
afraid to say anything more.

''Considering what, Nurse Banks?'' By giving her the
professional courtesy of addressing her by title, Sam was
showing respect for her position, putting them on an equal
footing so that she would feel more comfortable opening
up to him.

It seemed to work. She closed the door and came back
into the room. ''I don't like breaking a confidence, but
this has been bothering me a great deal ever since Emily
disappeared.'' She glanced at Abby, then lowered her
voice, as if her words were for Sam alone. ''She came to
me right after school started, very distraught. She was new
in town, new on the job, and I don't think she had anyone
else to talk to. I've always been good with people. A nurse
has to be.''

Sam nodded.

''It was clear to me that something was eating that poor
girl up inside. It took awhile, but I finally got her to open
up to me.'' She fingered the smiley-face pin uncon-
sciously. ''When she was seventeen years old, she worked
as a counselor at a summer camp. She fell madly in love
with a boy there, another counselor, and she told me that
was the happiest time of her life. But at the end of the
summer when she went home, she found out she was
pregnant. Her family talked her into putting the baby up
for adoption, but it tormented her. She said she dreamed
about the baby, a little girl, almost every night, and that
sometimes she could hear the child calling out to her,
crying for her. Vickie gave birth five years ago. You see
what I'm getting at, don't you? Her child, the one she
gave up, is the same age as Emily and Sara Beth.''

"IF YOU'RE LOOKING for Vickie, she's not home," a woman called up to Sam and Abby. Abby had seen her when they'd first approached the apartment complex, but the woman had been careful not to make eye contact. She'd waited until they'd knocked on Vickie's door before speaking up.

Abby stared over the railing into the courtyard. "Any idea where she might have gone?"

The woman shrugged.

"When did she leave?"

"Hauled ass before sunup. Parking lot's right outside my bedroom window." The woman aimed the nozzle of a garden hose toward the bed of wilting petunias.

Sam and Abby retraced their steps down the stairs and walked into the courtyard. The woman turned off the hose and came over to meet them. "She's not in any kind of trouble, is she?"

"No, not that we know of. We're talking to everyone at Fairhaven Academy about the recent disappearances."

The woman shook her head. "Those poor little girls. Who would do such a thing?"

Abby said noncommittally, "We're doing everything we can to find them and bring them back home safe and sound, Ms.—"

"Flo Crowder. Florence actually, but everyone calls me Flo. My husband's Ernie Crowder. Used to work for the railroad, but he's retired now. Supposed to be helping me manage this place, but he doesn't do anything but sit in his recliner all day and watch the stories."

Sam nodded sympathetically, hiding his impatience. "Mrs. Crowder, did you see anyone with Vickie Wilder when she left?"

"No, she was alone. But she had a suitcase. I figured she might be going to visit her mama for the weekend."

"Where does her mother live?"

"Memphis, I think."

"Do you have an address?"

"No, can't say as I do." The woman's expression grew sober. "Look, Vickie's a nice girl, okay? I understand that you've got to talk to anybody and everybody you can about those kidnappings, but she's taking this real hard. And I don't think her sister helped matters any."

"Her sister?"

Flo nodded. "She came to stay with Vickie a few days before all this happened, but then she just up and left. Like she didn't want to stay and support Vickie when she was having a hard time."

"What's this sister's name?"

"I don't know. I never really met her, just saw her once in a while. She didn't work, and she kept to herself during the day. A real standoffish type. Wouldn't even speak to me if she met me on the stairs. Nothing like Vickie. They don't look alike, either. I wouldn't have guessed they were sisters if Vickie hadn't told me."

"Has Vickie talked to you about the disappearances?" Abby asked.

"Some. She was the teacher in charge of the playground when that first little girl went missing. What was her name? Emily something-or-other?"

"Campbell."

"Yeah, Campbell, that's it. Vickie said that kid was just the sweetest little thing you ever did see. Never caused a bit of trouble in school. But I got the impression the other one was her favorite."

"Sara Beth Brodie?"

Mrs. Crowder nodded. She reached into the pocket of her house dress and pulled out a pack of cigarettes. "You mind? I can't smoke in the house on account of Ernie's allergies. Never used to bother him,'' she grumbled under her breath. Abby got the distinct impression that Ernie's retirement was not sitting too well with his wife. She shook out a cigarette almost viciously and lit up. Dragging hard, she closed her eyes, seeming for a moment to be caught up in nicotine ecstasy.

"Where was I?" she asked, exhaling a long stream of smoke.

"You said you thought Sara Beth was Vickie's favorite."

"Oh, yeah. I mean, she was cut up enough when the first little girl disappeared, feeling responsible and all, but when she heard about Sara Beth—" She paused to take another drag. "Sara Beth was a little hellion in school, Vickie said, but that didn't mean she wasn't just as sweet as her other kids. That's how Vickie talked about them. She called them 'her kids.' Anyway, she thought Sara Beth's home life might not be so good. That's why the kid acted up at school. If I heard her say it once, I heard her say it a dozen times, 'Miss Flo'—that's what she calls me—'some days I wish I could just bring all those kids home with me. Especially the troubled ones. Especially the ones who need a little extra love.'"

Abby glanced at Sam. His mouth tightened slightly. "We appreciate your help, Mrs. Crowder."

"I'm glad to do what I can." She tossed her cigarette into the wet flower bed, then started to leave.

"One other thing," Sam said. "This sister—what kind of car does she drive?"

Flo turned to stare at him. "I didn't think she had a car at first. She didn't keep one here. Always used Vickie's when she needed to go someplace. I figured that's why she stayed cooped up in the apartment all day, but then I saw her one day in a different car, a few blocks over from here. I was walking home from the grocery story, and she pretended like she didn't see me so she wouldn't have to offer me a ride. But I'm pretty sure it was her."

"What kind of car was it?"

"I couldn't tell you the make or the model, but I think it was white. Or maybe a real pale yellow. It had a lot of dust on it, like maybe she'd been driving out in the country."

"Do you remember what day this was?"

She screwed up her face, trying to remember. "You know, I do. It was the same day that second little girl disappeared. I remember, because I'd stopped by the bank before going to the grocery store, and I saw Karen Brodie. Later that night, when I heard about the kidnapping on the news, it came back to me that I'd seen Karen earlier that day, and that she hadn't known then what was about to happen to her little girl."

THE FORENSICS TECHNICIANS were thorough. They went through every room of Vickie Wilder's apartment, studying the contents of the cabinets, opening closets, examining pictures. They left nothing unchecked, no book unopened, no drawer unsearched. They took the slipcovers off the furniture and looked under the cushions. They even pulled up the carpet and checked behind baseboards, but they found nothing to connect Vickie Wilder to the missing children.

"Nothing," Abby told Sam later when he'd met her back at the sheriff's station. "Not one piece of physical evidence we can use." Discouraged, she pushed her hair back from her face. "How about you? Did you have any better luck with the Memphis field office?"

"Two things they found out strike me as interesting. One, Vickie's sister and her husband live in Australia. They haven't been back to the States in three years. Secondly, while Vickie was in college at Memphis State, her roommate was arrested on a second-degree murder charge."

Abby's mouth dropped open. *"Murder!"*

"Her name was Greta Henley, and apparently her boy-friend turned up dead after an altercation at her and Vickie's apartment. He was stabbed, and Henley claimed it was self defense."

"Was Vickie involved?"

"She was never arrested, but she was under suspicion for a while. There were some inconsistencies in her state-ment. But get this, Abby. Greta Henley jumped bail. She disappeared, and the Memphis PD have never been able to track her down."

"You think it's possible she could be the woman Vickie claimed was her sister?"

"It makes sense," Sam said. "If Vickie wanted one or both of those children, she'd need an accomplice. Some-one who not only made the grab, but stayed with Sara Beth and/or Emily while Vickie remained behind playing the part of the distraught teacher."

Abby shook her head. "She seemed so genuinely upset. If she was lying, I bought the act hook, line and sinker."

IT WAS THE FIRST concrete lead they'd had in days, and the atmosphere inside the command center bristled with excitement as Abby briefed the other police personnel, including Special Agent Carter, about what she and Sam had learned. Even Carter seemed impressed and cau-tiously optimistic that the case was finally about to break.

As Abby walked out to the parking lot late that after-noon, Sam caught up with her. He hadn't been present at the briefing because he was doing exactly what she'd asked—keeping a low profile. But she'd made no secret of the fact that the information concerning Greta Henley had been derived through the Memphis field office via Sam. On that point, Special Agent Carter had expressed concern.

"I don't see what the problem is," Abby said. "You have the same connections that Sam Burke has. More so, because you're still with the Bureau. You could have picked up the phone and been in contact with both the FBI and the local police in Memphis, but you didn't. I think we should be grateful to Sam Burke that he had the foresight to do so."

Special Agent Carter had responded by turning on his heel and exiting the room without further comment.

So be it, Abby thought. This was her case. This was her town. No one could care more about the safety of those children than she. If Talbot Carter's ego had been bruised, then that was just too damn bad.

"Anything wrong?" Sam asked, gazing down at her.

She shrugged. "You FBI types get on my nerves sometimes, that's all."

"Carter giving you a hard time?"

"It doesn't matter. What matters is that we're getting close, Sam. I can feel it."

He nodded, but his eyes were troubled. "Vickie Wilder is looking like a solid suspect. I'll give you that. But we haven't found one piece of physical evidence linking her to the crimes. What we have is all circumstantial."

"If you're trying to cheer me up, please stop," Abby grumbled.

His gaze on her deepened. "I just want you to realize this is far from over. This case could still take an unexpected turn."

His words seemed ominous to Abby. Almost portentous. "Do you know something I don't?"

He shook his head. "No. But I've had a lot of experience. And when things start to look bright in a case like this, it's usually right before they get darkest."

Chapter Eleven

It was almost nine by the time Abby finally got home. She called in a pizza order before stripping and heading for the shower.

Her bedroom and bathroom were the only rooms in the house she'd changed from her grandmother's time. The Jacuzzi tub and separate shower were extravagances Abby could ill afford on her salary, but she'd justified the drain on her savings by reminding herself that she indulged in very few vices. Other than an occasional glass of wine, she didn't drink. She didn't smoke, take drugs or go clubbing. Her social life was actually pretty pathetic, but she was a lot better off than the other women in her family.

Single mothers, all of them, they'd had to give up their dreams at an early age to be both mother and father to their children. But growing up, Abby had never felt slighted by the arrangement because she'd always known how much her mother loved her.

When her mother wasn't around, there was her grandmother to take up the slack. Grandmother Eulalia, who'd toiled in the cotton fields for years, and then later had put in long, exhausting hours bent over her sewing machine, trying to provide for her family. But Abby had never heard her complain. Not once. Her grandmother had accepted her lot in life, including her mistakes, and she'd concentrated on making the most of it.

So had Abby's mother, for that matter. And her sister. Not one of them had ever allowed herself the luxury of wallowing in self-pity. Had ever wasted precious time worrying about what might have been. Even after Sadie's disappearance, Naomi hadn't let the grief destroy her. She'd founded an organization to help other parents of missing children. She'd used her tragedy to benefit others.

And what had Abby done?

She'd played by all the rules. She'd never let herself succumb to her impulses. She'd struggled mightily to keep her life on track, to avoid all the pitfalls, so why, all of a sudden, was she the one who was feeling so discontent tonight? Why was she the one who was lonely?

I'm probably just tired, she thought as she got out of the shower and dried off. Exhausted, heartsick, worried. A case like this was not just physically tiring, but emotionally draining as well. No wonder her thoughts were a bit maudlin tonight. She was entitled, wasn't she?

In the bedroom, she slipped on a cotton sundress in favor of the jeans she'd been wearing lately, because the fabric was much lighter and cooler. More practical in the heat.

The glass vial Mama Evie had given her yesterday lay on her dresser, and, removing the stopper, Abby waved the contents under her nose. She recognized some of the notes in the perfume: honeysuckle, roses, patchouli. But the undertones were harder to define. They were a little darker, a little more mysterious. A little forbidden, even.

She put a drop on her fingertip and dabbed it behind her ears, keeping in mind Mama Evie's warning to use it sparingly. Good advice, Abby thought, wrinkling her nose. The scent was a little overpowering as it mingled with the air. She tried to wipe it off with a towel, but the fragrance lingered.

Stepping outside, she let the night air whisk away the remnants of the scent. The back garden, her grand-mother's passion, always soothed Abby's overwrought nerves, even though she wasn't the least bit keen on yard work herself. She'd done little beyond weeding and mow-ing, and Grandmother Eulalia's carefully cultivated flower beds had grown into a riotous jungle of color. Abby liked it that way. It brought out an untamed aspect of her per-sonality she tried very hard to keep hidden. Better to let her impulses roam free in the backyard than in the bed-room, she'd always thought.

Settling herself in the swing, she pushed off with one foot, letting the gentle motion lull her for a moment. She watched the gray cat she'd brought home from Fairhaven stalk an invisible prey for a moment, then she laid her head back and closed her eyes. Nice, she thought drows-ily. Very nice.

A moment later, she was startled awake by the squeak-ing of the wrought-iron gate. Her gaze flew across the yard to where Sam stood just inside the fence. Her heart started to pound in slow, measured beats.

"What are you doing here?" she asked almost breath-lessly. "And how in the world did you know where to find me?"

"I asked around." His gaze moved over the yard. Day-light was gone, but the moon was up, illuminating the explosion of color in the flower beds, the honeysuckle that crept up the fence row, the trumpet vine that threatened to smother the oak tree that held the swing.

He walked toward Abby in the falling darkness. "I guess there really is a garden of Eden."

AND THERE was Eve, looking more tempting than ever.

She wore a soft, floral dress that bared her shoulders and legs, and in the fading light, her skin gleamed like moonbeams.

Something powerful stirred inside Sam. Something he needed to deny but couldn't. He wanted Abby. He couldn't remember wanting a woman so badly.

He walked over to the swing, and she shifted so that he could sit beside her. "I knocked on the front door, but I guess you didn't hear me."

"I dozed off," she admitted sheepishly. "What made you think to look around here?"

"Just a hunch."

She pushed off again, rocking them slightly. The back-and-forth movement was a little distracting, given Sam's mood.

"What are you doing here, Sam?"

"I came to ask you to dinner."

Her brows rose. "Dinner? This late?"

"You've already eaten?"

"No," she admitted. "But I ordered a pizza. Do…you want to share it?"

"Sounds great." The invitation had been so reluctant Sam wasn't certain he should have accepted. But then again, the way she looked tonight, he didn't think he wanted to leave. He was suddenly very aware of the way she was dressed, of the way her hair curled slightly at her bare shoulders. Of the way she was looking at him.

Their gazes met in the moonlight. The movement of the swing ceased, and in the silence, Sam thought he heard her catch her breath. His heart thudded against his chest, and he had to remind himself that he was too old to be doing this.

But he heard himself saying, unwisely, "You're a very beautiful woman, Abby."

Her gaze widened, as if he'd taken her completely by surprise. "I'm not. I mean, it's nice of you to say that and all, but I'm not. You should see my sister. If you think I'm pretty, you should see her. She's gorgeous, absolutely breathtaking—"

"Abby?"

She stopped and took a breath. "Yes?"

"You're babbling."

"No, I'm not." She settled her skirt around her. "I only babble when I'm nervous, and I'm not nervous."

"I am."

That stopped her again. "You…are? Why?"

"Because we're playing with fire."

"Then why did you come here tonight?"

"You know why," he said softly.

She turned to stare at him in the moonlight. "We went all through this before, Sam. I'm not going to sleep with you. I mean that."

"I know you do."

"Then that's the end of it. There's no need to talk about it any more."

"Okay." Was it really that easy for her? Could she simply block out her feelings? Ignore the attraction that had been building between them since the moment they'd first met?

If so she was a stronger person than he, Sam thought grimly.

He turned back to the garden. "This place is incredible. You must have a green thumb."

She gave a wry laugh. The sound seemed to drift on the darkness. "Hardly. This is what's left of my grandmother's garden. Since I moved in here, I've pretty much just let nature take its course.''

"Sometimes that's the way it should be," he murmured. "I've heard you talk about your sister and your mother and your grandmother, but what about the men in your family?''

"There aren't any."

"None?" He gave her an incredulous look. "There had to have been at one time."

"Not for long. Just long enough to propagate the species and ruin a few lives. The women in my family have very bad judgment when it comes to men."

"Is that why you're not married?"

She pushed off, rocking the swing slightly. "I just didn't want to repeat their mistakes. My grandmother and my mother and my sister were all tied down with kids by the time they were twenty. All three of them struggled to be both mother and father, both caregiver and provider. It's not an ideal way to raise a family."

"I wonder if there is an ideal way," Sam mused.

Abby glanced at him. "What about you?"

"I was married." He wasn't certain he wanted to talk about his marriage. He didn't think he wanted to bring Norah into this conversation. Into this garden. Into his relationship with Abby. If there was a relationship.

"For how long?" she asked curiously.

"Fifteen years."

That seemed to take her aback. "Wow. That's a long time."

"Yeah, but it's not forever." Sam couldn't keep a note of regret out of his voice. He hadn't loved Norah in a very long time, but he'd once loved her. He'd once made her a promise that he hadn't been able to keep. It was not something he liked to think about.

"No kids?" Abby asked softly.

Sam closed his eyes as he thought about Jonathan. As he watched him play for a moment in this very garden. Then the image faded. "We had a son. He died." He didn't look at Abby, but he could feel her gaze on him. Feel the warmth of her sympathy wrapping around him like a comforting embrace. He'd never talked about his son's death with anyone. He didn't understand why he wanted to tell Abby about him now. Why her pity wasn't something he felt he had to turn away from.

"What happened...unless you don't want to talk about it?"

"It's not easy to talk about." He gazed at the garden. "Jonathan had leukemia. He was only nine years old when he died. My wife and I divorced two years later."

She touched his hand. "I'm sorry."

He glanced at her, their gazes meeting in the darkness. "It was a long time ago."

It didn't matter. The pain was still just as fresh as the day his son had died, Abby thought. The grief would never go away. She still missed her mother and her grandmother terribly, but she couldn't imagine what it would be like to lose a child.

She thought again of the two recent kidnappings and of Sadie, and Abby's eyes burned with unshed tears. She wanted to find Sara Beth and Emily. More than anything, she wanted to return them safe and sound to their loved ones, but Sam's son would never be coming back.

No matter how hard she tried, no matter how fierce her dedication, Abby could never give him that.

WHEN THE PIZZA finally arrived, Abby cleared off a space on the coffee table, and, after bringing in plates, napkins, glasses, and a bottle of wine from the kitchen, she sat down on the floor and tucked her legs beneath her.

"Hope you don't mind. Since you're here, we may as well get some work done, and this is where I do my best thinking."

"Uh, no. It's fine."

He wasn't exactly the type to recline on the floor, Abby thought in amusement. When he started to sit down beside her, she said, "Don't you ever relax? At least take off your jacket."

Shrugging out of his suit jacket, he tossed it onto the back of the sofa, then loosened his tie and rolled up his shirtsleeves. Giving Abby a wry look, he slipped off his shoes. "See? I'm relaxed." He slid down on the floor beside her and took the glass of wine she offered him.

"I've got beer if you'd prefer it."

"No, this is good. Thanks."

They helped themselves to pizza, and Abby picked up one of the folders she'd brought home from work. "I've got some background information here you might like to take a look at. I'd be interested in hearing some of your impressions of the people we interviewed today." She opened the folder and scanned the top sheet. "Let's start with Lois Sheridan."

"A perfectionist. Rigid. Inflexible. An obsessive compulsive personality disorder. Not to be confused with an obsessive compulsive disorder. Probably has an active fantasy life."

Abby looked up in surprise. "Really?" Lois Sheridan hadn't struck her as the type of woman prone to fantasies. At least not the good kind.

"She likes control," Sam said. "She's manipulated her environment so that she has complete autonomy. She probably had a very disorganized childhood. Raised in foster homes, maybe, or an orphanage."

Abby's mouth opened slightly. "According to her background check, you nailed her dead on."

He gave her a wry look. "You sound surprised."

"No, it's just…impressive, that's all." She picked up another folder and opened it. "Willa Banks."

"The nurse? Interesting personality."

"How so?"

"She enjoyed the interview. Answering our questions gave her a sense of importance, maybe even power. She wanted us to think she was nervous, but she wasn't. And contrary to what she said, she wasn't the least bit hesitant about breaking Vickie Wilder's confidence. I suspect she has an avid interest in police work. Maybe someone close to her was in law enforcement at one time. Maybe she even fantasized about being a cop. She lives alone, no family to speak of."

"Okay, now you're showing off." Abby nibbled on a piece of crust. She opened the next folder and stared down at a picture of Vickie Wilder, trying to recall her initial impression of the young woman. Nondescript in both her demeanor and appearance. Could she really have kidnapped Sara Beth and Emily?

Abby handed the folder to Sam and watched as he studied Vickie's picture. Something flickered across his features.

"What?" Abby asked him.

He shrugged, but his gaze never left the picture.

"You suspected Vickie when we interviewed her, didn't you? Why didn't you say so?"

"I did. I told you I thought she was holding something back."

"But there was something else, too, wasn't there?"

He hesitated. "I'm not sure. She seemed almost familiar, but I know I've never met her."

Abby glanced at him in surprise. "I felt that, too. Not about her, necessarily, but about a photograph I saw in her apartment. It seemed familiar to me, but I couldn't figure out why."

He closed the folder and laid it aside. "Maybe she just has one of those faces that makes you think you've seen her before." But Abby didn't think he sounded convinced.

"In a way, I hope Vickie is the one," Abby said. "Because I don't believe she'd harm those children. If she took them as a substitute for the baby she had to give up, then they're still alive."

"Assuming the same suspect took both children," Sam said. "But you've never believed that, and neither do I. I think we still have to treat the cases separately. Otherwise, we could overlook something extremely important."

With a shock, Abby realized he was right. Ever since she'd learned about Vickie's background, she'd merged the two cases. She'd been going under the assumption that if Vickie had taken one child as a replacement for her baby, she'd taken both of them. But that wasn't necessarily the case. In fact, it didn't seem very likely.

She reached for the next folder and opened it. "Curtis Brodie."

"No reason to suspect him in Emily's abduction, but I wouldn't rule him out in Sara Beth's." Sam took a long sip of his wine. "Parents are always prime suspects, and in Curtis's case, I think he's a sociopath. He has a need to control and manipulate those around him for his own personal gain or satisfaction. He knows right from wrong, but he doesn't care. He feels no guilt or compassion. He's arrogant, self important, but he's also got enough charm to con his victims. At least for a while."

Abby had seen that charm at work earlier today. And the manipulation. "You think he could be violent?"

"Given the right circumstances, yes."

"I want to talk to him again," Abby said. "I want to ask him some questions about his financial trouble, especially regarding the IRS. I'd like to know just how desperate his situation is."

"Be careful," Sam warned. "I've seen firsthand what men like him are capable of if they feel threatened."

His ominous words sent a shiver up Abby's spine. "What about your sister? Do you think Karen's capable of violence?"

"No." No equivocation on his part whatsoever.

Abby frowned. "Could it be that you just don't want to believe it?"

"What are you getting at, Abby?"

"I'm not saying she's lying. I'm not saying she's capable of violence. But there's something about her reaction to this whole thing that bothers me."

"In what way?"

"I'm not sure I can put my finger on it exactly. Maybe it's because when she learned about Sara Beth's disappearance, she didn't fall apart the way Naomi did when she learned that Sadie had been taken. Or the way Tess Campbell did. I realize comparisons are unfair, because everyone reacts differently in situations like this. That's why I've hesitated to say much."

Sam shrugged, but his expression tightened. "You're entitled to your opinion, but I don't believe for a minute that Karen would ever hurt Sara Beth. She loves that little girl."

Abby wished she could share his conviction, but the truth of the matter was, she didn't trust Karen Brodie. Abby might not have Sam's insight, his ability to read people, but she trusted her own instincts, and something was telling her to take a harder look at Karen Brodie even as the evidence pointed to Vickie Wilder.

Given his relationship to Karen, Abby wondered if she'd made a mistake bringing Sam in on this case.

Pushing her plate aside, she picked up the last folder. "Luanne Plimpton."

Sam grimaced. "A narcissist. Classic case. Craves admiration, has a sense of entitlement, lacks empathy."

"Even I could have told you that much." Abby closed the folder and handed it to him. "Sara Beth was in her care when the child went missing. Luanne says she stopped at that particular drugstore because it was on the way home, but there's a Big Star Pharmacy just two blocks over," she said, referring to one of the large chains. "Hardly anyone out of the immediate neighborhood shops at Ferguson's anymore. I don't even know how the old man stays in business. The store is always empty. Maybe that's why she stopped there. Maybe she knew there'd be no one around, no witnesses."

"She'd need an accomplice, too. Someone who knew about the stop ahead of time."

"Someone like Curtis," Abby said. "Maybe he and Luanne cooked this whole thing up together."

Sam glanced down at her folder. "Then if I were Luanne, I'd be pretty damned worried. If Curtis was desperate enough and cold-blooded enough to kidnap his own child, it's a safe bet he wouldn't have qualms about eliminating any witnesses."

"But supposing Curtis had nothing to do with it. It's pretty obvious Luanne has plans of becoming the next Mrs. Curtis Brodie. If she perceived Sara Beth as an obstacle, she'd want to remove her, wouldn't she?"

Sam eyed her approvingly. "You've given this a lot of

thought, haven't you? You're searching for deeper motives aside from the obvious.''

"Yes, but you're the expert." Abby reached across him to retrieve the wine bottle. She replenished both of their glasses. "We've established means, motive, and opportunity for virtually every adult who came into contact with Sara Beth—and to a lesser extent, Emily. We have to narrow the list, and that's where your expertise comes in. Have you worked up a profile?''

"I'm working on it. From everything I've seen and read in the reports, I believe your niece Sadie was taken ten years ago by a woman, a Caucasian, somewhere between the ages of twenty and forty-five, possibly a little older. The abductor was someone familiar with this town. She lived here either at the time or at some time in the past, or she had relatives here. She deliberately chose the location and the time of the abduction because she knew she would be able to move about freely without suspicion. A lot of people were coming and going from the grounds after school. Chances were good she wouldn't be noticed. Choosing Sadie was also very deliberate. Her age, her physical appearance. The child was taken to fill some kind of void.''

Abby clung to his words in fascination. "You mean because the abductor's own child might have died? Or had been put up for adoption?''

"Something like that. But remember, Vickie Wilder was only a child herself ten years ago.''

"What about Emily?''

"Sadie's and Emily's abductions are connected. We may be dealing with one UNSUB in their disappearances.''

Abby thought for a moment. "But if the abductor took

Sadie as a replacement for her child, or *a* child, why did she come back ten years later and take Emily?''

Sam didn't answer, and Abby said, almost in a whisper, ''You think she took Emily as a replacement for Sadie, don't you? Because something happened to Sadie. You think she's dead.''

''I'm sorry, Abby, but after ten years, you have to know that's a very real possibility. If I'm right, chances are good that Emily could still be alive.''

Abby closed her eyes. She prayed with all her heart that Emily was alive. Safe and unharmed. That they would find her soon. But if Sam was right, Sadie would never be found.

A fist of fear closed around Abby's heart as images bombarded her. Images of Sadie and Naomi. Images of innocence lost.

Ten years was a long time to grieve. A long time to cling to hope. There'd been times when Abby had thought to herself that a resolution, no matter how devastating, would be better than the awful purgatory of not knowing. Of forever waiting. But now she wasn't so sure.

To think of Sadie gone forever…

To think of having to tell Naomi…

''I could be wrong,'' Sam said softly. ''It could be that someone just wants us to think Emily and Sadie's disappearances are connected.''

''What about Sara Beth? Do you have a profile of her abductor?''

He frowned into his glass. ''No. Not yet.''

Was he telling her everything? Abby wondered. Or was he holding back on her? Was he afraid to face the truth?

''We don't really know anything, do we?'' she asked him. ''We speculate, we have hunches, but we don't have anything concrete. All these people we've talked to—any one of them could have taken Sara Beth or Emily, but we don't know much more than we did six days ago when Emily first disappeared. And the trail is getting colder every second.''

"It's not like you to give up."

"I'm not giving up," she said almost angrily. "I'll never give up. It's just…I'm scared."

"I know."

"I'm scared we won't find them in time."

"You will. You're one of the best investigators I've ever worked with, Abby. And if you care a little too much at times…it's better than the opposite. Believe me."

"You care, Sam. You just don't want anyone knowing it. Even yourself."

"Don't try to make me into someone I'm not. I'm burned out, Abby. There are times when I feel like an old man."

"You're not old."

He gave her an ironic smile. "Too old for you."

Abby very carefully placed her wineglass on the coffee table, then turned back to face him. "Why don't you let me be the judge of that?"

Chapter Twelve

Sam wasn't quite certain how it happened so quickly. One moment he was staring into her eyes, and the next thing he knew, he was kissing her long and deep. And she was kissing him back. He touched her all over, and she touched him back. Touched him in a way that made him burn for her.

"Abby—"

"I know," she whispered. "I know."

He fumbled with her clothes and then with his own, ripping off the items and discarding them in an untidy heap on the living-room floor. They fell back against the rug, arms and legs entwined. Abby's body was hot and straining against his. Lush. Soft as silk. She was incredible. Sam wanted to restrain himself. Wanted to hold back and make it good for her, but it had been so damn long. And Abby was so damn sexy. And he needed her so badly…wanted her more than he could ever remember wanting anything.

"Yes," she whispered, encouraging him, moving against him until control was out of the question. Until all he could do was hold her tightly, kiss her deeply and let nature takes its course.

ABBY HAD ONLY meant to kiss him. She'd only meant to draw comfort from the feel of his arms around her. But the moment his lips met hers, she'd wanted more. Needed more.

His touch was so electric. His body pressed against hers sent heat waves pulsing through her. It was wrong, of course. Irresponsible and foolish, and Abby made no excuses for herself. She simply wanted Sam at that moment, and she meant to have him. For once in her life, she was not going to put up roadblocks to her most secret desires.

She might have still if it had been anyone but Sam. But, oh, did he know how to kiss! How to move. He knew just where to touch her to leave her gasping for more. The pleasure was so intense Abby couldn't help but cry out.

Her hands moved to his shoulders, trailed down his chest. His skin was so hot. His body so hard…

"Are you sure you want this, Abby?"

Her mind said no, but her body said yes. A thousand times, yes. She clutched his arms. "I've never wanted anything so badly in my life," she whispered.

His gaze darkened knowingly as he lowered himself over her, and his body claimed hers in a slow dance of desire that left Abby shuddering. And wanting more…

THEY LAY ON THEIR BACKS, staring at the ceiling. Finally Sam rolled over and propped himself on his elbow to gaze down at her. "That was—"

"Stupid," Abby said, squeezing her eyes closed. "Really, really, really stupid."

Ouch. Nothing like a little brutal honesty to quell the afterglow. "Sorry," Sam muttered, not knowing what else to say.

"Don't apologize. It wasn't your fault. No more than it was mine." She lifted her hands to her face. "I can't believe I let that happen. I don't do that kind of thing. I know I just did…but I don't…'' She trailed off helplessly. ''What I mean is, I don't have casual sex with strangers. At least, I *didn't* until tonight. That's how all the women in my family turned up pregnant.''

''You're not going to get pregnant,'' Sam pointed out reasonably. ''We took care of that, remember?''

''That makes me feel so much better. I just had *safe*, casual sex with a stranger.''

''We're not exactly strangers.'' Sam rolled over onto his back. He was getting a little annoyed by her attitude. Granted, he was rusty, but it hadn't been *that* bad, had it?

As if sensing she'd gone a little too far, Abby said quickly, ''Look, it's nothing personal. But that's just the point. It wasn't personal. We hardly know each other.''

Maybe not, but Sam had opened up more to Abby in the past few hours than he had to anyone in years. He didn't know why. He just knew that she wasn't like any woman he'd ever met before. He just knew that he trusted her in a way he hadn't trusted anyone in a long, long time.

And what they'd done…what they'd shared had been incredible. Why was she trying to deny it?

''I'm not going to lie and say I don't know what came over me,'' she said. ''I knew what I was doing. I did it because I wanted to. It felt good. And for a little while…''

It made you forget about two missing little girls. Sam understood. Better than she did. Sometimes being with someone was the only way to make the darkness go away.

Abby reached up to the sofa and grabbed a quilt from the back. She cocooned herself in it, and Sam suddenly became overly aware of his own nudity. He worked out. He kept in shape. But he was forty-three. A lot older than the men Abby was probably used to. Men like Special Agent Carter. Or like Dave Conyers. He'd seen the way both of them had looked at Abby today at the station. Hell, he couldn't blame them. She was a very desirable woman, and any normal, red-blooded male would want her.

But the thought of Abby with another man, any man, wasn't something Sam cared to dwell on. He reached for his clothes as she got up and moved to the window to stare out. Pulling on his pants, he walked over and put his hands on her arms.

An hour ago, even thirty minutes ago, such an intimacy would have been unthinkable. But they'd just made love, and whether Abby wanted to admit it or not, it hadn't been casual. It hadn't been wrong.

He bent and kissed her neck. "Abby, don't you think you're overreacting? We're both adults. We're both free. What did we do that was so wrong?"

"Just because something feels good doesn't make it right, Sam."

"I know that. But at the risk of sounding indelicate, that wasn't your first time, was it?"

"No."

"Then what's so different about being with me?"

She turned and gazed up at him. "I'm not like the women you're used to. I'm old-fashioned. I think a man and woman should at least be in love before they make love."

"Were you in love with the others?"

"Other. And, yes, I thought I was. But there's no question with you and me, is there? You aren't in love with me any more than I am with you."

Sam felt a strange, unsettled sensation in his stomach. "No, I guess not."

"So that makes what we did no more than casual sex."

"Stop saying that." He dropped his hands from her

arms and moved back into the room, picking up his shirt from the floor and drawing it on.

She turned and stared at him in confusion.

"What? I can't be angry?" he snapped. "For your information, what we did wasn't the least bit casual to me. We may not know each other very well, and we may not be in love, but I do care about you, Abby. What we shared meant something to me. I'm sorry it meant so little to you."

She looked almost shocked by his words. "You care about me?"

"Why should that surprise you? There was something between us the moment we laid eyes on each other."

"Physical attraction, yes, but—"

"It was more than that and you know it."

She seemed at a loss. "I don't know what to say."

"Good." He jerked on his tie. "Because in my opinion you've said too damn much already."

"I'm sorry." She sounded wounded. "I guess I just wanted you to know that...I don't expect anything from you."

"You mean there isn't going to be some gun-toting cousin showing up on my doorstep to try and make an honest man of me?" He looked around. "Damn. I can't find my other sock."

Abby's mouth twitched. "For your information, we don't do shotgun weddings down here. Hardly ever anymore, and besides, I told you before—there are no men in my family. The only person you have to worry about is my sister, Naomi. And if she gets wind of this—" She stopped short. "Sam, if anyone finds out about this, my reputation, my career—"

"No one's going to find out."

She drew a long breath. "It can't happen again. You know that, don't you?"

"I guess I kind of figured." He finished buttoning his shirt as he slipped into his shoes.

Once he was dressed, they stood awkwardly apart. "I should probably get going." Sam wasn't quite sure what to do. Should he try to kiss her? Given her mood, she might just smack him. And not in a good way.

As if sensing his trepidation, she pulled the quilt more tightly around her. "It is getting late."

He nodded, but he still couldn't quite make himself head for the door. "Are you going to be okay?"

She gave him a little smile that made him want to kiss her even more badly. Agitated, in the throes of remorse, she still looked pretty damn sexy. "I'll be fine. A little repentance is good for the soul."

"Don't be too hard on yourself."

She nodded as she reached a hand up to push back her mussed hair. The quilt slipped a little, revealing one creamy shoulder and a tantalizing glimpse of cleavage.

Sam gritted his teeth and headed toward the door, but she stopped him. "Sam?"

He turned and took a step back into the room. "Yeah?"

"All those things I said…" She paused, biting her lip. "With the guilt and all, I might not have mentioned that you were pretty amazing."

He gave her a brief smile. "I wasn't sure. It's been a while and…things happened a little quickly—"

"Sam?"

"Yeah?"

"You're babbling."

"I never babble," he said quite seriously.

She nodded. "Right. And I never have casual sex with a stranger."

ABBY HAD JUST CLIMBED out of the shower and was slipping into bed when her phone rang. For a moment, she had the irrational hope that it might be Sam, wanting to come back over. For another half second, she debated with herself on what to tell him. Yes. No. Maybe. Then she jerked up the phone and lifted it to her ear. When she heard Sheriff Mooney's voice, disappointment darted through her. And then fear.

Oh, God, they've found one of the children. Please let her be alive.

"What is it, Sheriff? What's happened?"

"Abby, I'm at the Brodie house. Get over here as fast as you can. Karen Brodie just got a ransom demand. By morning, the damn place is going to be crawling with feds."

ABBY BREATHED a sigh of relief when she pulled up to the Brodie house and saw that there were no news vans parked at the curb or reporters milling about in the yard. The media hadn't yet gotten wind of this new development, and the longer they could be kept at bay, the better.

Sheriff Mooney was inside, along with the deputy who had monitored the call. There were a few others standing around, but it was clear to everyone present that Special Agent Carter had assumed an elevated role in the investigation. It would continue to be a joint effort between the feds and the locals, but the Bureau's presence from now on would be a lot more prominent because the ransom note had changed the dynamics of the case.

Carter sat at the kitchen table, listening to the taped message with a tense but excited look on his face.

"Hello, Mrs. Brodie," the distorted voice greeted. "Sara Beth says she wants to come home, but it's not going to be that easy. You have until the close of work on Monday to put together $500,000 in small, unmarked bills—''

"Oh, my God!" Karen Brodie's voice on the tape, shocked and desperate, interrupted the kidnapper. "Who are you? Who *are* you?"

But there'd been no one on the other end by that time.

Abby glanced at Carter. "That's it?"

He nodded grimly. "But it's more than we had a few hours ago, Sergeant Cross. Now, if you'll excuse me, I need to speak with Mrs. Brodie."

He couldn't have dismissed her more curtly if he'd shoved her in the back. Abby walked over to Sheriff Mooney. "What time did the call come in?"

"Around 10:30."

Abby tried to calculate what she'd been doing at that time. Had she and Sam still been in the throes of passion, or had regret already set in?

"Did we get a trace?"

"The call was made from a pay phone on Highway 240 between here and Alma," he said, referring to a tiny, rural community about ten miles south of Eden. "We've got a team on the way down there to dust for prints and canvass the area, but I doubt anyone saw anything. There's nothing but woods out there for miles."

"You send our people or theirs?" she asked, nodding toward Carter.

"It's a joint effort."

Yeah, right, Abby thought. The feds would use local personnel for the grunt work, but if the outcome of the case was favorable, you could be certain they'd take full credit. They always did.

She glanced back at the table where Carter was still

talking to Karen Brodie. Her face was pale, her demeanor almost rigid. She looked as if she was using every last ounce of her strength to hold herself together.

She's in shock, Abby thought. Sara Beth had been missing since Wednesday. A ransom call at this late date hadn't been expected, but it could be good news. It could mean she was still alive. But Karen Brodie didn't seem to comprehend that yet.

The back door opened and Sam walked in. Abby's heart jumped to her throat at the sight of him. At the memory of him.

Their gazes met and a shiver rolled over her.

My, oh my, she thought. *Just a short while ago, I was making love to this man.*

Her face beet red, Abby turned away, unable to hold his gaze. She hoped, prayed, no one else had noticed her discomfort.

He moved across the room and sat down at the table beside Karen. Putting his arm around her shoulders, he spoke to her in low tones, which Special Agent Carter didn't seem to appreciate. He was in charge here. He was the hero here.

"Feds," Abby muttered.

"What?" Sheriff Mooney asked sharply.

"What's Carter telling her?"

"Probably running her through the pros and cons of paying the ransom."

As any cop knew, paying a ransom didn't automatically guarantee the safe return of the victim. More often than not, just the opposite was true. A kidnapper didn't like to leave witnesses. But if a drop wasn't made and the victim died, then the guilt could be overwhelming.

Abby shuddered, thinking of Karen Brodie's choices.

"I DON'T UNDERSTAND," Karen murmured. She clung to Sam's hand. "How can this be happening? *Why* is it happening?"

She was hanging on by a thread. Sam had never seen anyone look so fragile.

She's not going to be able to do this, he thought. She could barely listen to Carter's instructions, much less make the decision on whether or not to pay the ransom.

And it was a call she had to make. She and Curtis. Sam could advise. He could tell her what his experience had been in such cases. He could give her the odds of Sara Beth coming out of this alive whether they paid the ransom or not, but the simple truth was, no one really knew the best course of action. Every case was different. Every kidnapper an individual, but the one thing Sam knew for sure was that the hours were ticking away. With every beat of the clock, the probability of Sara Beth's safe return grew dimmer.

He looked up and saw Abby. Except for the moment when he'd first arrived, she'd avoided eye contact with him. His stomach tightened as he stared at her for a moment, willing her to meet his gaze.

Karen's grasp tightened on his, and Sam tore his attention away from Abby. If possible, his sister's face had grown even whiter. A look of dread came over her features. She stared at the doorway that led into the dining room, where a man's voice had risen in anger. Her hand trembled inside Sam's. Her lips parted, but she said nothing.

Sam turned to the doorway just as Curtis strode through.

BEFORE ANYONE could stop her, before anyone realized she'd even moved, Karen Brodie launched herself across the room toward her husband. She raked her fingernails down his face, drawing blood, before he could grab her wrists.

"You did this!" she screamed in fury. "You did this just to torment me! If you hurt her, I swear I'll kill you. Do you hear me? I'll kill you!"

She tried to go for his face again, but Curtis held on to her wrists and flung her away from him. But this time, Sam had come around the table and grabbed Karen. She tried to struggle away from him, but then the adrenaline seemed to gush out of her and she collapsed against him, sobbing. She couldn't seem to stop.

Curtis eyed her in disgust. "Keep her away from me," he said through clenched teeth. He turned to Sheriff Mooney. "Now do you see what I have to put up with? She's crazy. You saw the way she came at me. Thank God she didn't have a knife this time. And you people call yourselves the law. Do your damn job. If anyone in this room is responsible for Sara Beth's disappearance, it's her." He stabbed a finger at Karen, who was still sobbing helplessly in Sam's arms. "What'd you do to her?" he yelled. "What did you do to Sara Beth, you crazy bi—"

"That's enough," Sam said, very quietly. But his voice, his eyes were as savage as Curtis's. And every bit as cold.

For a moment, Curtis bristled. His hands balled into fists, but something he saw in Sam's face, in that frigid gaze, must have discouraged him from a confrontation. He turned away, muttering, "Just keep her away from me."

Abby felt a little shell-shocked by the scene. She'd broken up brawls before, even a knife fight once between two grown men. She'd witnessed domestic quarrels, tangled with suspects who resisted arrest, experienced violence in varying degrees. But something about the ugly fray between Curtis and Karen Brodie left her almost physically ill.

...when things start to look bright in a case like this, it's usually right before they get darkest.

Sam's words came back to haunt her, and Abby had to wonder if they'd stemmed from more than just his experiences on cases like this. More than just his insights into human nature. Was it possible that Sam had known then the case was far from being solved? Had Vickie Wilder been a way to throw Abby off track?

Someone took her elbow, and Abby started.

Dave Conyers grinned down at her. "Jumpy tonight, aren't you?"

She rubbed her temple, where a headache was starting to throb. "It's this case. Just when I thought I might be figuring it out, a ransom call comes in. Vickie Wilder has disappeared, and the Brodies are literally at each other's throats. So, yeah, I'm a little jumpy." She glanced up at him. "What's up?"

"I just came from the station. I thought you might want to know that Sheriff McElroy down in Palisades is trying to get in touch with you. Says he tried you at home, but he didn't get an answer. I guess you were already on your way over here."

"What he'd say?"

"He said to tell you he finally remembered the name of the woman Bobby Lee Hatcher married. Says it just came to him out of the blue."

Yeah, Abby thought. It had come to him after he'd decided he couldn't make any political capital out of it. "Well?" she prompted Dave.

"Are you sure you're ready for this?"

The adrenaline started to pump. ''Not Vickie Wilder?''

Dave Conyers grinned. ''Close, but no cigar. Mrs. Bobby Lee Hatcher is none other than one Luanne Plimpton.''

Chapter Thirteen

Abby's mouth went dry in shock. Just like that, she had Bobby Lee Hatcher's connection to Eden. He'd followed Luanne up here. When he'd seen her with Sara Beth—

Or were they in this together? Had one of them made the ransom call tonight?

Abby's mind whirled. "We need to talk to her ASAP."

"No time like the present," Dave said cheerfully. He wore black slacks and a blue silk shirt opened at the collar. His clubbing clothes, he called them. Abby wondered if he'd been working in the station all night, or if he'd dropped in after spending a few hours in a bar. He hadn't been drinking, though. His blue eyes were clear and alert.

Abby glanced at her watch. "It's late. Maybe we should bring her down to the station in the morning."

Dave shook his head. "Why wait? Better to catch her by surprise, before she has time to make up a story."

He was right about that. "Let's go then."

Dave drove, and on the way to Luanne Plimpton's house, he gave Abby a sly gaze. "Say, what's up with you and Sam Burke?"

Abby's face flamed in the darkness. "Nothing is up with us. Why do you ask?"

Dave shrugged. "Because I've seen the way he looks

at you. You'd have to be blind or stupid not to pick up on the fact that the guy has the hots for you, and you aren't either one. So give it to me straight, Abby. You two going at it?''

"Shut up!" Abby grumbled, not confirming or denying Dave's question. This was exactly what she'd been afraid of, what she knew would happen. She could just imagine the buzz around the sheriff's station by morning.

"Hey," Dave said, shrugging. "I don't care. It's none of my business. I just wondered if that's the reason you went to bat for Burke with the sheriff."

"I went to bat for him because I thought he could benefit these cases." Abby stared straight ahead, trying to keep her voice and her expression neutral. But she had a bad feeling she'd already given herself away to Dave. "There's nobody on these cases—in the whole country— that has more experience or expertise than he does. I didn't think we could afford not to use his help."

"There's the matter of his conflict of interest," Dave pointed out.

Abby shrugged. "He's not investigating. He's consulting. He's working up profiles. There's a big difference."

"Still, Special Agent Carter wasn't too happy to hear about Sheriff Mooney's decision."

"I don't see why he should have a problem with Sam Burke. He said himself that even the FBI still uses Sam as a consultant. And he teaches criminal profiling at the Academy. If Carter could get someone else down here with even half as much experience, we'd be lucky."

"You don't have to convince me," Dave said. "I happen to agree with you. But he's doing a little more than consulting, Abby. You took him with you on interviews. You let him talk to witnesses."

"Because he asked questions I never even thought of.

Because he listens to more than just their answers. He observes their expressions, their inflections. He knows what he's doing,'' she said a little defensively.

"Yeah," Dave muttered. "But I wonder if you do."

Instead of asking him what he meant, Abby changed the subject. "Anything new with Emily's case?"

His expression turned grim in the dash lights. "Other than Vickie Wilder, I don't have one solid suspect. And the evidence against her is pretty damn weak."

"What about the mother? Tess Campbell?"

He gave Abby a reproachful look. "Look, I know we both think she may not have been exactly square with us about her past, but you know as well as I do that she's not capable of harming her own kid. I've never seen anyone so torn up in my life."

Abby had to agree. She didn't know Tess as well as Naomi did, but from what she'd seen, the woman's grief was genuine. And as for her past, well, they all had things they weren't particularly proud of. In Tess's case, Abby suspected her reticence had something to do with a relationship gone bad. Tess was a few years younger than Abby, but she vaguely recalled rumors about Tess and a man from one of the well-to-do families across the lake. Tess had left town suddenly, only to return a few years later a young widow with a child. It didn't take much imagination to figure out what might have happened. When Tess had gotten pregnant, the man had refused to marry her. The scenario was not unfamiliar to Abby. No wonder Naomi and Tess had grown so close. They had a lot in common, apart from their missing children.

It was true cops had been fooled before, but Abby had the same gut instinct as Dave. No way Tess Campbell would have harmed her child.

Abby wished her instincts were as strong regarding

Sara Beth's parents, but unfortunately, the scene earlier had only reinforced for Abby that both Karen and Curtis Brodie had serious problems—and not just with each other.

She told Dave about the profile Sam had given her earlier on Sadie's kidnapper and on Emily's. "He's convinced the same person kidnapped both children. But not Sara Beth."

"That's pretty much in line with what you've said from the first." Dave scowled at the road. "But if the same person took both Sadie and Emily—ten years apart—then that rules out Vickie Wilder. Ten years ago she was, what? Twelve, thirteen?"

"It doesn't rule her out in Sara Beth's abduction. But it's always possible Sam's profile could be off. Profiling is not an exact science."

"Which Special Agent Carter likes to keep pointing out," Dave said with a grin.

He pulled to the curb in front of Luanne Plimpton's home and turned off the engine. They got out, and Abby glanced around. The houses along the street were modest, but the neighborhood overall was upscale, with lots of trees and well-manicured yards.

"This place is nice," Dave said admiringly as they headed up the walkway.

"I wonder how she affords it on a secretary's salary."

Dave thumbed the doorbell. "Bonuses, obviously."

Several minutes later, a curtain parted at a front window, then a voice said from the other side of the door, "Who is it?"

"Lieutenant Conyers and Sergeant Cross with the Jefferson County's Sheriff's Department. We need to speak with you, Miss Plimpton."

The door drew back on its chain lock. "It's very late. Can't it wait until morning?"

Strange, Abby thought. As close as Luanne Plimpton was to one of the kidnappings and one of the victims, you would think her first assumption, on seeing two cops at her door in the middle of the night, would be that Sara Beth had been found. But she hadn't even asked about the child.

Abby and Dave exchanged glances as he said, "This is extremely important. Please open the door, Miss Plimpton."

Reluctantly, she slid off the chain, then drew back the door. She wore a white silk robe and slippers, and her hair and makeup were perfect. She was dressed for bed, Abby thought, but not for sleep. Was she waiting for Curtis Brodie? Or someone else? Her ex-husband, perhaps?

She led them into a small, but well-appointed living room. Like the woman herself, the furnishings were expensive and attractive. She didn't take a seat, nor did she offer them one. Instead, she strode to the fireplace, picked up a pack of cigarettes from the mantel, shook one out, and lit up. "Look, I was just on my way to bed. What's this all about?" She eyed them coolly through a haze of blue smoke.

"We'd like to talk to you about Bobby Lee Hatcher," Abby said.

The woman's face immediately went white. It was amazing to watch. Her expression never changed. Her eyes didn't even blink. But the color literally drained from her complexion. Then she tried to cover. "Who?"

"Bobby Lee Hatcher. Your ex-husband. Or are the two of you still married?"

She flicked a speck of tobacco from her tongue. "I don't have a husband. I've never been married."

"Before you make any further denials, you should know that I spent yesterday afternoon in Palisades," Abby told her. "I spoke with Sheriff McElroy and with Bobby Lee's grandmother."

At last the woman flinched. "How is the old battle-ax?"

"Then you're not denying you know her?"

Luanne stubbed out her cigarette almost viciously. She walked over and sat down heavily on the sofa. "Okay," she said. "It's true. Bobby Lee and I were married. But that was a long time ago. I was just a kid. I didn't know what I was doing, or believe me, I never would have gotten mixed up with that bunch. They're crazy. Every last one of them. If I didn't know it before, I sure as hell knew it after he kidnapped that girl."

"Mrs. Hatcher hinted that you might have had something to do with the kidnapping."

Luanne laughed bitterly. "I'm sure she did more than hint. She accused me to my face of making Bobby Lee do it. As if I could make him do anything. If I even so much as suggested what shirt he should wear, he was just as apt to backhand me as not." She glanced up at them, her face rigid. "I didn't talk him into kidnapping that girl. But I wasn't sorry when they sent him up. Otherwise, I never would have gotten away from him."

"Has Bobby Lee tried to get in touch with you since he got out of prison?" Dave asked.

"Lord, no. I didn't even know he'd been released." Suddenly, Luanne Plimpton didn't look particularly expensive or attractive. What she looked was scared.

"He hasn't called you, sent you a letter, anything?"

She shook her head. "No. He doesn't know where to find me, thank God, and I intend to keep it that way."

"What about his cousin, Marvin?" Abby asked. "You know where we can find him?"

Luanne frowned. "Why do you want to find Marvin? He's as crazy at the rest of the Hatchers."

"Sheriff McElroy seemed to think that Bobby Lee might be wherever Marvin is."

"I don't know where any of the Hatchers are, and I'd like to keep it that way."

"If Bobby Lee does make contact, you let us know." Abby scribbled her home number on the back of her card and handed it to the woman. "Call me anytime, day or night."

Luanne took the card, but she didn't even glance at it. "If I thought there was any chance Bobby Lee could find me, do you think I'd still be here?"

A FEW MINUTES later, Dave dropped Abby back at the Brodie house before heading home. There was still a lot of activity inside, but some of the cops had left. Abby sought out Sheriff Mooney and briefed him on what she and Dave had learned.

"You run Marvin Hatcher's name through the computer?"

Abby nodded. "If he drives a car, he didn't register it."

"Well, keep looking. This afternoon I would have put my money on the Wilder woman, but after this ransom call, I'm not so certain. This is one of the most frustrating cases I've ever worked on, Abby. I feel like I've aged twenty years since last Monday."

Abby knew exactly what he meant. Every tick of the clock was starting to seem a little too much like a death knell.

ABBY FOUND Curtis Brodie alone in the living room. He'd poured himself a drink and stood staring out at the pool.

"Mr. Brodie?"

He turned at the sound of her voice. His gaze raked her from head to toe. "Well, if it isn't Sergeant Cross. Bungled any more cases lately?"

She gritted her teeth and ignored the dig. "I wonder if I might ask you a few questions."

"The FBI is in charge now. I don't have to talk to you."

"It's a joint effort with the sheriff's department."

"Oh, well, that's a relief," he said sarcastically. "I'm glad you're still involved."

"I'd like to ask you some questions about your secretary, Luanne Plimpton."

He looked mildly surprised. "Luanne? You don't honestly think she had anything to do with Sara Beth's disappearance, do you?"

"We're not ruling out any suspects at this point."

"Look," he said, whirling on her. "Luanne had nothing to do with this. I've told you people all along where to look. You want to find out what happened to my daughter, take my wife down to that station house of yours and grill her. Make her sweat a little. Make her tell you what she did with Sara Beth. But you're not going to do that, are you? Because you perceive her as the victim in all this, just the way she planned it."

"Mr. Brodie, I understand your frustration, but we're doing everything we can to find Sara Beth and bring her back safely."

"Then you're wasting your time." He swirled ice in his drink. "Sara Beth's not coming back alive. We all know that."

Something curled in Abby's stomach. "What makes you think that?"

"How many missing kids ever come back in one piece?" he asked harshly. He turned back to the window to stare out. After a moment, he said, "What was it you wanted to ask me about Luanne?"

"How did she come to work for you?"

"She has a cousin who used to work for me as a mechanic. He gave her a recommendation."

"Did you have a background check run on her?"

"Hell, she answers my phones. It's not exactly rocket science."

"Did you know that Luanne was married ten years ago to a man named Robert Lee Hatcher? Has she ever mentioned him to you?"

The glass in Curtis Brodie's hand shattered, but his facial expression never changed. Except for his eyes. Abby had never seen such fury.

"Married?" he said through clenched teeth. "Why, that lying bitch."

ABBY DIDN'T GET home until after two o'clock in the morning. Exhausted, she tumbled onto her bed fully clothed and was already half asleep when the telephone roused her.

"Hello?" she muttered.

"Abby?"

Sam's voice brought her immediately awake. She sat up, cradling the phone against her ear as she leaned back against the headboard. "What's wrong? Is Karen all right? Did she get another ransom call?"

"No, it's nothing like that. I just got back to my hotel. Sheriff Mooney filled me in about Luanne Plimpton. I must say, I hadn't anticipated that."

"I don't think anyone did." Abby brushed back her hair.

"It certainly gives Bobby Lee a reason for being in Eden." Sam paused. "But that's not why I called."

Abby moistened her lips. "It isn't?"

"I wanted to tell you—" He broke off.

"Yes?"

Another pause. "Earlier, at your place—"

Abby's heart started to flail like the wings of a caged bird. "We don't need to talk about this," she said quickly.

"I think we do."

"We both agreed it was a mistake. Can't we just leave it at that?"

"I never said it was a mistake. In fact, I can't remember when I've had such a pleasurable evening."

Abby felt her cheeks burn even though she was completely alone in her darkened bedroom. But Sam's voice, his words, conjured up such powerful images. Such *pleasurable* images…

And it had been pleasurable for her, too. Abby couldn't deny that. She'd lost herself in Sam's kisses, his embraces, and no amount of guilt and remorse were ever going to change that fact.

"Abby? Are you still there?"

She clutched the phone. "I'm here."

"I should let you get some sleep."

They both needed to rest. Tomorrow the media would descend on them in droves. It would take a lot of patience and fortitude to deal with the frenzy, but at the moment, all Abby wanted to do was lie back on her bed and talk to her lover on the phone.

But Sam wasn't her lover, she reminded herself. They'd made love once. That didn't make him her lover.

Then what did it make him? A one-night stand? A mistake?

Suddenly, it didn't seem like so much of a mistake to her anymore. And Sam didn't seem like a stranger. He seemed more like a colleague. A friend. And, yes, a lover.

"Good night, Abby," he said very softly.

The intimacy in his voice sent a shiver up her backbone. She pressed the phone against her ear and closed her eyes. "Good night, Sam."

ABBY COULDN'T get back to sleep. She tossed and turned, and then finally gave it up. Getting out of bed, she walked into her grandmother's sewing room and sat down in the rocking chair by the window. Staring out at the darkness, she went back over the events of the past few days, trying to sort it all out in her mind.

Vickie Wilder remained a strong suspect. For one thing, she'd apparently fled. That always looked bad. A Be-On-The-Lookout had been issued for her car, but so far she hadn't been apprehended. Secondly, the unknown woman claiming to be Vickie's sister was seen in a white car that might or might not match the description of the vehicle spotted near the crime scene. And the woman might or might not be Vickie's college roommate who was on the lam.

Then there was Vickie's confession to Willa Banks, the school nurse, about a baby Vickie had given up for adoption. Alleged confession, Abby amended. They only had Willa Banks's word that Vickie had given up a baby who would now be the same age as Sara Beth and Emily. However, if the claim was true, then Vickie fit Sam's profile. She was between the ages of twenty and forty-five. She was familiar with Eden and with the school. She could move about freely without arousing suspicion. And she had experienced a loss in her life, a child she might have tried to replace.

The fly in the ointment, of course, was that Sam thought Sadie and Emily's kidnapper were one and the same. Which would rule out Vickie Wilder because she would have been too young at the time of Sadie's abduction.

Bobby Lee Hatcher. He'd spent nine years in prison for aggravated assault and kidnapping, having gone into the slammer after Sadie disappeared and been released a month before Sara Beth and Emily went missing. And now Abby could tie him to Eden through Luanne Plimpton.

Had Luanne's fear of Bobby Lee been genuine tonight, or had she been afraid that her involvement in the kidnapping was about to be exposed? Sara Beth had been with Luanne at the time of the kidnapping. They'd stopped at a drugstore off the beaten track, one that never had many customers. Once inside, Luanne had let Sara Beth go off on her own to look at coloring books while she went to the back of the store where the pharmacy was located. She claimed she hadn't heard the bell over the door ring. She claimed she hadn't seen anyone else come into the drugstore. But was she telling the truth? Had she and Bobby Lee cooked up the scheme together? Had one of them made the call tonight from the phone booth near Alma?

And what about Karen and Curtis Brodie? They had still accused each other of harming the child, even in the face of a ransom demand.

Karen's accusation rang in Abby's ears. *You did this! You did this just to torment me! If you hurt her, I swear I'll kill you. Do you hear me? I'll kill you!*

And Curtis Brodie, answering her, *She's crazy. You saw*

the way she came at me. Thank God she didn't have a knife this time.

What did you do to Sara Beth, you crazy bi—

Sara Beth's not coming back alive. We all know that. How many missing kids ever come back in one piece?

Abby massaged her face, trying to rub away the tension and the terrible dread Curtis Brodie's words had conjured. There was only one way he could be that certain his daughter was dead.

"No," she whispered in the darkness. "Please, no."

Don't let us be too late, she silently prayed.

She forced herself to go back over that conversation with Curtis Brodie. Something, aside from his assertion about Sara Beth, niggled at Abby. What was it? What was she missing?

And then she had it. She stared out the window in dismay. Why hadn't she seen it before? Why hadn't she made the connection before? They'd assumed that Luanne Plimpton had divorced Bobby Lee Hatcher during his nine years in prison. But what if she hadn't? What if, in spite of her protestations to the contrary, she'd kept in touch with some of Bobby Lee's family—namely, Bobby Lee's cousin, Marvin, an auto mechanic.

How did she come to work for you?

She has a cousin who used to work for me as a mechanic. He gave her a recommendation.

Chapter Fourteen

Sunday

Abby slapped at a mosquito on her neck as she gazed at the old farmhouse. It wasn't unlike the Hatcher place down in Palisades, but at least there wasn't a swamp within miles, and, she hoped, no cage full of snakes.

Curtis Brodie had provided them with an address for the man who had given Luanne a recommendation: one Marvin Hatcher, who resided in Alma. Curtis had put it together almost immediately, his fury boiling over at the thought of an ex-employee being involved in his daughter's kidnapping. "I'll kill him," he vowed. "I'll kill that scumbag myself." And then he'd raged at the sheriff's department, taunting them that the kidnapper had been right under their incompetent noses the whole time.

Then he'd gone down to the command center and made a statement to the press.

"Jerk," Abby muttered, remembering Curtis's angry tirade against her, against Sheriff Mooney, against the whole lousy FBI, as he'd put it. At least he hadn't discriminated, she thought, but thanks to him, the media knew they had a new lead. The reporters who'd set up camp outside the sheriff's station and the command center were in a feeding frenzy, and Abby wouldn't have been surprised to see a news van pull up beside her now, courtesy of Curtis Brodie.

The house was a shotgun-style, accessible only by a narrow gravel road that would be nearly impassable in the winter or after a good hard rain. Two deputies accompanied Sheriff Mooney and Abby, along with two FBI agents and Special Agent Carter. They all wore Kevlar vests since they couldn't predict what they'd find at the house, or how volatile the situation could turn out to be. If Sara Beth was inside, they had no idea what her condition might be or if force would be required to get her out. What they did know was that time was of the essence.

Before they started across the weed-infested yard, Sheriff Mooney grabbed a twelve-gauge shotgun from his trunk. At Special Agent Carter's nod, they moved in. He, Abby, Sheriff Mooney, and one of the deputies took the front, while the other deputy and the two agents slipped around back. At the porch steps, Abby and Sheriff Mooney separated, covering the windows while Special Agent Carter strode up the steps, flanked by his own man.

He knocked on the door. "This is the FBI! Open up! We're here to talk to Robert Lee Hatcher!"

No answer. Nothing stirred. The countryside was eerily silent. Abby turned and scanned the woods that surrounded the house. So many places to hide. For all they knew, Bobby Lee Hatcher could be out there somewhere now, watching them.

"We have a search warrant!" Carter called out. "Open up, now!"

"Don't look like he's home," the deputy remarked.

Carter turned toward the sheriff. "You got a battering ram in your trunk?"

"Yeah, but we don't need one." He nodded toward the

deputy beside him. Randy Selway was a bear of a man who moonlighted on weekends as a bouncer at a particularly rowdy roadhouse on the outskirts of town. "See what you can do."

The FBI agents gave him some room, and Randy gave a powerful kick against the door. The whole thing went crashing inward, landing with a loud *whack* against the floor. He looked at Special Agent Carter and flinched. "Sorry."

"We're in, at least," Carter muttered.

He entered first, weapon drawn, and the others came in behind him, stepping around the ruined door. The way the house was built, Abby could see the back door from the front of the house.

Sheriff Mooney held the shotgun at his side and gazed around. "This is a regular little crap hole, ain't it?"

Abby had to agree. The house was filthy and stank to high heaven. Flies buzzed around dirty dishes stacked in the sink and on containers of food that had been left sitting out for no telling how long. It gave her a sick feeling to think of one of those children being held in such a place.

The house was tiny with one room serving as a living and kitchen area, and the bedrooms and bathroom straight back. No hallways. No closets. No place much to hide.

The floorboards creaked as the large deputy moved to the back of the house. Abby walked around the living room. There was a couch, a TV and not much else. Sunlight poured in through a narrow window, and dust motes danced in the brilliance. Something glinted underneath the TV, and Abby knelt to fish it out with a pen she pulled from her pocket.

She snagged it on the end of her pen and held it up. A child's hair clip glistened in the sunlight. Pink plastic with kittens peeking over the edges. The kind that Sara Beth had been wearing in her school picture.

Abby's heart gave a painful thud. She started to call out to the sheriff, but just then, Selway's voice boomed from the back bedroom.

"Oh, God. Oh, my God! Sheriff! You better get back here quick."

SAM WATCHED as the forensics team scoured the house for trace evidence. He wasn't allowed inside the room where Luanne Plimpton's body had been discovered, but Abby had shot Polaroids of the crime scene and the body, and Sam had spent several minutes studying them while forensics finished their work.

Actually, photos of the crime scene and victim, along with the police reports and witness accounts, were usually all he ever had to work from. It was rare for a profiler to witness an actual crime scene, to be involved in a case in the early stages. Most of the time, the Investigative Support Unit wasn't called until a case had gone unsolved for months, sometimes years. And even then, the local authorities often approached them with a fair amount of skepticism. How could someone unfamiliar with the case, who hadn't spent untold man hours tracking down leads, look at photos and reports and be able to tell a seasoned cop who he was looking for, sometimes right down to the kind of clothes the suspect would be wearing when the cop apprehended him?

But it had happened. More than once, and there was nothing like the rush that came with nailing an UNSUB so accurately. Sam felt that same rush of excitement now, and for a moment, he forgot about the dark side of profiling: the hundreds of suspects who were never apprehended, who continued night after night to feed their grue-some appetites.

He gazed down at the photos. This was not the kind of crime he normally dealt with. No serial killer was at work here. Luanne Plimpton had been murdered by someone who knew her. Someone in a terrible rage against her. She'd been stabbed and beaten, her face battered so badly it was almost unrecognizable. When the body was dam-aged so severely around the facial area, it almost always meant that the victim knew her assailant. The attack was personal. But there was no mutilation of the breasts or genitals which suggested to Sam that sex hadn't been a motivation.

Then what was the motivation? Who had hated Luanne Plimpton enough to kill her?

Bobby Lee Hatcher?

Curtis Brodie?

Another possibility presented itself to Sam. He remem-bered clearly Luanne Plimpton telling him that Karen could be violent. That she had tried to kill Curtis once with a butcher knife.

And he also remembered how Karen's hands had balled into fists when Abby had asked her about Luanne.

She couldn't have done this, Sam thought. In such an act of rage, the perpetrator was almost always a man.

But Sam could think of a few exceptions, and he knew he couldn't afford to overlook any possibility. The suspect had to be apprehended, and quickly, because if the hair clip that Abby had found was any indication, the killer had Sara Beth.

WHILE FORENSICS did their thing inside, Abby and several deputies scoured the immediate area around the house. The FBI agents held back and let the sheriff's department conduct the search because a homicide was under the jurisdiction of the locals.

Fifty yards or so from the back of the house, a row of falling down buildings—chicken coops, an old outhouse, a tool shed—marked the perimeter of the woods. They each took a building to search, joking about which one would get the outhouse.

Behind the tool shed, a path led back into the woods. Abby started down it, glancing back to make sure the buildings and the deputies were still in her sight. The sun was fully up and hot, but the trees dappled the light. Humidity thickened the air, and she could feel perspiration running down her back. The mosquitoes were out, too. She wished she'd taken the time to use a repellent, but it was too late to worry about that now.

The path narrowed, and for a moment, Abby thought it simply disappeared into the woods. She started to turn back, but then through a thicket of honeysuckle and bramble, she glimpsed the weathered wood of another shed. She glanced back. She could no longer see the outbuildings behind the house, but she could still hear the deputies.

The structure had been a smokehouse, by the looks of it, a place where bacon and ham had once been cured. But she had no idea what it had been used for last, and for a moment, the image of all those writhing snakes made her feel queasy in the heat, but she shoved the discomfort aside and continued toward the structure. Ray Dean Hatcher and his snakes were a long way from here, and she hoped neither his brother nor his cousin shared the same pastime.

Slipping her gun from her shoulder holster, she flicked off the safety. That was better, she decided. The gun in

her hand was like an old friend, and she was suddenly
thankful for all the hours she'd put in at the firing range.

Abby moved slowly through the briar that tore at her
clothing. Perspiration ran down the side of her face, and
she used her shoulder to wipe it away.

In the distance she could hear the deputies continuing
their search. The only other noise was a faint breeze that
whispered through the trees. Abby didn't know why, but
she was suddenly scared, and not of snakes. She was
afraid that someone would be waiting for her inside that
shed. Afraid that no one would be there. Afraid that the
hair clip she'd found in the house belonged to Sara Beth.
Afraid that it didn't. Afraid that even with the discovery
of Luanne Plimpton's body, Bobby Lee Hatcher was going to turn out to be another false lead. And that when all
was said and done, they would still be no closer to finding
Sara Beth or Emily.

There was a window in the shed, but it was too high
for Abby to see through it. Moving as quietly as she
could, she rounded the corner to the front of the building.
The door sagged on its hinges and was held shut by a
wooden latch that swiveled on a nail. The latch had been
turned upward, but the door didn't hang open. It remained
closed, as if someone were holding it from inside.

Abby's heart started to pound. She gripped her gun.
"Police!" she yelled. "Come out with your hands up!"

No sound but the ruffle of leaves in the wind. Then
behind her, she heard someone yell.

Abby called over her shoulder, "Down here! There's a
path—"

The door of the shed shot open and a man rushed out,
striking Abby with the full force of his weight. She fell
backward to the ground, the breath knocked out of her.
The gun flew out of her hand.

Abby had only a brief impression of the man as she rolled over. Gasping for air, she reached frantically for her gun. Whoever he was, he was big. Tall. Muscular. Dark hair. He fit the description they had of Bobby Lee Hatcher.

Bobby Lee Hatcher, who'd been in prison for aggravated assault and kidnapping....

Bobby Lee Hatcher, who might have killed his own wife....

Who might have kidnapped Sara Beth and Emily...

The heel of his work boot came down hard on Abby's wrist. She screamed in pain as she tried to roll away. He flung himself on top of her, and his knee crushed her wounded wrist. He pinned her other arm beneath her, trapping her. She could smell sweat, sour and nauseating, as he reached for her gun.

A wave of blackness washed through Abby, but she fought the dizziness. Tried to block out the pain. The worst thing she could do was panic.

She tried to remember her training, but even apart from the man's size, the odds were against her. He now had her weapon.

"I won't go back," he rasped. His breath was hot and fetid against her face. He had a tattoo, a huge, fanged snake, that wrapped around his neck. It seemed to move as his veins bulged in agitation. "You hear me? I'm not going back!"

Their gazes met as he lifted the gun. His finger squeezed the trigger. Abby heard the shot, but for a moment, nothing seemed to register. Then she saw the bloom of red on his chest a second before he fell backward.

Ignoring the pain in her wrist, Abby struggled from underneath him. Footsteps came out of the brambles toward her. She looked up. Curtis Brodie stood over her,

.38 Special pointed down at her. Then he took aim at Bobby Lee Hatcher, who was lying prone in the dirt.

"No!" Abby screamed. "Don't! He may be the only one who can tell us where your daughter is!"

For a split second, Curtis hesitated, then he tossed his gun to the ground and spat. "I hope the son of a bitch rots in hell." He turned and started back toward the house.

ABBY LAY ON HER BACK in the emergency-room cubicle and stared at the ceiling as she waited for the doctor who'd set her broken wrist to sign her release papers. She'd been here for hours it seemed, and the inaction was driving her crazy. She hated not being down at the station where all hell was breaking loose.

Luanne Plimpton was dead. Bobby Lee Hatcher was dead. The two people who, it now appeared, had kidnapped Sara Beth would never be able to give up the whereabouts of their tiny victim.

Abby squeezed her eyes closed. She couldn't help feeling partly responsible. If she hadn't let Bobby Lee surprise her like that, and if she hadn't lost her gun, she might have been able to prevent Curtis from shooting him.

Curtis Brodie's sudden appearance on the scene was still under investigation. He hadn't been charged, and, given the circumstances, the fact that he'd saved Abby's life, it was doubtful that he would be.

He'd provided a statement without hesitation and without benefit of counsel. He swore that he'd driven out to that house thinking Sara Beth was there. Thinking he might be able to save his daughter. Who could blame him for that? When he saw Hatcher with Abby's gun, he'd reacted without thinking. He saw the man he thought was his daughter's kidnapper trying to kill a law-enforcement officer, and his instincts had taken over.

Abby was hard pressed to believe that Curtis's motive had been that heroic. She still wasn't convinced that he'd shot Bobby Lee in order to save her.

Then why? Out of revenge?

She heard voices outside her room, and she hoped it was the doctor with her release papers. When Sam walked in, her breath left her in a painful rush.

Their gazes met, and Abby felt tears sting her eyes unexpectedly. Which was crazy. No reason for Sam's presence to make her so misty. No reason that she should be almost pathetically glad to see him.

He crossed the room to her bed. "Hey."

She gave him a weak smile. "Hey."

"How do you feel?"

She held up her cast. "Doctor says I'll be good as new in six weeks." But they both knew a broken wrist could have dire consequences for a police officer. If the bone didn't heal properly, it could affect her ability to shoot a weapon accurately. Abby didn't want to think about that now. She didn't know what she'd do if she couldn't be a cop.

"Did you just come from the station?" she asked him.

"Yeah. The place is crawling with reporters."

Abby had expected that. She stared at the ceiling. "I can't help feeling responsible for all this. If I hadn't let Hatcher get the jump on me—"

"Don't beat yourself up over this," Sam said. "You were doing your job. You can't go back and change what happened."

"I know that." The tears threatened again, and Abby struggled to blink them away. "But if I hadn't lost my weapon…if I'd been quicker to react…if I'd seen Curtis coming…" She trailed off. "Luanne's dead. Hatcher's dead. What if they hid Sara Beth or Emily away someplace where we'll never find them? What if—'' She broke off again, unable to put into words the horror that was running through her mind. Those tiny little girls alone somewhere. Frightened. Hungry. Maybe hurt. If they didn't find them soon—

Sam took her hand. ''We'll find them, Abby.''

''I want to believe that,'' she said softly. ''I've thought all along that if I just put in enough hours, if I just gave it all I had, I'd be able to find them in time. But now I'm not so sure. Now I'm thinking, what if those children are lost forever because of something I did or didn't do?''

Sam sat down on the edge of the bed, and before Abby could protest, he pulled her into his arms and held her tightly.

And for the first time in a very long time, Abby wanted to put her faith in someone else. Wanted to believe that something good could come from all this, that maybe, just maybe, Sam was meant to come into her life. And that she was meant to fall in love with him.

If she would only let herself.

Chapter Fifteen

Abby protested all the way home from the hospital. She wanted to go back to the station, but Sam was adamant. "You're in no shape to go back to work today. A wounded cop is a danger to himself—or herself—and others."

"It's just a broken wrist." But he was right, and besides, her wrist was throbbing. Abby refused to take another painkiller, though, because she didn't like losing control of her faculties.

Naomi's car was parked in the drive when Sam pulled up, and Abby let out a long sigh. "Oh, boy. Looks like the general's here."

Sam gave her a skeptical look. "Who?"

"My sister." Abby reached for the door handle, forgetting about her hand. She knocked the cast against the arm rest and winced. "Damn."

"Here, just wait a minute. I'll come around and open the door."

"That's ridiculous. I can do it myself."

But before Abby could manage with her left hand, Sam reached across her and opened the door. For a second, their mouths were only inches apart, and Abby was bombarded with memories of how he had kissed her last night. Everywhere.

Their gazes clung for the longest time, and Abby wondered if he was going to kiss her again. She leaned toward him slightly, issuing an unmistakable invitation, but just then, the front door of the house flew open and Naomi came out on the porch. She waved to them anxiously.

"Thank God, you're all right! I've been worried sick ever since Dave called!"

Abby and Sam climbed out of the car and started toward the porch. "Dave Conyers called you?" Abby asked in surprise. That didn't sound much like Dave.

"He said you were going to be all right, but I wanted to see for myself." Naomi opened the screen and stepped back for them to enter. A tantalizing aroma drifted out from the kitchen.

Abby sniffed appreciatively. "You've been cooking."

"I didn't know what else to do." Naomi dried her hands on her apron. She glanced at Sam expectantly. "By the way, I'm Abby's sister."

Sam actually seemed speechless for a moment as he gazed at Naomi. He wore the same awestruck look on his face that Abby had seen on every other male who had come into contact with Naomi since she'd hit puberty.

She was beautiful without even trying to be. Her short, sleek hairstyle made her brown eyes look even larger and warmer and complemented a peaches-and-cream complexion that almost looked air-brushed. She was tall, slender, and even when she was wearing blue jeans and a simple cotton shirt the word *elegant* immediately came to mind.

Sam caught himself and thrust out his hand. "Sam Burke."

Naomi's brows rose. "The profiler? I've heard about you."

"That worries me a little," he murmured, shooting Abby a glance.

"Naomi helped found the Missing Children's Network," she told him. "She's also helped to organize the volunteers down at the command post."

Sam looked impressed. "I've heard of your organization. You do good work."

Naomi smiled. "Thanks." She turned to Abby and took her arm. "Let's get you off your feet, young lady."

Abby held up her cast. "My wrist is hurt, not my feet."

"Don't argue." Naomi settled Abby on the sofa and bustled around plumping pillows and fetching a footstool. "There. Comfy?" When Abby nodded wryly, Naomi glanced at Sam. "I've cooked enough food to feed an army. You'll stay and eat with us, won't you, Sam?"

He glanced at Abby, raising his eyebrows slightly.

She shrugged. "You're welcome to stay. Naomi's a great cook."

"Unlike some folks we know." Naomi tweaked Abby's cheek.

Sam said, "I'd love that, but if you'll excuse me, I need to make a phone call first."

After he'd disappeared through the front door, Naomi went to the window to peek out. "So what gives?"

"About what?" Abby asked innocently.

Naomi gave her a sharp glance. "Don't be dense. About you and Sam Burke."

"Nothing gives," Abby lied. "We're working together on a case, that's all."

Naomi came back to sit beside her on the sofa. "It's more than that. I saw the way he looked at you. That man's crazy about you, Abby."

Dave Conyers had said something to that effect last night, but Naomi's words still shocked Abby. "Don't be ridiculous. He barely knows me."

"He knows you well enough, I'd say." Naomi hesitated, frowning. "Are you sleeping with him, Abby?"

"Naomi!"

"Well, are you?"

"Lord, why don't you just make sure the whole neighborhood hears you?" Abby grumbled. "Much less Sam."

Naomi looked worried. "I'm your big sister. I have a right to know these things."

"No, you don't."

"Okay, so I don't have a right. But I can be concerned about you, can't I? He's a lot older than you, Abby."

"What difference does that make?" She was tired of hearing that argument—first from Sam, and now from her sister. "Besides, there's nothing serious going on between Sam Burke and me anyway."

"But there could be, if you'd let it."

Abby sighed. "You're such a romantic. Look, it wouldn't matter even if we were serious about each other. Which we aren't. Nothing could come of it. He lives in Virginia. I live in Mississippi. He has his life, I have mine. It wouldn't work out."

"Sounds like you've thought about it, though." Again Naomi hesitated. "I can see why. There is something about him," she murmured.

Naomi had noticed it, too. That indefinable quality that made Sam Burke dark and mysterious and pretty much irresistible.

Abby felt a little prickle of jealousy. Naomi was so beautiful and so smart and so sweet. And Abby was just...Abby. No reason for Sam to think of her as anything special. No reason for him to remember her, when he got back home, as anything but a pleasant interlude on one hot summer night.

No reason for Abby to think, suddenly, about the time when Sam would no longer be in her life.

SAM PUT AWAY his cell phone as he came back inside. He turned toward her, his expression tense. "I'm sorry, Abby, but I can't stay for dinner after all. I really need to be with Karen right now."

"I understand." And she did, even though she couldn't help feeling disappointed. She'd wanted to have dinner with him, maybe linger over a glass of wine. And then after Naomi went home...

Something flickered for just an instant in Sam's eyes, an emotion Abby couldn't quite define. Then he said grimly, "Karen and Curtis have been at it again, this time over whether to pay the ransom. Curtis claims he can't come up with the money by tomorrow. He's insisting Karen somehow work it out with the bank."

"There may not be a need for ransom money. If Luanne and Bobby Lee were responsible for Sara Beth's kidnapping, then there won't be another ransom demand."

Sam's mouth tightened almost imperceptibly. "I realize that. Abby—" he put his hands on her shoulders "—there's something I need to talk to you about."

"I'm listening."

"No, not now. I really do have to go. But later...if it's not too late..." He trailed off, bending swiftly to kiss her on the lips before he turned and left the house.

Abby was so dazed by the kiss that it took several moments for his final words to sink in.

...if it's not too late...

Too late for what?

ABBY TOUCHED very little of the food Naomi had prepared, and was sorry after she'd gone to so much trouble. But her sister had merely shrugged, put everything into plastic containers and stored it in the fridge, remarking that at least Abby would have something decent to eat for a few days.

After Naomi had cleaned up the kitchen, which made Abby feel even worse, she'd left, making Abby promise to take care of herself. "Don't even think about going in to the station," she'd warned.

Abby couldn't have even if she'd wanted to. She couldn't drive with her right hand out of commission, let alone handle a gun.

Her wrist still throbbed, but Abby resisted the pain pills. She lay on the couch and studied the ceiling, trying to ignore the ache.

After a while, a car pulled up in her drive, but she didn't bother getting up. It was probably Naomi coming back to check on her. Or scold her for something.

"Abby?"

Half asleep, she recognized Dave Conyer's voice calling to her through the door, and Abby swung her legs over the side of the couch and got up to let him in.

"What are you doing here?" she asked in surprise.

Dave opened the screen door and stepped inside, wearing jeans and a casual shirt. He didn't bother hiding his shoulder holster and weapon under a jacket.

"I just came by to make sure you're all right."

Abby's gaze narrowed. "I've never known you to be so solicitous. Especially over a simple broken wrist."

He shrugged. "Okay. So I have an ulterior motive. I thought you might want to know that the State Highway Patrol picked up Greta Henley in Biloxi a few hours ago.

She was driving a white 1992 Chevy Caprice. They think she was heading for Florida.''

Abby's heart thudded against her chest. "What about the children? Or Vickie Wilder?"

"She was alone. And so far, she's denying any knowledge of Vickie Wilder or the kidnappings."

"I want to talk to her."

"Get in line," Dave said grimly. "We all want a go at her, but the Memphis PD has asked that she be turned over to them. It looks like we may have to wait our turn."

"No way," Abby said vehemently. "We have to get a picture of Greta Henley over to Florence Crowder. If she makes a positive ID, then there's no way in hell Henley is going back to Memphis. Not until she tells us what she knows about Vickie Wilder. And about those missing children."

SAM HAD FINALLY got Karen calmed down, and she was in her bedroom resting. When he'd first arrived, she'd been in a terrible state of agitation. Someone from the sheriff's department had brought over the hair clip for her to identify, and she'd taken one look at the pink plastic bauble and collapsed into near hysteria. Sam had thought for a moment he might have to call a doctor, but Karen wouldn't let him.

She'd clung to him desperately. "He did this. Don't you see? Curtis is responsible for all this. I crossed him and now he's making me pay."

Sam had tried to reason with her. When he tried to remind her that Luanne Plimpton and Bobby Lee Hatcher were the prime suspects now, she'd become even more frantic. "They didn't do it," she said over and over. "He wants it to look that way, but they didn't take her. I know they didn't. He killed them, Sam. Just like he's threatened to kill me. I thought I could protect Sara Beth from him, but now I know I can't. He'll do anything to keep me away from her.''

Finally, she'd worn herself down, and Sam had convinced her to go into her bedroom and rest for a while. A deputy still monitored the phone in the kitchen, and Sam nodded to him as he poured himself a glass of water. Then, going back into the living room, he opened Sara Beth's file, flipping through copies of witness statements, detectives' notes—most of them Abby's—photographs of the drugstore and parking lot, FBI documents. There were background checks on the family, namely Karen and Curtis. It had been Sam's experience that the background reports on the immediate family were where clues often turned up. Deep debt. A history of violence. It pained him to think that Karen, his own sister, was almost as much of a stranger to him as Curtis was. Her past was certainly as troubled.

Sam read back over the statements given by Luanne Plimpton and all the school personnel, including Vickie Wilder.

Something had been bothering him ever since he'd interviewed Vickie. He'd told Abby he thought Vickie was holding out on them, but it was more than that. Sam couldn't put his finger on it exactly, but there was something a little familiar-looking about her. He hadn't met her before that day. He knew that. But it was as if he'd caught a glimpse of her somewhere, just a brief glance that had formed a subliminal impression.

He closed the folders and decided to go check on Karen. Opening the bedroom door, he glanced inside. The bed was neatly made. It didn't appear as if anyone had lain on top of it, much less crawled beneath the covers.

Maybe Karen had straightened the spread when she got up. Maybe she was in the bathroom.

Sam listened for a moment. He couldn't hear water running, so he didn't think she was in the shower. He knocked on the bathroom door. "Karen?"

No answer. He knocked again, then pushed open the door. The bathroom was empty. He went back into the bedroom and glanced around. Atrium doors opened onto the patio, and Sam walked over to check the locks. One of them was open.

Karen had slipped out without his knowing.

And suddenly, a memory came crashing over him. In a flash Sam knew exactly where he'd seen Vickie Wilder.

WHEN ABBY couldn't reach Sam on his cell phone, she dialed Karen Brodie's number. A deputy answered, and Abby identified herself, then asked to speak to Sam.

"He's not here, Sergeant Cross. He left a little while ago."

"Did he say where he was going?"

"No, but he kind of left in a hurry."

Abby frowned. "What about Mrs. Brodie?"

"She's in her bedroom resting. Should I get her up?"

"No, don't disturb her. She needs her rest."

Abby hung up, then tried Sam's hotel room. He wasn't there, nor was he at the station or command post. No one had seen him, and he still wasn't answering his cell phone.

Fresh out of ideas, Abby called Naomi. "Can you come back over?"

Naomi was instantly alarmed. "Why? What's wrong? Do you need to go back to the hospital?"

"It's nothing like that," Abby assured her. "I need you to drive me somewhere."

Naomi was immediately suspicious. "Where?"

"Just come over. I'll tell you when you get here."

"Abby—"

"Hurry, Naomi. I think I may have figured out where Sara Beth Brodie is."

She heard the sharp intake of Naomi's breath. "I'll be there in ten minutes."

She made it in five.

Abby was waiting for her out in the driveway. She wore a lightweight jacket over her shoulder holster, but she knew the gun wouldn't do her much good since she couldn't use her right hand. Still, the weight of it was comforting as she maneuvered the door handle with her left hand and slid inside.

Naomi gave her an anxious look. "Where are we going? The sheriff's station? The command post?"

"No. We're going to Vickie Wilder's apartment."

Naomi lifted her brows as she backed out of the driveway. "Why are we going to her apartment?"

"Because I'm trying to find a missing little girl."

"I got that part. But why do you think Vickie Wilder has her in her apartment?"

"Not in her apartment. But somewhere."

Naomi scowled at the road. "I thought Luanne Plimpton and Bobby Lee Hatcher were the kidnappers. Their pictures have been all over the news today."

"That's what someone wanted us to think. And that same someone killed Luanne and Bobby Lee to keep us from finding out the truth."

Naomi drove in silence for a moment. "Abby, I don't like this. I think we should call Sheriff Mooney. Or Sam."

"I couldn't find Sam. But don't worry. I'm not going to do anything to put either one of us in danger, okay? I'm just playing a hunch. If it pans out, then I'll call Sheriff Mooney. He's got enough to worry about right now, dealing with the press after today's debacle. I don't want to waste his time until I have something concrete."

"All right," Naomi agreed. "I guess I can see your logic. But how are we going to get into Vickie's apartment?"

"You let me worry about that."

As it turned out, that wasn't much of an obstacle after all. Florence Crowder remembered Abby, and she put up little more than a token resistance about letting her back into Vickie's apartment.

"What'd you find in there, anyway?" Mrs. Crowder asked as she led them up the stairs.

"I just want to have another look around, that's all."

"That's what your partner said when he came by earlier, but I know how cops operate. If there wasn't something mighty suspicious about Vickie's apartment, you wouldn't be wasting time coming back here."

"My partner?"

"Yeah, the tall fella. Dark hair. Receding hairline. Kind of reminds me a little of Bruce Willis. I've had a thing for him ever since that first *Die Hard* movie came out."

Naomi and Abby exchanged glances.

"When was he here?" Abby asked.

"Just a little while ago. We'd just finished eating. Ernie's in there right now stretched out in his recliner watching *X-Files*." She let them in with her passkey, then stood back. "Be sure and lock up when you're finished."

"We will."

"You have any idea when she's coming back?"

"Vickie?" Abby shook her head. "No."

Mrs. Crowder gave her a hard look. "Did she take those little girls?"

"We don't know who took them, Mrs. Crowder, but we're not leaving any stone unturned until we find them."

"I never would have thought it of her, you know. She had me buffaloed. Just goes to show you, I guess. Seemed like such a sweet girl." She shook her head sadly. "And she just loves kids to death."

Abby winced at the woman's unfortunate choice of words.

ABBY AND NAOMI studied the picture of Vickie and her boyfriend, the same photograph that had puzzled Abby the first time she saw it.

"What a sweet couple," Naomi murmured. "And she looks so sincere. I can't believe she'd do anything to harm an innocent child."

Abby didn't want to remind her sister that some of the most pleasant-looking people in the world were also the most hardened criminals.

"There's something about that picture that bothers me," she said. "But I can't put my finger on it."

"Oh, I know what it is."

Abby looked at her sister in surprise. "You do?"

Naomi nodded. "Of course. You probably recognize that cabin in the background."

Abby stared at her sister in confusion. "What?"

"Sure, you do. It's Half Moon Bay Camp, out by the lake. See the crescent moon on the building? And, look, you can even see the emblem on their shirts." When Abby still didn't respond, Naomi said impatiently, "Don't you remember? Mama sent you there one summer, and you hated it. You pitched such a fit, she had to go get you the second day. You swore you'd never go back."

Willa Banks's words came back to Abby. *When she was seventeen years old, she worked as a counselor at a summer camp. She fell madly in love with a boy there,*

another counselor, and she told me that was the happiest
time of her life.

Of course, Abby thought. Half Moon Bay Camp, where
Vickie Wilder had fallen in love the summer she turned
seventeen. The place where her child had been conceived.
The place where she'd spent the happiest time of her life.

Abby hadn't thought about that camp in years. It was
run by a local church, but it would be closed now for the
season. No one would be there.

She conjured an image. Remote, deserted, surrounded
by woods on three sides and the lake on the other.

The perfect place to hide a child.

Chapter Sixteen

Twilight had fallen by the time they got to the narrow lane that led back through the woods to the campground. Naomi pulled to the side of the road and parked. "I haven't been out here in years. I'd forgotten how spooky it is."

The countryside *was* a little eerie, Abby thought. Or maybe it was just their frame of mind.

"Now do we call Sheriff Mooney?" Naomi pressed her.

"Give me ten minutes," Abby said. "I want to take a look before we get squad cars charging down through here. If Vickie has Sara Beth in one of those cabins, I don't want to risk her making a run for it. Or worse, panicking. I don't want to put Sara Beth in the line of fire."

"Abby, this is crazy," Naomi said a little desperately. "You can't go traipsing off through those woods alone."

"I'm not alone. You're going to wait for me right here, and if I'm not back in ten minutes, you're going to call Sheriff Mooney. Come on, Naomi, give me a little credit here. I'm a cop."

"A wounded cop. You can't even use your weapon."

"I hope I won't need to." Abby opened the door and

got out. ''Pull the car up around that bend so if anyone comes along, they won't see you. And for goodness' sake, keep your doors locked.''

''I'll roast in here if I don't roll the windows down,'' Naomi complained.

''And you'll get eaten alive by mosquitoes if you do,'' Abby warned.

''Oh, just go.'' Naomi gave her an impatient wave. ''I'll manage. Just hurry up. And Abby, you be careful, you hear me? You're all I've got left in this world.''

Abby started to return the sentiment, but then she thought about Sam. She didn't have him, but it was becoming painfully apparent that she wanted him.

THE WOODS were heavy with darkness, but Abby didn't dare turn her flashlight on because she didn't want to alert anyone to her presence.

Through patches in the trees, she could see light glinting on water. Somewhere in the distance, a boat motored across the lake. The sound grew louder for a moment, then faded, and the silence seemed magnified in the aftermath.

A mosquito buzzed her face, and Abby swatted it away. But there were plenty more where that one came from. She thought about Naomi sitting in the car, either sweltering or putting up a valiant battle against the pesky insects.

Naomi, waiting for her.

Naomi, waiting all these years for Sadie to come home.

Abby felt the familiar pain inside her chest. She couldn't bring back Sadie, but she could find Sara Beth. Please God, she could find Sara Beth, and then Emily.

The cabins loomed ahead of her. Surrounded by woods, they were set back about fifty yards from the lake. As

Abby approached the nearest one, she could hear water lapping against the dock, and for a moment, she could have sworn she heard voices, the sound of a child, but she knew it was her imagination. Her desperation to find the missing girls.

The cabins were all dark. Abby moved silently between them, glancing in windows, trying to detect some movement, no matter how slight, in the inky blackness of their interiors.

There were six cabins all together, and the last one was set a little farther back into the woods. Abby paused, listening to her surroundings. She'd heard something again, a sound too slight to startle, but she knew how vulnerable she was out here. She didn't want to take any chances.

Glancing around, she calmed her nerves. All was silent. All was still. And then, as she turned back to the cabin, she saw something flicker in the window. A tiny thread of light where a blackout blind hadn't been pulled all the way to the sill.

Her heart pounding, Abby started toward the light. She drew her weapon, but in her left hand, it was virtually useless.

She made her way up to the cabin. The opening beneath the blind was so small, she couldn't see inside the room. After a moment, she pressed her ear to the glass. She heard nothing at first, but then, like the tinkle of a wind chime, came the sound of a child's voice.

Abby's pulse thundered in her ears. She wanted to rush inside that cabin and sweep the child up into her arms, hold onto her tightly until they were both safe and far away from this place.

But then another sound came from inside. A voice that sent a chill up Abby's spine.

Sam's voice...

But what was he doing inside the cabin with Sara Beth? How had he found her?

When had he found her?

Or had he always known where she was? Abby wondered, a sickening betrayal washing over her.

Had he known, and deliberately steered her in the wrong direction, as Sheriff Mooney had warned her? Had he fed her information that would keep her away from the truth?

Distracted by the revelation, by her shock, Abby was too late to react to the snapping of a twig behind her. She whirled, but at that exact moment, something collided with her right temple, hard enough to drop her to her knees.

And for a moment, she saw nothing but darkness.

SAM KNEW that he would never forget the sound of the cabin door being kicked open or the look of betrayal on Abby's face as she stood in the doorway. He'd automatically reached for his weapon, but when he saw Abby, he'd hesitated. And then it was too late.

He registered the blood streaming down the side of her face at the same moment he saw a shadow move behind her. And then she was shoved violently into the room and landed sprawling at his feet.

He went for his gun again, but Curtis Brodie said coldly, "Don't do it. Don't even think about it. I'll drop you where you stand if you make one false move."

Sam glanced back down at Abby. Her eyes were closed. She wasn't moving. *Dear God…*

Out of the corner of his eye, he saw a scurrying movement beneath one of the bunks. At the first sign of danger, Sara Beth had gone immediately to her hiding place. Just as she'd been instructed.

In another corner of the cabin, Karen and Vickie Wilder stared in terror at Curtis Brodie.

"Well, well, well," he said, gazing around. "What a cozy little setup we have here." Keeping Sam in his line of sight, he crossed the room to Karen and placed the gun against her temple. He grabbed her arm and jerked her to her feet. "Did you think I wouldn't know you were the one who took her? Did you think I wouldn't find out where you were keeping her? God, you're so stupid and pathetic. So easy to figure out. All I had to do was up the ante. Make you sweat a little. After the ransom demand, you knew you had to move fast, didn't you? All I had to do was watch and wait."

"You *were* behind the call," Karen said, her voice surprisingly defiant. "But don't pretend you did it to find Sara Beth. You wanted the money. That's why you said you couldn't raise it, that I'd have to get a loan from the bank."

Curtis gave a low laugh. "Maybe you're not so dumb after all. I needed a little extra cash to get me started somewhere else. Someplace where the IRS has no jurisdiction. Mexico sounds pretty good."

Sam, conscious that Abby still lay prone at his feet, said, "So you recruited Luanne Plimpton to help you."

Curtis laughed again. "Didn't take much convincing, considering her greed. And her taste for the finer things in life. She told me she knew someone who'd be willing to pick the money up at the drop for a small cut. An old friend, she said. Someone we could let take the fall if things went bad."

"Sounds like a good plan." Sam let a little admiration creep into his tone. First rule when interviewing even the most brutal killer. Don't let him see your disgust. Don't let him think you're passing judgment. You're his friend, his confidant, his best buddy. "What went wrong?"

"They were planning a little double cross, that's what went wrong. The bitch lied to me. She and Hatcher were planning to skip town with the money. I caught on after Sergeant Cross over there told me Luanne was married to Hatcher. I drove to the house where Hatcher was staying that night, and found them together. So I made a phone call, got Hatcher out of the house, and then I went in and had a little talk with Luanne."

"But you didn't do much talking, did you?" Sam said. "Did you plant Sara Beth's barrette in the house after you killed Luanne?"

"A stroke of genius, if I do say so myself," Curtis bragged. "But don't feel too sorry for Luanne. She had it coming. They all do. I wouldn't have minded seeing Hatcher blow away that nosy little detective over there, but I couldn't afford the luxury. I didn't want him talking. But enough of this. It's time to get what I came for." He jammed the gun to the base of Karen's neck. "Where is she? Where's my daughter?"

"Just leave her alone," Karen whispered. "Please. You don't love her. You don't love anyone but yourself."

"I sure as hell don't love you." He wrapped his arm around her neck and drew her to him. The gun barrel flicked toward Vickie Wilder, cowering in the corner. "All these years, I thought you were another cold fish, but maybe it was just that I didn't have the right kind of equipment to excite you. Is that it?"

Karen's hands curled around his arm. "It's not like that. Vickie's just a friend."

"A friend who helped you kidnap my daughter. How'd you talk her into that?"

"She saw the way Sara Beth acted with you. How

frightened she was. She knew something was wrong, so she came to talk to me about it. I told her we were divorcing, and that I was trying to get full custody of Sara Beth. But I knew you'd never let her go. You would use her to hurt me any way you could.''

''So you took my daughter.'' He said this to Vickie, and for the first time, she seemed to come alive.

''I would do anything to protect an innocent child from a monster like you.'' She spat the words, and for a moment, Curtis actually seemed taken aback by her vehemence.

Then his eyes narrowed. His expression grew rigid. ''You had it all figured out, didn't you? Even got your brother to come down here to make sure the cops were looking in all the wrong places.''

Out of the corner of his eye, Sam saw Abby move, very slightly. Her left hand balled into a fist.

She thought the same thing, that he'd betrayed her, but at the moment, all Sam could think was that, thank God, she was alive.

''Sara Beth!'' Curtis called. ''Come out here to Daddy. I want to talk to you.''

No answer. No movement.

Sam imagined the child curling more deeply into the shadows underneath her bed.

''Sara Beth,'' Curtis said more sternly. ''If you don't do as I say, I'm going to have to punish your mother. You don't want that, do you?''

''No!'' Karen screamed. ''Don't come out, Sara Beth.''

But the child was already scrambling from beneath the bed. Curtis flung Karen aside. ''Come over here, Sara Beth. You and Daddy are going to take a little trip together.''

''Please, no,'' Karen pleaded. ''She's just a baby.''

"She's my daughter. Do you think I'd let someone like you raise her?"

Sara Beth stood looking up at him with solemn little eyes. "Don't hurt Mama."

"I won't. Not if you do as I say. Now, come here."

She started toward him. A distant sound echoed through the darkness. So faint Sam couldn't be sure he wasn't imagining it. But it sounded like a siren....

Had Abby managed to call for backup before Curtis spotted her?

"Come on," Curtis coaxed Sara Beth. "Daddy's got a boat waiting at the dock. You like boat rides."

The child started to cry, obliterating the sound of the siren. Sam didn't think Curtis had heard it yet. If Sam could just keep him talking...

Directly behind Curtis, the glass in the window exploded. Curtis, caught off guard, spun toward the sound, then whirled back around. But in that split second, Sam had pulled his weapon. He fired just as Abby lunged for Sara Beth. She knocked the child to the floor, shielding Sara Beth's body with hers.

But it was all over. Curtis Brodie, a man very much like Sam's father, lay dead on the cabin floor.

ABBY SAT in the same emergency room cubicle she'd been in earlier that day, but now instead of getting her wrist set she was having the gash in her head stitched.

"This is getting to be a regular habit with you," the doctor said sternly. He'd given her a local, but it still hurt like hell.

Naomi hovered nearby, reluctant to leave Abby's side. As it turned out, she hadn't waited ten minutes to call Sheriff Mooney. She'd barely waited ten seconds, and then she'd followed Abby into the woods. When she'd seen the cabin, heard what was going on inside, she'd thrown a rock through the window to create a diversion. She might actually have saved all of their lives, but she'd shrugged off the notion when Abby suggested it.

"I didn't think, I just reacted," Naomi said. "It could have gone the other way. He could have just started shooting. Oh, my God, when I think what could have happened—"

"But it didn't," Abby said. "We're all safe. And Sara Beth is back with her mother, in no small part thanks to you."

And at that, tears had filled Naomi's eyes.

After the doctor finished and left the room, Naomi came to stand beside Abby. "Have you talked to Sam yet?"

"No. I'm not sure I want to."

"I think you're being a little hard on him, Abby. Are you ticked because he figured out everything before you did?"

Abby drew back, hurt. "No! Of course, not. I'm angry because he must have had suspicions all along about his sister. He's a profiler, Naomi. He knows how to read people. You think he didn't know?"

"Maybe he did have suspicions. But he didn't have proof. He did exactly what you would have done in his shoes," Naomi insisted. "He looked at other suspects. He left no stone unturned. And to tell you the truth, I'm not so sure I wouldn't have done what Karen did if I were in her place. If I'd ever thought Sadie was threatened…if I'd been given a chance to save her…" She glanced away, her eyes filling again.

"I know. But don't you see?" Tears welled in Abby's eyes, too. "If I hadn't found that cabin, if Curtis hadn't shown up when he did, I don't know what would have happened, and I can't help wondering what the outcome would have been. Did Sam go there to convince Karen to turn herself in, or did he go there with the intent of helping her to get away?''

''I don't know, Abby. All I know is that I don't think I'm in any position to judge either one of them.''

Maybe not, but for most of her life, Abby had always been so sure she knew right from wrong. That life was all black and white with no shades of gray in between. But now everything had been turned upside down, and she knew that for her there would always be doubts. There would always be lingering suspicions about Sam's actions this night.

Chapter Seventeen

Monday

Sam was waiting for her outside the sheriff's station the next morning. Abby got out of her car and walked slowly toward him.

"How's Sara Beth doing?" she asked him.

"Amazingly well, considering. She's going to have some rough times ahead of her, but she'll be all right. We'll make sure she is."

"What about Karen?"

His gaze clouded a little. "She's in for some rough times, too. We still don't know if she, Vickie Wilder and Greta Henley are all going to be charged with kidnapping. At any rate, Greta Henley will have to stand trial in Memphis for the outstanding charges against her."

Both Karen and Vickie had given statements last night. Emily's abduction had given them the idea to 'kidnap' Sara Beth in order to get her away from Curtis. Vickie had stayed in touch all these years with her old roommate, and she'd enlisted Greta's help. Greta had followed Sara Beth and Luanne Plimpton from school that day, hoping for a chance to grab her. The drugstore stop had provided the perfect opportunity. She'd taken Sara Beth to the cabin where she was to stay with her until Vickie could help Karen make the necessary arrangements for new identities for her and Sara Beth. But Greta had gotten cold feet and fled. That's why Vickie had disappeared. She'd been forced to tip her hand because someone had to stay with Sara Beth.

"If the feds charge them, won't you have some pull?" Abby asked.

"No. Not under the circumstances. But even if they have to stand trial, I think a judge and jury will be lenient, considering Curtis's actions. Karen had good reason for fearing for her child's safety."

"I hope you're right," Abby said. "I think the best thing for Sara Beth is to be with her mother. Although what she did was very reckless."

"I know."

"She had us all fooled, you know. She was so upset after the ransom demand. It's hard to believe she could be that good of an actress."

"It wasn't an act," Sam said. "You can imagine how terrified and confused she must have been when she got the call. She thought she had Sara Beth tucked away all safe and sound—and then someone calls demanding a ransom. She knew Curtis was behind it somehow, but she couldn't call Vickie and alert her because her telephone calls were being monitored. Karen was afraid that Curtis had figured out where she'd taken Sara Beth, and that he'd do something to her before Karen could get out there to stop him."

"If only she'd told us the truth," Abby murmured.

"It's easy to play Monday morning quarterback," Sam said.

"I guess."

Their gazes met and held for just a moment before Sam glanced away. "About last night…" He paused, then started again. "I know you think I had it all figured out from the first, but I didn't. It all came together for me just about the same time it did for you."

"But you must have had suspicions, Sam. You had to have had doubts."

"Maybe. Maybe it was like you said the other night. I was afraid of the truth. But I never misled you, Abby. I promise you that."

"I guess I can't help wondering if you would have turned Karen in if I hadn't shown up, or if you would have helped her escape with Sara Beth."

"I guess I'm wondering that myself," Sam murmured. "The truth is, I don't know the answer."

Abby wasn't certain she could live with that. "How *did* you figure it out?"

"Remember when I told you that Vickie Wilder seemed familiar to me that day we interviewed her? But I knew I'd never met her. Last night I finally figured out why. I saw her the day I first got to town. She was driving down the street, away from Karen's house, just as I was arriving. I barely glanced at her, and I didn't even know then that she'd been to see Karen. But there was something about the way she stared at me, as if she were frightened of me, that made me remember her, at least vaguely. Now, I realize Karen must have told her that I was coming, and Vickie was afraid I'd find out what happened."

"How did you find out about the cabin?"

"I caught up with Karen after she'd stepped out of the house, and I followed her just the way Curtis did."

They stood silently for a moment, and then Sam said

tentatively, "I'm going back to Quantico, Abby. I'm going to try and salvage what's left of my career. And while I'm there, I'd like to write a letter of recommendation to the Academy on your behalf."

Abby gazed at him in shock. "I can't leave. We found Sara Beth, but Emily is still missing."

"I understand that. But once she's found—"

"Sadie will still be missing."

His gaze on her deepened. "It's been ten years. You can't keep searching forever."

"I know that. But if there's a chance, no matter how slim…" Abby trailed off, knowing that after all this time, Sadie was probably lost to them.

"You can't keep using Sadie as an excuse," Sam said softly.

Abby's gaze flew to his. "That's not what I'm doing!"

"Isn't it? I've seen the way your eyes light up when you talk about the FBI. I know how fascinated you are by profiling. But you've let Sadie's disappearance keep you here in Eden because you're afraid. You're scared you can't cut it out there in the real world."

A wave of anger rolled over Abby, even though she knew there was some truth in what he said. "Maybe you're right," she said coolly. "But when all is said and done, this is where I belong."

"Then I guess there's nothing else left to say except good-bye."

THE STATION WAS abuzz when Abby walked in. Dave was in with Sheriff Mooney, and when they saw her, they both motioned her inside.

"What's going on?"

"Close the door, Abby."

Her heart sank. What was this, an ambush?

Sheriff Mooney was somber as usual, but there was an air of excitement about Dave Conyers. She glanced from one to the other. "What is it?"

"We got a break in the Campbell case, " Dave said. "At long last."

Abby felt the familiar jump start of adrenaline in her bloodstream. "What is it? What happened?"

"Your sister was just in here," Dave told her. "She'd been to see Tess Campbell this morning. When she came outside, a note had been left on her windshield."

Abby's heart skidded against her chest. "A ransom note?"

"No. A note from a child. We think it's from Emily." Sheriff Mooney handed her a plastic evidence bag.

Abby scanned the note inside. It was painstakingly written in crude block letters: I com hom soon, mama.

"Oh, my God." She glanced up. "It was found on my sister's car?"

"Yes, but we think there's a reason for that," Dave said. "Her SUV is similar to Tess Campbell's. Same color, same body style. But Tess's SUV was parked in the garage, out of sight. The kidnapper must have mistaken Naomi's vehicle for Tess's."

"The lab will check for fingerprints," Sheriff Mooney said. "The paper and ink will have to be analyzed, as well as the handwriting. This could turn out to be nothing more than hoax."

"Or it could be a sign that Emily is still alive," Abby said.

"That's what we all want to believe," the sheriff said quietly. And it seemed to Abby that for the first time since she'd known him, Fred Mooney was almost moved to tears.

NAOMI WAS WAITING for Abby in the cubicle that was her office.

"They told you about the note?" When Abby nodded, Naomi sat down in a chair across from Abby's desk. "Oh, Abby, I can't tell you what I first thought when I saw it. For a moment, I thought it was from—" She broke off, glancing away.

"I know," Abby said softly. "But it's been ten years, Naomi."

She nodded. "I've been reminding myself of that all morning. And I've been doing a lot of thinking. About Sadie. About my life. About you and Sam."

"There is no Sam and me, Naomi. He's on his way back to Quantico."

"And you're letting him go, just like that?"

Abby gazed helplessly at her sister. "He lives in Virginia. My home is here in Eden."

"But it doesn't have to be." Naomi leaned forward, her gaze earnest. Troubled. "I've always wondered if the reason you stayed here was because of me. Because of Sadie. I've kept you looking for her all these years, haven't I? I've been so selfish."

Abby took her sister's hand. "I've stayed because I wanted to. I've wanted so badly to find her, Naomi."

"I know. But maybe it's time we both faced reality. Maybe it's time we both let go."

"Naomi—"

"Don't throw away a chance for happiness, Abby. Don't keep your life on hold any longer. It's time to move on."

Abby swallowed past a sudden lump in her throat. "I don't know if I can. What if it doesn't work out?"

Naomi smiled. "And what if it turns out to be something quite wonderful?"

AFTER ALL THIS TIME, he would already be gone, Abby thought as she rushed through the station, oblivious to the curious gazes that followed her. He'd already be on his way out of town, and then Abby would have to get in a squad car and chase him down. How embarrassing would that be? Especially if he chose not to stop—

He was still in the parking lot, leaning against his car. Standing in virtually the same position he'd been in when Abby had left him thirty minutes ago.

She slowed her steps as she approached him. "You didn't get far."

"No, I didn't. I kept hoping you'd change your mind."

"About the Academy?"

Something flickered in his eyes. "For one thing."

Abby drew a long breath. "I can't leave yet, Sam. There's been a break in Emily's case."

"Yes, I know. I just talked to Dave Conyers. And I understand that even though it's not your case, you can't go until it's resolved. But when Emily's found?"

He was right, Abby thought. Not if, but when. "I'd like to take you up on your offer. I'd like to see if I can cut it at Quantico."

"It won't be easy," Sam warned. "I can write you a letter of recommendation, but that's all I can do. You'll have to make it on your own merits."

"I wouldn't want it any other way."

He nodded. "When you get through training, you'll be assigned to a field office somewhere. There's nothing I can do about that, either."

"I understand."

"But after you've paid your dues, I'll see that you get a shot at profiling. I do still have clout at the Investigative Support Unit, but I don't think you'll need my help. You're a natural, Abby."

She gave him a tentative smile. "And just where will you be during this time?"

"I'll be at Quantico, teaching classes at the Academy. I may even get to teach you a thing or two. And then, on weekends, I'd like to be in whatever city you're assigned to."

Abby's heart started to pound. She took a step toward him. "This is never going to work, you know."

"Probably not."

"We're too different."

"I'm too old for you."

She was only inches from him now. Abby felt her breath catch at his nearness. "I told you once that I'd be the judge of that."

"Right. But you never gave me the verdict."

Her brows lifted slightly. "I thought my actions that night spoke louder than words."

A memory passed between them. A moment of heat. Then tenderness.

After a while, Sam said softly, "Someday, I'd like to tell you about Jonathan."

"I'd love to hear about him."

Sam pulled her into his arms and rested his chin on her head. "He loved baseball."

"Did he?"

"And pizza. And German Shepherds. He was a great kid, Abby."

She closed her eyes. "I'm sure he was. Especially if he was anything like his father."

Sam's arms tightened around her, and Abby confessed a little breathlessly, "I think I'm falling in love with you, Sam."

He gave a wry chuckle. "That's good. Because I think I fell for you the moment I first laid eyes on you."

Look for THE TEMPTED,
the second book in
Amanda Stevens's
exciting trilogy

EDEN'S CHILDREN

Wherever Harlequin Intrigue
books are sold.

Chapter One

"Mama?" Five-year-old Emily Campbell sat up in bed and rubbed her eyes as she tried to peer through the darkness. Someone was sitting beside her bed.

"Your mother's not here. Go back to sleep."

"I want my mama."

"She's not here, I said. Now hush."

Emily began to cry. "I want to go home. Why can't I go home?"

"Because your mother had to go away for a while, so she asked me to look after you. Remember? I told you that."

Yes, but Emily still didn't believe it. Her mama would never go away and leave her for this long. Where was she? Where was Grandma JoJo? Why hadn't they come for her? A terrifying thought struck Emily. What if something had happened to them? "I'm scared," she whimpered.

"Why are you scared? You're not hurt, are you? You're not sick. I'm taking real good care of you, just like I promised I would. And look at all these pretty dolls...I got them just for you."

It was true. Emily hadn't been hurt. She'd been taken care of, although sometimes she was left alone for long periods of time, locked in this room. And she did have lots of toys to play with. They just weren't her toys.

"Can I have Brown Bear?" she asked in a tiny voice. A soft, cuddly toy was placed in her arms, but Emily pushed it away. "I want *my* Brown Bear."

A frustrated sigh. "Are we going to have to go through this every night?"

Emily began to wail. "I want my Brown Bear! I want my mama!"

"Stop that!"

Emily felt a hand touch her arm in the darkness, and she tried to flinch away.

"I'm not going to hurt you. It's a picture of your mother. Put it under your pillow and it'll make you feel all better."

The picture was slipped into her hand, but Emily didn't want it. She didn't want it anywhere near her. The lady in that photograph wasn't her mother, no matter how many times she was told differently.

Look at your mama. Isn't she pretty?

That's not my mama.

Sure it is. It's just been so long since you saw her, you've forgotten what she looks like, that's all.

It *had* been a long time since Emily had seen her mother. So very long. But she still remembered what her mother looked like. She had long, glorious hair, just like the lady in the fairy tale Emily loved so much, and a smile that made Emily feel all warm inside. The woman in the picture looked nothing like Emily's mother.

But she didn't put up a fuss this time. She took the picture and stuffed it underneath her pillow without a word because she didn't want the light to be turned on. In the dark, she could make believe this really was her room and that her mother was just down the hallway.

Sniffing back her tears, Emily lay down and curled up beneath the covers, closing her eyes and pretending to fall back asleep. She tried to imagine her mama sitting beside her on the bed, reading to her from the book that had been Emily's favorite since she was little. *Goodnight stars, goodnight moon…*

"Goodnight, Mama," she whispered, so softly no one in the darkness could hear her.

Psst...

INTRIGUE®

has an even *bigger* secret—

but it's

CONFIDENTIAL

till September 2001!

*Harlequin truly does
make any time special. . . .
This year we are celebrating
weddings in style!*

To help us celebrate, we want you to tell us how wearing the Harlequin wedding gown will make your wedding day special. As the grand prize, Harlequin will offer one lucky bride the chance to **"Walk Down the Aisle"** in the Harlequin wedding gown!

There's more...

For her honeymoon, she and her groom will spend five nights at the **Hyatt Regency Maui.** As part of this five-night honeymoon at the hotel renowned for its romantic attractions, the couple will enjoy a candlelit dinner for two in Swan Court, a sunset sail on the hotel's catamaran, and duet spa treatments.

To enter, please write, in, 250 words or less, how wearing the Harlequin wedding gown will make your wedding day special. The entry will be judged based on its emotionally compelling nature, its originality and creativity, and its sincerity. This contest is open to Canadian and U.S. residents only and to those who are 18 years of age and older. There is no purchase necessary to enter. Void where prohibited. See further contest rules attached. Please send your entry to:

Walk Down the Aisle Contest

In Canada
P.O. Box 637
Fort Erie, Ontario
L2A 5X3

In U.S.A.
P.O. Box 9076
3010 Walden Ave.
Buffalo, NY 14269-9076

You can also enter by visiting www.eHarlequin.com
Win the Harlequin wedding gown and the vacation of a lifetime!
The deadline for entries is October 1, 2001.

PHWDACONT1

HARLEQUIN WALK DOWN THE AISLE TO MAUI CONTEST 1197
OFFICIAL RULES
NO PURCHASE NECESSARY TO ENTER

1. To enter, follow directions published in the offer to which you are responding. Contest begins April 2, 2001, and ends on October 1, 2001. Method of entry may vary. Mailed entries must be postmarked by October 1, 2001, and received by October 8, 2001.

2. Contest entry may be, at times, presented via the Internet, but will be restricted solely to residents of certain georgraphic areas that are disclosed on the Web site. To enter via the Internet, if permissible, access the Harlequin Web site (www.eHarlequin.com) and follow the directions displayed online. Online entries must be received by 11:59 p.m. E.S.T. on October 1, 2001.

   In lieu of submitting an entry online, enter by mail by hand-printing (or typing) on an 8½" x 11" plain piece of paper, your name, address (including zip code), Contest number/name and in 250 words or fewer, why winning a Harlequin wedding dress would make your wedding day special. Mail via first-class mail to: Harlequin Walk Down the Aisle Contest 1197, (in the U.S.) P.O. Box 9076, 3010 Walden Avenue, Buffalo, NY 14269-9076, (in Canada) P.O. Box 637, Fort Erie, Ontario L2A 5X3, Canada.

   Limit one entry per person, household address and e-mail address. Online and/or mailed entries received from persons residing in geographic areas in which Internet entry is not permissible will be disqualified.

3. Contests will be judged by a panel of members of the Harlequin editorial, marketing and public relations staff based on the following criteria:

   - Originality and Creativity—50%
   - Emotionally Compelling—25%
   - Sincerity—25%

   In the event of a tie, duplicate prizes will be awarded. Decisions of the judges are final.

4. All entries become the property of Torstar Corp. and will not be returned. No responsibility is assumed for lost, late, illegible, incomplete, inaccurate, nondelivered or misdirected mail or misdirected e-mail, for technical, hardware or software failures of any kind, lost or unavailable network connections, or failed, incomplete, garbled or delayed computer transmission or any human error which may occur in the receipt or processing of the entries in this Contest.

5. Contest open only to residents of the U.S. (except Puerto Rico) and Canada, who are 18 years of age or older, and is void wherever prohibited by law; all applicable laws and regulations apply. Any litigation within the Province of Quebec respecting the conduct or organization of a publicity contest may be submitted to the Régie des alcools, des courses et des jeux for a ruling. Any litigation respecting the awarding of a prize may be submitted to the Régie des alcools, des courses et des jeux only for the purpose of helping the parties reach a settlement. Employees and immediate family members of Torstar Corp. and D. L. Blair, Inc., their affiliates, subsidiaries and all other agencies, entities and persons connected with the use, marketing or conduct of this Contest are not eligible to enter. Taxes on prizes are the sole responsibility of winners. Acceptance of any prize offered constitutes permission to use winner's name, photograph or other likeness for the purposes of advertising, trade and promotion on behalf of Torstar Corp., its affiliates and subsidiaries without further compensation to the winner, unless prohibited by law.

6. Winners will be determined no later than November 15, 2001, and will be notified by mail. Winners will be required to sign and return an Affidavit of Eligibility form within 15 days after winner notification. Noncompliance within that time period may result in disqualification and an alternative winner may be selected. Winners of trip must execute a Release of Liability prior to ticketing and must possess required travel documents (e.g. passport, photo ID) where applicable. Trip must be completed by November 2002. No substitution of prize permitted by winner. Torstar Corp. and D. L. Blair, Inc., their parents, affiliates, and subsidiaries are not responsible for errors in printing or electronic presentation of Contest, entries and/or game pieces. In the event of printing or other errors which may result in unintended prize values or duplication of prizes, all affected game pieces or entries shall be null and void. If for any reason the Internet portion of the Contest is not capable of running as planned, including infection by computer virus, bugs, tampering, unauthorized intervention, fraud, technical failures, or any other causes beyond the control of Torstar Corp. which corrupt or affect the administration, secrecy, fairness, integrity or proper conduct of the Contest, Torstar Corp. reserves the right, at its sole discretion, to disqualify any individual who tampers with the entry process and to cancel, terminate, modify or suspend the Contest or the Internet portion thereof. In the event of a dispute regarding an online entry, the entry will be deemed submitted by the authorized holder of the e-mail account submitted at the time of entry. Authorized account holder is defined as the natural person who is assigned to an e-mail address by an Internet access provider, online service provider or other organization that is responsible for arranging e-mail address for the domain associated with the submitted e-mail address. **Purchase or acceptance of a product offer does not improve your chances of winning.**

7. Prizes: (1) Grand Prize—A Harlequin wedding dress (approximate retail value: $3,500) and a 5-night/6-day honeymoon trip to Maui, HI, including round-trip air transportation provided by Maui Visitors Bureau from Los Angeles International Airport (winner is responsible for transportation to and from Los Angeles International Airport) and a Harlequin Romance Package, including hotel accomodations (double occupancy) at the Hyatt Regency Maui Resort and Spa, dinner for (2) two at Swan Court, a sunset sail on Kiele V and a spa treatment for the winner (approximate retail value: $4,000); (5) Five runner-up prizes of a $1000 gift certificate to selected retail outlets to be determined by Sponsor (retail value $1000 ea.). Prizes consist of only those items listed as part of the prize. Limit one prize per person. All prizes are valued in U.S. currency.

8. For a list of winners (available after December 17, 2001) send a self-addressed, stamped envelope to: Harlequin Walk Down the Aisle Contest 1197 Winners, P.O. Box 4200 Blair, NE 68009-4200 or you may access the www.eHarlequin.com Web site through January 15, 2002.

Contest sponsored by Torstar Corp., P.O. Box 9042, Buffalo, NY 14269-9042, U.S.A.

HARLEQUIN®
INTRIGUE®

and HARPER ALLEN present

Bound by the ties they forged as soldiers
of fortune, these agents fearlessly put their
lives on the line for a worthy cause.
But now they're about to face their
greatest challenge—love!

August 2001
GUARDING JANE DOE

September 2001
SULLIVAN'S LAST STAND

Available at your favorite retail outlet.

Makes any time special ®